Helen

Enjoy the read!

Baby's Breath

JP Nelson

JP Nelson

BOONDOGGLER PRESS

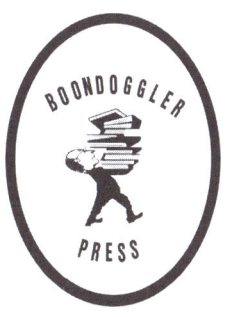

"We're not wasting words here"

Dear Reader,

Would you ever jump into a tannin-tainted river laden with hungry piranha if it might save your life? What about climb aboard a two-seater Cessna piloted by a lunatic you swore-off ever flying with again, if it could help find a missing colleague? Would you willingly take an ad hoc hallucinogenic snuff mixed by a mysterious shaman for a chance to learn the truth? Could you catch a trusted friend in lie? Could you shoot someone before they shot you? Would you turn your back on everyone you cared about for a chance at immortality?

Baby's Breath is a novel filled with such inner conflicts. A story, I believe, crafted with a comparable blend of speculative science, provocative issues, and intriguing characters amassed within an exotic setting so as to have tension on every page. Once you read the novel, I am confident you will too.

Find out if Kyle Preston, not only survives, but can also overcome his losses – and most of all – enjoy the read!

JP Nelson

JP Nelson

Sale of this book without a front cover may be unauthorized. If this book has no cover, it may have been reported to the publisher as "unsold" or "destroyed" and neither the author nor the publisher may have received payment for it.

Baby's Breath is a work of fiction. Names, characters, places, and incidents are the products of the author's imagination or are used fictitiously. Any resemblance to actual events, locales, or persons, living or dead, is entirely coincidental.

© Copyright 2006

ISBN: 0-9776847-0-9

Library of Congress Control Number: 2006901463

First North America print rights granted to Boondoggler Press, Inc.

All rights reserved, including the right to reproduce this book or portions thereof in any form whatsoever.

For information regarding discounts for bulk purchases, please contact the sales department of Boondoggler Press at sales@boondogglerpress.com

Boondoggler Press, Inc.
4501 Manatee Ave West
Suite 251
Bradenton, Fl 34209

Cover design by Scott Polzen
Cover model: Isaias Ramos
Printed in Canada

To my wife,

and the beauty of the mountain girl within her
may happiness fall upon you
as the rains of Amazonas.
always, anywhere, and the ties between two friends

to family and friends

Baby's Breath

Frozen in a moment, alone, bitter, and cold
Life viewed not from the green mountain
but from an iced shoal
passing time in which one's misfortunes are retold,
Bound to a damnation that devours the soul
Lie beneath thy marker – remembered to my grave.

Prologue
KINDRED SPIRITS

Expedition: Day 57

If anyone, including myself at some point later in life, should ever read from these pages, I hold no ill-will for the questioning of my words. With the boat scheduled to arrive tomorrow, I am compelled to write – despite the hour – despite my fatigue – despite my drunkenness – despite my state of mind.

For the last two months Brooklyn and I have collected samples from a snake-riddled heap of thorns known as a liana forest. Work, if not torture, no one should ever endure. And yet, I would gladly leave our base camp right now, in the dark of night with all its peril, and trek back through the jungle to the field site for a chance to experience the acts of magic one can find in such a place, when that is your calling.

If possible, I would, but that magic has been robbed of me by news of my mentor's death. Stolen is my joy, and my excitement, and of the importance, and of the very reason for this expedition. More than any of these things though, I have lost a part of myself because Professor Lowery and I shared a kindred spirit – a bond between two men even the best of friends and perhaps most brothers never know.

And yet, such a bond, rare as a rainbow, I have with Brooklyn. The two of us, from very different worlds with an even greater distance between our beliefs, connect on a colorful path that has led us to that same pot of gold. A treasure I fear to be robbed of as well.

Tomorrow I will travel home, back to a place far different than this one with the uncertainty of never seeing the people and things I leave behind – almost as if abandoning them for I know without a doubt, Brooklyn and his success is an exception and not the rule.

For that reason I am troubled because it is in my charge to teach people about his world. Somehow I must reach kids who bathe in scalding hot water and eat foods wrapped in designer packaging at their leisure. Most of them frown upon the indigenous people of the world as uncivilized and backward. They look down upon their culture as secondary and disposable. Science, Medicine, and Art – each exist here and yet are considered insignificant by modern standards when that is the furthest from the truth.

Brooklyn speaks of a spirit world and how one cannot really hold it. With those words I am reminded of the virtual worlds my students thrive upon inside their computers, satisfied with projections instead of what's real. I wonder what will happen to my friend – will he survive in this age of gizmos and gadgets or will I all too soon mourn the loss of him as I do my mentor.

AN EDEN WITHOUT ITS APPLE

Kyle Preston drank last night beyond the point of politeness and shared things about himself he regretted telling now that morning arrived. His sweat-soaked clothes reeked of the harsh malted rum that loosened his tongue. A "white man's" response to hot northern days but useless in the tropics where it clung to him as the vines upon the surrounding trees. Together the sweat and stench added to his grief. Grief along with his lingering hangover that refused to go away.

Onboard the *Anna Maria* and headed downstream to Manaus, Kyle Preston's grief robbed him of his accomplishment. The field site for his expedition produced some very interesting samples. A thorough review still needed to be performed but in all, Kyle, along with his indian guide, Brooklyn, collected twenty-three distinct varieties of lianas within the same hectare. Of these, one matched an unidentified species his colleague back at

UNC, Dr. Stephen Lowery, received recently from the Biosphere Reserve in Pico de Neblina, three hundred kilometers to the north. Kyle felt so certain the vines were identical that he informed Lowery of the find only to learn a week later of his mentor's unfortunate passing.

Despite Kyle Preston's heartfelt acknowledgement of Stephen Lowery as his mentor, the ethnobotanist's peers recognized him as an authority and rightly so. At age twenty-six and already his eleventh expedition to South America, Kyle had carved out a niche for himself studying lianas. The thorn-riddled woody vines he fancied differed greatly from the more eye-catching varieties of plants his colleagues and other botanists adored. A fact not gone unnoticed by the skipper of the transport boat.

"Senhor Preston – you are not like most estrangeiros who come here," Captain Jack noted in an ad hoc mixture of both English and Portuguese. "No one else shows such interest in our weeds," he admitted as he watched the lanky, white-bread American record details about one of the vines in a tattered, leather-bound journal. "Dois meses?" he asked pointing towards the large wooden crates stowed near the bow of the boat. "Two months and that's all there is?"

"Every rose has a thorn – at least that's what we say in my country," Kyle replied then put down his pen and grabbed the bandana wrapped around his neck. "You'd be surprised," he added after wiping the sweat from his unshaven face, "what medicines come from plants like these."

"Sim, sim – I think I understand what you say," the skipper said as he leaned up against the wheel and let his big round belly stir the boat through a straightaway. "We too have our sayings, though they are about our fiery women and not our weeds. Still, I mean no disrespect when I say, you are different from most foreigners who travel here – they don't really want to know this place," Captain Jack shared with a sigh. "They come all this way just to stay in fancy resorts that only they can afford. They come to Amazonas and never see it as it really is."

"It's hard to imagine any of my neighbors ever coming out here," Kyle declared as he thought about the quaint brick homes back in Chapel Hill with their manicured lawns. "Most of them won't cut their own grass let alone hack through the jungle."

"You were," Captain Jack stated as he reached up and rubbed the neck of his pet monkey, Nonie, who sat in the rafters of the wheelhouse eating an apple. "You were willing to come see for yourself."

"My work brought me out here," Kyle said as he stood up and walked over to the crate nearest him that contained both the dried voucher samples and those preserved in either chloroform or alcohol. "That's all," he added still mired down in glum. "Besides, I couldn't have done it without Brooklyn's help."

"No Senhor," the Captain scoffed while adjusting course to avoid a patch of blackened stumps rising above the water's surface. "You should never have brought him," he added with a dismissive, if not disdainful, glance towards Brooklyn, who sat in the back of the boat playing a flute with his dog curled up beside him. "He's "sem fe."

Kyle hardly seemed surprised to hear Captain Jack say Brooklyn should never have come. After all, the skipper almost backed out of his agreement to transport them after learning Kyle's guide was not only an indian but also a shaman. What did interest Kyle though, was how Captain Jack said Brooklyn was without faith. It showed him just how much religion still overshadowed life in Amazonas and made Kyle wonder whether Brooklyn's equal mistrust of the skipper and his two boathands might stem from the very same thing.

"His religion is just different," Kyle said in defense of his friend.

"You know as well as I that there is only one true God," Captain Jack proclaimed. "Heathens like him are worthless."

"If you gave him a chance – you'd be surprised – he knows quite a bit."

"Black magic is all he knows," the Captain snorted as he crossed himself. "I want no part of it and neither should you. Now excuse me Senhor Preston," the skipper said after looking east and noticing some small islands on the horizon, "Perhaps one day these two worthless boys of my brother will turn into men but until then, I must nag as a mother for them to keep a look out for stumps and hidden shallows, especially now as we approach Anavilhanas."

At latitude 1.45° south and longitude 63.05° west the *Anna Maria* reached the western boundary of Anavilhanas. For the next nineteen kilometers the strength and definition of the Rio Negro conceded to this beautiful yet treacherous archipelago of over four hundred islands. A natural labyrinth ridded with winding passages and abrupt dead-ends to which each isle played a role.

The first of these islands the *Anna Maria* passed were mere bird roosts. Smidgens of land covered only by mangroves with the weight of anhingas and roseate spoonbills bending the bushes' branches down to the water line. Within a kilometer though they grew in stature with vast beds of giant water lilies and flowering hyacinths afloat nearby. Then, as the boat traveled further into the archipelago, the islands splintered the Rio Negro into several channels with no distinction in its course. A course, just as Captain Jack forewarned, filled with sandbars, charred remnants of trees, and other hidden dangers lurking in the shallows.

Ahead of the *Anna Maria*, two long but narrow islands split the main channel yet again. They tapered towards one another to form a teardrop-shaped cove with a small opening at the far end. Lush exotic growth ran along the ridge of each isle with a handful of emergents sprinkled about like watchful sentries. Below them lay two enormous beaches where the water of the Rio Negro lapped against the pristine shores.

"Do you remember this place?" Captain Jack shouted

back to Kyle as the skipper maneuvered the *Anna Maria* between the two isles.

"Should I?" KP replied as he stood back up from where he sat next to Brooklyn then looked over the side of the boat.

For a moment Kyle Preston felt they stumbled upon an eighth wonder of the world. The cove's beauty overwhelmed him. Its purity humbled him. In every direction Kyle saw something awe inspiring to behold. Even Brooklyn seemed taken aback a bit by the shear beauty of the place when a pair of pink dolphins surfaced at the bow of the boat then again at the stern before disappearing just as quickly as they appeared.

"It looks very different from before with the river this low," the skipper acknowledged, "but remember – we passed through here on the way to your camp. I told you then about the giant turtles coming ashore here to lay their eggs."

"Wow," Kyle said, "I don't recall it looking like this – it's truly an Eden."

"It is," the skipper remarked with pride. "If you're lucky you may see some hatchlings breaking out of their nests."

"How much has the water dropped from before?"

"Nearly six meters," the skipper guessed. "That's why there's so much beach now and why the pass ahead is so much narrower but don't worry – the river runs very deep through the middle all year long. We always make it through even with the rainy season still a month away."

"Something I'm not sorry to miss," Kyle remarked because he timed his expedition to coincide with the driest months of the year in order to work within the liana forest. "Hopefully all these weeds I'm bringing back won't weigh us down," he joked while fumbling around in his knapsack for his journal to make some notes about the cove. "God forbid, we get stuck out here – even if it is an Eden – I'm ready to go home."

"We'll do just fine," Captain Jack vowed as he reached forward and rubbed Nonie's neck. "I have faith in the Lord."

"Silencio!" the oldest of the brothers hissed from the bow of the boat then spun back around.

Kyle looked up to find both Mattice and Marcos standing with rifles drawn and aimed at either island. Each poised to bring down any creature careless enough to be caught off-guard at the water's edge. A chance relished by the brothers to impress their demanding uncle and maybe earn some extra money by selling their unsuspecting quarry in Manaus at the city's open market.

"Quem de barco?" Captain Jack roared back then bristled as any lion would at a challenge to his authority.

The skipper added a long sneer to reinforce his disapproval over being hushed on his own boat. For several minutes afterwards he seemed quite taken with himself until he saw something large move up ahead on the island to the left.

"Ali," Captain Jack clamored then cut the boat's engine. "I'm not sure what it was," the skipper whispered as he came around to the side of the wheel to get a better look, "but whatever it was – it moved from the shoreline up into the shadows of the trees."

Both Mattice and Marcos turned to look to where their uncle pointed but the glare coming off the water made it hard for them to see much of anything in that direction. Within a few seconds though, a flock of spindle-tailed loons jetted out from a stand of Bebedor trees from that exact spot.

"Facil, facil – easy, easy," Mattice said to his younger brother in dismiss of the moderate payoff the loons' feathers would bring for a chance at whatever scared the birds.

Marcos held up and lowered his gun as well then both boathands watched as the birds flew overhead.

Thump!!

Captain Jack clutched his throat while blood squirted from his veins, out of the wound, and through his fingers. He tried to call for help but instead choked upon the warm trickle. For a moment he righted himself upon the boat's wheel but then collapsed to the floor. Afterwards, Nonie jumped down to the deck, tapping the skipper's face and grunting affectionately at him.

At the back of the boat Kyle closed his journal and reached for his knapsack then heard a thud over at the wheelhouse. He turned to look but without warning something knocked him off his feet and sent him sailing breathless through the air as a rag doll tossed to the side.

Pummeled into the Rio Negro, Kyle's momentum

carried him almost two meters down before the ethnobotanist even realized he had been thrown overboard. Afterwards, he kicked with his arms and legs but, despite being a better-than-average swimmer, only slipped further away from the surface and a needed breath. Downward he spiraled with a continual tug at his ankle. A burden that, once he reached down and felt the entanglement, seemed all too familiar.

For all the times Kyle Preston carried his knapsack through the jungle he knew the feel of those straps. The way the leather turned slimy when wet. Hell, his shoulders still ached from where the straps rubbed his skin raw. Somehow the pack also ended up in the water and then Kyle remembered grabbing it to stuff his journal back inside just before being thrown overboard.

For a moment a vision of each sample from every plant, tagged and ready to be studied, ran through his mind. Kyle recalled how hard Brooklyn and he worked to collect them and the treacheries they faced while in the liana forest. Moreover, the ethnobotanist had stashed the ones he prized the most within his knapsack, which made him sick to think they would be lost at the bottom of the river – lost forever because Kyle Preston knew he was about to die.

2
CHUM

The surprise and subtlety of those first shots yielded to sheer brute force as a speedboat whirled towards the *Anna Maria* from the other side of the pass. Along with the roar of the incoming boat's twin outboard engines came the incessant crackle of gunfire. The barrage of bullets whittled away at the *Anna Maria*'s bow where Mattice and Marcos still stood in disbelief they were under attack.

"Movimento," Mattice finally clamored after his right arm was grazed.

Seconds later, another thunderous salvo peppered the deck right after Mattice ducked behind one of the storage crates. He buried his head while the wooden planks all around him splintered into toothpicks. The boathand then heard several large splashes towards the back of the boat off starboard and afterwards a loud thump to his side.

"Olhar," Marcos yelled followed by a laugh as he crouched behind the other box.

"Que?" Mattice grumbled then twisted around so his back was pressed up against the crate. "O que e assim engracado?" the older brother asked as he pulled off his shirt and bound his wound the best he could.

"Muito," Marcos declared despite all the bullets a whiz around them. "Mas especial isto," he added followed by an even hardier laugh.

Mattice looked over in time to see Marcos pull a thin wooden dart out of his neck from just below the ear. A four-inch spear studded with a blackened tip and a wad of fibers balled around the back end. At first Marcos still seemed amused by the dart as he rolled it between his fingers. Then his hands trembled and for a time beyond infinity the two brothers just stared at one another.

"Eu sou muito bem," Marcos said even as the tremors worsened. "Realmente," he insisted. "Muito b—"

Helpless to do anything while the gunfire kept him at bay, Mattice could only watch as his brother slumped over then fell unconscious upon the deck. White foamy drool slid from the young boathand's mouth. The rise and fall of his chest faded if not stopped all together and his heart labored erratic. All the while, blood, dark as midnight and spoiled by the darts poison, dribbled from his wound. Then as if possessed, Marcos' body seized and stiffened beyond its natural limits with his fingers clinched around the dart.

"Voca a seguro agora," Mattice whispered after a lull

finally came in the shooting and he crawled over to his brother's side. "You're safe now," he repeated with their faces just inches apart. "You're safe now."

Kind and precious words, but a lie left unfinished because Marcos erupted as violent as a volcano filled with blood then fell dormant. In a state of sheer panic Mattice crossed first his brother then himself. Afterwards, he wiped the blood from his bewildered face, grabbed his rifle and headed back towards the wheelhouse.

After a mad scramble to get inside, Mattice found his uncle sprawled out upon the wheelhouse floor, face down in a pool of blood. The skin on the back of the skipper's neck was obliterated with shredded muscles and shattered vertebrae splattered throughout the cabin. A horrible site made even worse when Mattice looked up and saw Nonie hanging from the rafters.

Blood-soaked from lying earlier in the skipper's blood, the monkey just hung there with her eyes fixed upon Mattice. As she did, blood dripped from her hands and feet down upon the boat's wheel. Then, when Mattice stepped over Captain Jack's body towards her, Nonie began to groan – each pathetic moan a little louder than the one before until she screamed at the top of her lungs.

Stepping back but still staring into Nonie's eyes, Mattice witnessed fear in its rawest form. The same overwhelming and uncontrollable fear he saw seconds ago in his brother's eyes. The very fear Mattice knew existed in his own eyes as well – not the fear of a brazen knock upon a door, or the beguiling scratch at a window, or the steady footsteps of a stranger across a floor – more than of what waited around the corner, or loomed within a dark closet, or lurked beneath the surface of the water. Mattice's fear arose not from the unknown, but from certainty – the certainty to face undeniable truth and absolute wrongs – to accept irrefutable proof and incontestable guilt – to receive final judgement.

Tormented within this purgatory, Mattice moved back towards the door and peered outside. For the first time since the attack began, he finally got a good look at the other boat. With less than fifty meters between them, the boathand counted three people onboard – one of them stood on that ship's bow firing a gun – an automatic rifle Mattice figured as another salvo of bullets ricocheted all around him.

As he ducked for cover yet again, Mattice realized he hadn't heard or seen either of the *Anna Maria*'s passengers. Despite the danger, he poked his head out of the wheelhouse and looked towards the back of the boat but saw no one. He then called out to Kyle and even Brooklyn several times but when no one answered, the boathand assumed the worse.

With his uncle's dead body at his feet and Nonie still screaming from above, Mattice knew he had to do something or would die there too. The boathand wondered whether these pirates would let him live if he surrendered but his gut told him otherwise. He then thought about restarting the boat's engine and making a break for it but knew that would only tip off the ambushers someone onboard still lived. The same was true about firing back even as his grip on the rifle tightened because of a desire to avenge his brother's death.

"Lord," Mattice beckoned as he dropped his rifle then kneeled upon the deck even as the pirates closed in, "I am neither righteous nor worthy enough to ask this of you but please Lord, please be my shepherd as you were David's and guide me through this valley of death I find myself in, for I do not want to die by the hands of these pirates. Humbly, I ask this of you."

After praying, Mattice recalled the splashes he heard earlier and looked behind the boat. There, about one hundred meters back, he spotted the shaman's dog swimming towards one of the islands. Mattice scanned for the others but saw no one and wondered if they already made it to shore? Regardless, he accepted this as a sign and in a leap of faith jumped overboard.

Once in the water, Mattice somehow eluded the ambushers as they circled about the *Anna Maria* several times before coming alongside. He wanted to swim as hard as he could but instead just let the current pull him along towards the pass where once through, he could swim to the backside of one of the islands. The slow pace alarmed him but at least he kept moving further away from the death and confusion. He would never be able to forget those haunting images – still Mattice thanked God for sparing him from that ruin.

The boathand only made it downstream as far as the spot where the birds first gave the pirates away when his wounded arm started to throb. Mattice had been wrong earlier – the gunshot penetrated deeper than it looked and the water aggravated the wound. Like a fisherman's chum line, a plume of blood trailed behind him all the way back to the boat. A trail gone unseen by Mattice, as well as the ambushers, but not by another of God's creatures.

Crazed by the blood rich water, they attacked all at once and with such overwhelming force, the boathand thought he had run into one of those blackened stumps submerged beneath the surface. Already wincing in pain from the bullet wound, the collision inflamed the fire within his shoulder. Shearing pain, numbing pain, blazed from his arm into the very core of his body. He tried to knock it away but his arm remained entangled. Then, in a moment of true terror, Mattice watched the river around him boil up as a pot upon a stove and he knew his horrid fate.

Powered by muscular jaws with razor sharp teeth, dozens of piranhas ripped Mattice's arm from its socket and carried it away towards the bottom of the Rio Negro. For one brief but ghastly second as his head slipped beneath the surface, the boathand saw pairs of red eyes coming towards him. Bite after bite they carved away at Mattice until his organs were exposed. Blood poured from his body and turned the water red as wine as they feasted upon him until nothing but bones remained.

3
MODUS PONENS

When the speedboat came alongside the *Anna Maria*, a man wearing a pair of shiny black leather boots first boarded. He stood rigid with an automatic rifle at his waist with the already smoking barrel out in front of him and his itchy finger upon the well-worn trigger. He then pivoted in a broad sweep of the deck, ready to cut down anything that moved. Once satisfied, he made his way towards the bow of the boat. The even stride of his gait reeked of his self-confidence with the resounding rap of his boot heels upon the wooden planks.

"Here's one," he announced after coming across Marcos lying behind the storage crate with the dart still in his hand. "Damn good shot but that's not him," he added after flipping the body over. "Start dowsing everything while I keep looking."

Another man, an indian with a bold red stripe running down the middle of his face, then crossed over to the *Anna Maria*. Draped over his shoulder hung the blowgun he used to bring down Marcos. For the moment though, in one hand he wielded a machete and in the other a plastic tank filled to the brim with gasoline. Without any fanfare, he did as told and poured the fuel out over the deck. All along, his body ached for someone to still be alive, even more so than his partner.

"Prey," the indian said when he reached the wheelhouse. "Prey – Prey," he repeated with a fiery look in his eyes that made it hard to tell whether he or the fuel was more volatile. "Prey – Prey."

"It's just that fat old slob of a captain," the man with the black boots shrugged after coming over and looking. "Him and his damn monkey."

"Are there any other bodies?" the driver of the speedboat inquired.

"No – but I know I shot him – he must have fallen overboard."

"Hurry up then," the driver insisted. "We'll have to look for him."

"Go back – I'll finish up here," the man with the black boots said to the indian with a finger pointed towards the speedboat.

Desperate for a release of the savage emotions that always besieged him, the indian stood his ground. Unsettled as quicksand he first glared over at his partner, then the driver of the speedboat, then shifted his sinister gaze back and forth between the two of them. For a moment he seemed poised to strike at them but eventually set the tank of fuel down then turned his attention towards Nonie, who still hung from the rafters of the wheel house.

Just as with Mattice, the wooly monkey screamed as the indian stepped over Captain Jack's dead body. Unlike before though, the fretful warning went unheeded because the indian reached up indifferent and plucked Nonie from her roost. Afterwards he brought the monkey outside then slung her across the deck.

Incensed by the flurry of brutality, Nonie rushed forward while the indian held his ground and savored the creature's response. As her scream turned into a snarl, his eyes grew wilder. As her muscles summoned their strength, his grip tightened firmer upon his machete. He saw not a lone monkey in front of him but a thousand images to despise, waiting until the last possible second then—

Swoosh!!

All the tension built up in the indian's body gushed out in one bone-crunching swipe of his razor sharp machete. It found the nape of Nonie's neck and separated the monkey's head from its body. The torso toppled within inches of the indian's feet while the head rolled back towards the wheelhouse. In a single motion the indian then scooped up his prize and raised the dead monkey's body high above him along with his blood stained machete.

"Ohanaa, toa ayaa freem," the indian triumphed in his native tongue. "Ohanaa, toa ayaa freem," he boasted over and over with an unmistakable sly smile towards his companions. "Rana, I am fierce!"

"Enough," the driver of the speedboat proclaimed.

"Oh, let him have his fun," the man wearing the black boots said after picking up the head and tossing it overboard but not before poking in jest at the eyes. "He needs that – it's like a stiff drink or a big old fat cigar – or a poke – that's just how he unwinds."

"His needs," the driver scoffed while preparing a flare to ignite the gasoline. "His needs are of no concern – finding that body – that's what you should be concerned about."

As the speedboat backed away from the *Anna Maria*, one by one the wooden planks fell as dominoes to the fire until the entire deck blazed out of control. Choking black smoke soon billowed up into the once pristine air. The smell of burning hair and flesh spoiled it as well. Then without warning, an enormous explosion blanketed the sky and echoed throughout the cove followed by another and then another until very little remained of Captain Jack's beloved boat.

"This will make people think twice about coming here," the man in the shiny black boots declared as he watched the fiery remnants of the *Anna Maria* float downstream until beaching near the pass.

"The work of pirates no less," the driver of the speedboat expounded while snapping several pictures. "But we still need to find that body – so keep an eye out as we head up stream."

As the boat barreled further up into the cove, the indian pointed to something floating in the water. The driver of the boat made an abrupt turn then rode the engines even harder as they headed over towards a patch of lilies and hyacinths just offshore of the southern island. Within seconds the ambushers reached the spot in hopes of finding Kyle Preston's body but instead found only a tattered leather-bound book.

"I told you I got him," the man in the black boots howled.

"Maybe," the driver cautioned while looking around, "or maybe he dropped that as he jumped overboard."

"No – I shot him," the man in the black boots insisted. "I shot him and killed him!"

"What about the other boathand or the indian or even his dog – none of them were onboard – does that mean you shot them as well?"

"Who cares about them – you yourself said the scientist was your only concern."

"He is," the driver remarked, "but you're forgetting what my associate said about returning without proof."

"We've got proof," the man in the black boots said as he retrieved the journal from the river.

"That won't do and you know it," the driver stated.

"It will have to because nothing survives for too long in these waters, especially once injured."

"Prey," the indian butted in as he pointed this time over to shore.

"You were saying," the driver of the speedboat blurted while watching a dog shake the water from its coat.

"Damn luck but that's about to change," the man with the black boots muttered while pulling a pistol out of its shoulder holster and taking aim at Cleto.

The gun crackled louder than thunder and drove out several blue-masked torrents hidden within the nearby patch of lilies and hyacinths. Two of the ducks rose no more than a few meters up into the air before the man in the shiny black boots took aim and dropped them. A third he let fly back behind him then turned and shot it as well. Afterwards, he put his gun back into its holster with the air choked with smoke, smoke and the unmistakable sound of a dog wincing in pain.

"Still have any doubts about whether I hit him?"

"We're going to circle around a couple more times," the driver said unfazed by the display of marksmanship. "Keep in mind, without real proof, you'll be going to the airport without me because I'll be in Manaus – just in case Kyle Preston did survive."

4
INDISPUTABLE

From its cruising altitude of thirty-seven thousand feet, a sleek Learjet slipped down below the clouds then made several turns in preparation of landing. Just minutes before a tumultuous thunderstorm from the southwest dropped over two inches of rain upon the Boa Vista International Airport before moving on. Now with the sun back overhead, steam rose from the surrounding asphalt as if expelled from newly formed volcanic rock. Intermixed with this primordial mist festered the noxious wash from several large commercial airliners lined up out upon the taxiway in wait for clearance to take off.

Reports by most of the major international carriers warned of delays in Boa Vista due to weather. Located at a natural boundary between the Guyana Highlands and the Amazon Basin, the city received more than its share of rain compared to neighboring towns along the same latitude. Most of the time the controllers up in the tower kept a pretty good handle on things but this last storm caught even them by surprise.

The storm signaled the Amazon's rainy season indeed approached and yet it was not of much consequence to the pilots of the Learjet as the plane flared just a few meters above the runway then touched down. These were experienced men accustomed to flying into places all around the world and in every imaginable condition, which was why SynRx paid them almost three times the going rate to retain their services. Money the company gladly paid to insure the safety of its executives as the jet came to rest in front of a private hangar.

With an imposing aura to match his gooseberry appearance, Nathan Briers seemed more executioner than executive. His eyes, large and hypnotic, sparkled a brilliant emerald green but shivered those who waded into their frostbitten depths. Clean-shaven only around the mouth and chin, he stroked his muttonchops whenever dispensing holier-than-thou judgements without the moral mettle himself. Sharp words fashioned within a tight framework of four precise yet pretentious tenets he shared with only his closest associates. Shared and followed with the clarity of zealots in answering the call of the martyr.

As Nathan Briers departed, he grabbed his luggage including a steel-sided case stamped with a logo identical to one on the side of the plane. As usual the SynRx executive said nothing to the pilots as he passed the cockpit but then stopped momentarily at the outer doorway and mouthed something to himself as he looked down upon the two men waiting for him at the bottom of the stairs.

Darkly tanned with clothes unspoiled by sweat, Ian Haleem appeared accustomed to the hot humid conditions of Amazonas. His golden hair, rugged jaw, and bright blue eyes juxtaposed a man of pure Aryan stock but his name betrayed that assumption and rightly so. Even Father Mario, the most forgiving of the local abbey's clergy, remarked he embodied a bastard in every sense of the word and appeared as unsettled as the seed that sewed him.

If only Ian's accomplishments mirrored his handsome looks or his reputation shined as bright as the black leather boots he wore but neither were the case. Instead, decent people avoided him altogether because they heard rumors, whispers of the horrible truth, that he would kill anyone for a price. A greed-driven man in a soulless profession where even the speed and ease of second nature meant coming in dead last. Only the whores of the brothels along the Rua da Uniao, the bartenders in the adjoining saloons, and the hustlers outside in the alleys enjoyed seeing him coming.

Next to the bounty hunter stood his fiery partner, Rana, whose reputation vilified him to be just as unsavory, if not more, but for far different reasons. He was an Yanomamo, a member of a tribe of indians indigenous to northwest Brazil near the Venezuelan border that anthropologists deemed the fiercest of people. Hot-tempered, deceptive, manipulative, and arrogant – traits all Yanomamo shared besides being excellent warriors. Rana's passion for killing however, exceeded even his own people's tolerance limit, and he had been forced to live as an outcast. A ruthless renegade fueled by a heart of brimstone with a penchant to dangle the severed heads of his victims from their own intestines.

More so than his inbred vile nature, Rana's appearance unnerved people. A wolf amongst sheep, his name-brand clothes couldn't hide the self-mutilated, concentric lines tattooed above and below his eyes. A feather from a keel-billed toucan poked through his right ear in two places with one of the bird's clawed, blue feet attached to the quill so that it dangled below the lobe as an earring. Moreover, several large knots on the top of his clean-shaven head showed off the battle scars from club fighting – each bump a testament to his fierceness from a ritual only the strongest Yanomamo survived.

Of everything though, the most unsettling thing about Rana's appearance stemmed from the bright red band that ran down the center of his face. Known as a "blood stripe," all Yanomamo wore such a mark with it rumored to be the blood from their last kill. Whether true or not, the effect went beyond intimidation. A mask that empowered his uncivilized eyes to express more in a single glare than any prose scripted by the best of poets.

"How was your flight?" Ian yelled into Nathan's ear as he stepped down from the plane and onto the tarmac.

"Suffice to say I'm here so spare me the small talk,"

Nathan retorted. He waited a minute for the deafening whine of the jet's twin turbine engines to subside then added. "What I want to know is why the attack did not go as planned?"

"It did," Ian proclaimed. "We waited out of sight on the other side of the pass then ambushed them when there was no chance of escape."

"Then why are just the two of you here," Nathan asked while stroking the whiskers of his muttonchops.

"Well," Ian explained, "your associate insisted on going to Manaus. If you ask me they over-reacted because I think—"

"You think, Nathan Briers growled stopping Ian in mid sentence just as one of the commercial airliners roared down the runway. "I'm not paying you to think!"

"We found this," Ian mentioned as he held the waterlogged journal out in front of him. "He must have dropped it when he fell overboard."

"That proves nothing," Nathan Briers said while at the same time snatching the log. "Did you look?", he then asked as he thumbed through the entries. "Some of these are still legible."

"No boss man," Ian stated without hesitation. "Now hand over the money," he said looking at the briefcase. "We did our part."

"Really," Nathan scoffed. "I told you when you took this job you'd have to bring back indisputable proof in order to get paid. Given your reputation as well as your partner's, I expected to see Kyle Preston's head right now

– maybe not served on a platter mind you but something close to it. Instead, you show me his tattered journal and expect me to accept that as proof you killed him. Tell me – what part of indisputable did you not understand?"

"Now what?" Ian asked a few minutes later after watching the last two jets delayed by the storm finally take off.

"Until hearing differently – we assume the worse," Nathan insisted. "We assume Mr. Preston is still alive."

"Well, if he is," Ian boasted as he wiped a smudge of clay off one of his boots, "he won't be for long!"

"First, there's a little unsettled business here to attend to," Nathan mentioned in passing. "Something I think you'll both enjoy."

5
IN THE THICKET OF THINGS

With his cherished knapsack dragging him into the murky depths of the Rio Negro, Kyle Preston struggled to free himself. Further and further he fell into a swill darker and more baleful than anything he ever imagined – a black soup where he feared piranhas and caimans hovered just inches from his face. A purée of predators brewed into a frenzy just for this moment – a moment in which he was to be served.

When the bag hit the bottom, a massive plume of sediment shot up into the water then fell back down like snow. Even with the new found slack though, Kyle could not untangle his leg from the strap because the leather had swelled and become too slimy for him to work the knots. He then tried to empty the bag but the zipper to the main compartment jammed. In desperation he held the bag within his arms and kicked with his legs but its burden was too great to overcome. The ethnobotanist knew then his destiny, if not his doom, to be devoured like everything else that disappeared into these black waters.

With that acceptance, Kyle wondered if he would know the exact moment of his death or whether it would just happen? Oddly, he rationalized an answer to that question tied to the burning in his lungs. That pain meant he still lived and even though surreal for him to do so, KP counted each second that passed. Counting as if collecting data, which made him think about Stephen Lowery and wonder if he might have done the very same thing before he died?

With the count at seventeen Kyle heard several clicks echo through the water. A second later something huge brushed up against him, sending a shiver down his spine. Halfheartedly, the ethnobotanist swatted in the darkness at whatever hovered there but couldn't defend himself as it tugged upon him.

Sketchy at best, Kyle's recollection of the next few seconds flirted with miracle. He couldn't remember at what point the tugging stopped, or how his leg became untangled, or even pushing off from the bottom. He only knew that he was free from the bag and rising quickly upwards – rising more and more with each passing second. Precious seconds, which begged the question, like his burning lungs – would he make it in time? Would he breathe again?

When Kyle broke the water's surface he expelled the spent air from his lungs and took a breath unlike any before. Each molecule of oxygen gushed with a dreamy sweetness as they brought life back into his failing body. He savored that smell as well as the sound and the feel of the fresh air rushing inside him. They were overwhelming sensations that cooled the burning in his lungs and quieted the pounding of his heart. Sensations that for the moment at least made him forget how close he came to dying.

As Kyle took a second and even deeper breath he felt overjoyed yet startled to see Brooklyn pop up next to him. The shaman forced a smile but couldn't hide something bothered him. Puzzled more as to how his friend rescued him, Kyle started to ask that very question when an enormous explosion erupted downstream. Both men turned and watched in horror as a huge fireball shot up into the sky. Two more explosions followed but by then Brooklyn grabbed Kyle by his shirt and yanked him beneath the surface.

Seconds later a speedboat rambled their way and Kyle watched as its shadow passed overhead. Afterwards, the two friends re-surfaced near one of the floating meadows growing out in the pass. Then after helping each other through a maze of long stringy roots from the plants above, they emerged within the thicket but covered with debris and algae.

Twenty meters wide and easily three times as long the patch provided excellent cover. Each of the lilies sprawled out almost a meter across in diameter – their edges rolled upwards with the rest of the spongy yellow-green pads lying flat upon the water's surface. The hyacinths on the other hand grew more bushy with glossy dark green leaves and vibrant purple blooms that rose up almost an half meter above the water. Collectively, the plants offered an excellent place to hide but the river still ran too deep for either Brooklyn or Kyle to touch the bottom.

"Ugh," Kyle blurted as he exhaled then wiped away some of the algae from around his eyes and nose. "I don't know how much more of this I can take. What the hell happened?"

"Shhh," Brooklyn squeaked as a mouse with his finger over his mouth.

"My god, that's the *Anna Maria* on fire – isn't it," Kyle Preston said as he looked downstream where the explosion occurred. "What about the others?"

"No talk," the shaman whispered while listening to the speedboat.

"But the others," Kyle pleaded with Brooklyn despite his repeated warning. "What about Captain Jack, Marcos, or Mattice – we should look for them."

"No – just us, now no more talk," Brooklyn insisted just as the speedboat idled within a few boat lengths of them.

Deep down, Kyle Preston knew his friend was right. In planning this expedition the ethnobotanist downplayed the dangers, especially the threat bandits posed because all of his previous trips to South America went so well. The worst crimes he envisioned revolved around someone stealing money or maybe a piece of equipment while at the airport or at the hotel in Manaus. Granted the thought occurred to him that their base camp would be vulnerable while they were off at the field site but he dismissed those concerns given how remote both sites were. Maybe he should have been more careful – more cautious about travelling the river. After all, KP had heard horror stories from some of his colleagues and read recent accounts in the newspapers about just how ruthless and desperate some pirates had become.

Such desperation tormented Kyle because it meant the others might very well be dead. He then wondered if Captain Jack or either of his nephews felt abandoned? Abandoned because Kyle now realized that Brooklyn must have sensed something was wrong and pushed him overboard just as the attack started. The two of them trailed behind the *Anna Maria* while those still onboard headed straight to their deaths. A fate Kyle felt he cheated but now found himself facing yet again with the speedboat just a stone's throw away.

"Can you hear what they're saying," Kyle whispered over to Brooklyn, breaking the short-lived silence between them.

"No," the shaman answered.

"Me neither – that engine is grumbling too loud to make anything out."

"There," one of ambushers yelled!

Time came to a stand still as the two friends tread water and waited for what would happen next. KP trembled so badly the plants around him began to shake as well. Brooklyn reached out with his arm and locked onto to Kyle's shoulder. Then together they steadied each other, knowing only that the kindred bond between grew stronger. A bond only death could break.

Kabaam!!

A single gunshot crackled louder than thunder with the bullet whizzing just above their heads. Then almost at the same time three blue-masked torrents hidden just to the right of Kyle darted out of the patch squawking as they took flight. Before two of the birds even got a few meters up into the air they were shot dead while the third raced farther up into the sky only to be killed as well. Then the gun fell silent with the air choked with smoke, smoke and the unmistakable sound of a dog wincing in pain.

"I'm sorry," was all that Kyle could say as the two of them continued to tread water and listen to the dog cry while the speedboat circled around in the cove. "I'm sorry for all of this."

6
CABOCLOS

As loyal as his dog, Brooklyn defined the phrase "friend for life." Despite their vast differences, Kyle never questioned his loyalty. Never doubted he would do anything without even being asked. The ethnobotanist even joked back home, Brooklyn exemplified the type of friend that would not bail you out of jail after trouble, but instead, would be right there with you in the cell.

Native to the northeastern part of Surinam, Brooklyn was a Tirio Indian accustomed to life in the forest. Unlike Kyle, who sweated each step he took, Brooklyn flowed along with a grace equal to any creature in the jungle. His sense of direction relied not upon some satellite in the sky but only subtle signs within the forest to guide him. Whereas Kyle swatted at things with his slingshot, Brooklyn could fillet his target with an arrow from his bow. There was just no pretense about him – Brooklyn could survive in the jungle under any condition.

Any one of these strengths would have been reason enough for Kyle to bring his friend along on this expedition but Brooklyn was also a shaman – a very unlikely position given his tribe's last medicine man had been his great grandfather nearly a half century earlier.

For the Tirio and many other indigenous people of Amazonas, their culture and heritage wavered on the brink of extinction until the approval of several landmark initiatives. One of those resolutions called for the formation of an institute to preserve the art of traditional healers known as The Shaman's Apprentice School. Located in Manaus on the grounds of an international research center, it resulted from an agreement brokered between large Western pharmaceutical companies and a federation of indigenous people known as IPOTA.

While most drug companies believed the potential of synthetic drugs remained limitless, they also knew one quarter of all prescription drugs came from plant derived chemicals for their active ingredients. The school therefore offered a centralized location of different remedies with a high probability for a profitable new drug. In return, all the various tribes could send representatives from their villages to learn traditional cures, which was where the two friends met.

Empowered by his ancestral heritage, Brooklyn could identify hundreds of plants and their use as foods, drugs, or poisons. He knew the craft of making potions – some for healing – some for soothing – some for dreaming – others for killing. All enshrouded by either a dance, or a chant, or a spell, and always with the summons of spirits. As a shaman he performed the role of doctor, scientist, and priest for his people.

Dressed in traditional Tirio attire, Brooklyn wore only a red breechcloth with a small, animal-hide satchel tied to his waist. His long jet black hair darted through the cross section of a decorated animal bone then ran down to his shoulders. Blue vertical lines striped his painted body while red dots in the form of triangles and diamonds embroidered his face. He stood only five feet tall – almost a foot shorter than Kyle but lacked nothing in terms of stature.

"How bad?" Kyle asked once they were ashore and Brooklyn had had a chance to look at Cleto.

"The ear is shredded but that is all," Brooklyn announced with a sigh of relief. "I will search for some Ajuna berries to stop the bleeding."

While Brooklyn attended to his dog's wound, Kyle rushed down the beach towards the pass to where the *Anna Maria* ran aground. Only the bow of the boat remained afloat although engulfed in flames. Kyle waded out to the wreck but the blistery heat from the fire forced him to retreat. Seconds later the batteries stowed away in one of the crates exploded and sent hot acid into the air. Afterwards, the remaining remnants of the expedition still onboard slid across the deck and sank into the water.

"Is anyone there," Kyle shouted in dismay with a sense the rest of the boat was about to go under. "Captain Jack, Mattice, Mar—"

Kyle's nose told him flesh and hair burned but it was one thing to smell such a foul and rancorous odor and another to see a body consumed in such a manner. At first he saw only an outstretched hand, charred and still smoldering, but a hand nonetheless. Afterwards the dubious corpse slid across the deck and into clear view but was so badly burned, Kyle could not recognize who it was.

When the bow of the *Anna Maria* finally slipped beneath the water, Kyle watched the bubbles from the wreck rise to the surface and hoped for a miracle. Eventually the gurgling subsided though and the black water of the Rio Negro once again flowed smoothly through the cove with the glimmer of sunlight. Still, for Kyle, this Eden had lost its luster as he tried to make sense out of the senselessness.

As Kyle Preston turned to head back, he noticed a case of Yoo-hoo floating upside down just a few meters from shore. He waded out into the water to retrieve the drinks with most of the bottles still intact. Somehow, with all that had just happened, a slight smile managed to break upon KP's somber face as he remembered losing a bet with his friend over the drinks. He then hoisted the case upon his shoulder, lowered his head, and started walking along the beach.

Halfway back, KP finally raised his head surprised to see someone in a small wooden dugout at the far end of the cove. The ethnobotanist waved but the stranger simply continued to paddle. Kyle then quickened his pace to reach Brooklyn before the newcomer arrived.

"Oi," the man said in Portuguese at first as he dragged his homemade canoe onto shore. "I am Ocho Jesus Candido," he then said in English after looking at Kyle and pegging him for an American.

Ocho's broad nose, dwarfish build and coppery complexion did not match his Old World pedigree. In the eyes of most Brazilians he was a Caboclos, an half-breed looked down upon because of having indian ancestry. Kyle found it an ironic bigotry, given the extent of intermixing by the descendants of the Portuguese explorers with other ethnic groups within the country. Still, Caboclos were despised, even more than the indigenous people, despite being honest and hard-working river folk who normally kept to themselves except to trade.

"Have you seen anyone else?" Kyle demanded. "There were five of us."

"No – what happened?"

"We were attacked," Kyle said, "our ship destroyed."

"Then we must leave at once," Ocho insisted as if from experience. "Many bad people on the river these days – very dangerous."

"I don't understand – all the supplies were still onboard – why didn't they take anything?"

"Maybe they wanted to protect what they already had," Ocho replied then added, "Could be Coca – could be guns."

"You mean it was just our damn luck that we ran

across them," Kyle smarted while looking back to where the *Anna Maria* had gone down.

"Maybe – or maybe it was meant to happen – it is best you come with me," Ocho declared while corralling them towards his dugout.

"We need to get to Manaus," Kyle stated before climbing into the boat. "Can you takes us?"

"Too far," the Caboclos replied. "Much too far."

"Please," Kyle begged. "I know it's a lot to ask."

"I will take you as far as Ariua," Ocho finally conceded. "From there you can make arrangements with the Tower's staff for their boat to take you. That is the best I can do."

"Thank you," Kyle said in earnest. "We're fortunate you came along when you did."

Ocho opened his mouth as if to say something but then changed his mind. Instead, he steadied the dugout while Brooklyn and Kyle climbed aboard then jumped in as well. The three of them were squashed as sardines up against one another with the shaman and his dog up front, Kyle in the middle sitting atop the case of Yoo-hoo, and Ocho in the back with the only paddle.

"Hey, whoa, wait a minute," Kyle blurted before they had even gotten underway. "We're already sinking," he said as water dribbled in over the sides of the canoe. "We'll never make it."

"Here," Ocho said as he tossed a small tin cup to Kyle. "Try to keep up."

7
MAGIC SPARKLING IN THEIR EYES

Around midday the small wooden dugout turned up a nameless meander of a creek that flowed into the Rio Negro along its southern shore. The stream soon narrowed to only the length of the canoe as if being squished and squeezed by the surrounding jungle. Overhead the lower canopy closed in as well, forcing Kyle and the others to push wads of stringy growth out of their way. At any moment it appeared the creek would come to an end and they would have to walk if they were to go any further. Then without rhyme or reason, the creek opened into a sprawling marsh full of cattails and spindly sedges with a flock of double-banded ibis trolling either shore for fresh water clams.

Across the way, Kyle could see a small shack sitting out over the water. Common practice among the river folk of Amazonas, the house floated freely upon several logs cut from mature Andiroba that had been debarked then coated with the trees own boiled-down sap.

Treated in this manner, these timbers could stay afloat for several years before becoming waterlogged but more importantly, they allowed the house to rise and fall with the seasonal variations in the river.

"Welcome, welcome," Ocho said after he tied the dugout to a narrow walkway built atop several metal barrels alongside the shack.

"How much further to Ariau?" Kyle asked disappointed that Ocho turned to come home, especially since their odds of finding someone going to Manaus dwindled, if not disappeared altogether, on this side creek.

"Another hour or so," Ocho answered as he helped Kyle and Brooklyn onto the dock.

"That close," Kyle noted. "And how long until nightfall?"

"Tonight you are my guest," Ocho insisted despite Kyle's anxious demeanor. "Tomorrow I will take you to the hotel."

Reluctant at first, KP followed Ocho onto shore then looked back at the Caboclos' home. The faded yellow shack seemed dabbed more with amazon clay than with paint. The roof resembled a mosaic of rusted tin fitted together as pieces in a jig saw puzzle. The walls connected just as shabbily with no glass in any of the windows. Instead, large wooden shutters dangled around each opening to stop the elements from coming inside when it rained. Right now, with the sun overhead, those shutters were flipped back and from the window closest to him, Kyle could see several pairs of eyes peering out at him.

"Oi!" the ethnobotanist called out but no one answered.

"Don't take it personally," Ocho yelled over to Kyle. "My family is very shy – in fact, my children have never seen an estrangeiros like yourself but I'm sure they'll come around."

From where they stood outside the doorway, Brooklyn and Kyle could hear Ocho describe to his wife the events of his morning. He told her about going over to the cove to check on some turtle traps and while there had done some fishing. Next he told her that after starting home he heard several gunshots and a couple of loud explosions soon followed by a massive plume of smoke rising up into the air. He decided to paddle back to see what happened. For her part, Ocho's wife seemed leery of inviting them inside but then Ocho mentioned someone's name and the conversation came to an abrupt halt.

"Come," Ocho invited once he reappeared at the door.

Once inside, seven pairs of eyes besieged Brooklyn and Kyle. Besides the Caboclos and his wife, five children under the age of twelve stood with only a pair of shorts on, including the younger girls. Each resembled the other with jet-black hair and eyes to match. Ocho did his best to introduce his family but as he called each one by name, they hesitated to step forward.

After the introductions, Kyle scanned the one room shack while the children continued to gawk at him and

Brooklyn. In the corner to his left a ripe bunch of plantains hung from the ceiling by a piece of heavy twine. Along those two walls, some wooden spikes driven into the supporting beams jutted out from which to hang hammocks. Overhead a rusted kerosene lantern swayed from another piece of twine while over in the far corner by a window a hodgepodge of spent candles littered a table forged from a shipping crate. Next to the crate, two rough-looking stools rested on the sand-covered floor along with a pile of hand-made trinkets fashioned from braided marsh grass and snail shells. To the right of the work area, another window provided more light followed by a framed picture of Christ and then another window. Then finally, over in the corner to his right, the ethnobotanist saw a small child dozing on a woven throw stretched out over the shack's wooden floor.

"That's Tatiana, my youngest daughter," Ocho offered before Kyle Preston could ask.

Kyle then recalled Ocho saying her name in the conversation with his wife. The little girl looked to be around three or four years old with long black hair down past her shoulders. For the moment though, her hair drooped ruffled and drenched with sweat. In fact, beads of moisture rolled off of her one right after the other despite a washcloth dowsed with water upon her head. Even more disturbing though was the condition of her right foot – it sagged swollen almost twice its normal size with the skin discolored the shade of a rotten plum.

"What happened," Kyle asked as he walked over and bent down beside her.

"She stepped on a stingray three days ago," Ocho said then continued. "The barb broke off inside her foot so we had to cut it out. Since then we've tried to keep the wound clean but yesterday morning she started to run a fever and by nightfall she stopped eating or drinking."

"Help her," Ocho's wife pleaded, stepping out in front of her husband. "I can not bear the thought of losing my baby."

Even before Kyle Preston had kneeled down, he knew the little girl would die unless she received immediate medical attention. A gloomy judgement confirmed by his examination of the wound while listening to the mother relay more details about Tatiana's condition. Then while pressing around the wound, Kyle forced some vile-smelling puss out, which gagged almost everyone in the room. Remarkably, the girl never flinched a muscle, which meant she had already lost feeling in her leg.

"Definitely *Clostridium*," Kyle noted but doubted Ocho and his wife knew what that meant. "Bacteria – it's in her bloodstream."

"She is the reason you were spared," Ocho proclaimed after removing the washcloth from his daughter's forehead. He then dipped it into a bucket of water and replaced it on her head. "I believe God allowed me to find you in order to save our Tatiana."

"Normally I could do something but I lost all of my medical supplies when our boat went down," Kyle apologized then turned and looked back at Brooklyn. "Can you?"

"Needs powerful medicines," the shaman stated from across the room, "Spirits too."

After spending several hours scouring the nearby forest, Brooklyn and Kyle returned and started to prepare for the healing ceremony. They placed several pouches made from banana leaves on the ground along with an array of leafy branches and clumps of various mosses. Next they made a bed out of palm fronds and pillows from marsh grass for both Tatiana's head and swollen foot. Then after building a fire, Brooklyn stoked the coals while Kyle fetched some water in a kettle Ocho's wife gave them.

"Is there anything else?" Kyle asked after returning from the river.

"No more can I ask of you," Brooklyn replied. "The rest is between me and the spirits."

With that said, Kyle Preston backed away and sat down on a log he pulled from a woodpile. A few minutes later KP realized all of Ocho's children hid nearby in the bushes and trees. The ethnobotanist thought for a second then stood up and walked over to the shack and out onto the dock. He grabbed the case of Yoo-hoo he salvaged from the wreck and brought it over to his makeshift seat.

"Delicioso," Kyle announced as he rubbed his stomach. He then reached down and grabbed another bottle and held it out in front of him.

One by one, children popped out of their hiding places and crept over to where Kyle sat. They stood lined up in front of him for the longest time until the eldest boy, who looked to be around ten years old, overcame his fear and reached for the drink. Kyle then held another bottle out in front of him and this time one of the younger girls stepped forward. Before long each child held an Yoo-hoo in their hands and mimicked Kyle by rubbing their tummies when they drank.

——Sizzle, Snap, Popped!!!

All at once, the children spun back around towards the fire and watched in amazement as a purplish plume rose out of the kettle. Then their noses, including Kyle's, began to twitch as a bittersweet vapor wandered past them. Almost as if a curtain call, each of them immediately found a place to sit and waited to see what would happen next.

From their front row seats the children watched as Brooklyn opened up the first pouch which contained a large orange and gray toad. He held it firmly by its back legs while still wrapped within the banana leaf. Chanting deep and slow, the shaman waived the amphibian over the pot and almost immediately a glossy mucus exuded from its back. The Tirio then grabbed a piece of moss and scraped some of the sticky fluid off the toad's back then released the animal back into the forest. Stopping his guttural chant, the shaman dropped the peculiar ingredient into the kettle, where upon hitting the water it produced a creamy white foam and another tickling smell.

At seeing this, one of the younger boys ran over to the house and yelled to his parents about what he had seen. In his high squeaky voice he spoke excitedly about the witch doctor, the tickling smoke, and the toad. He seemed thrilled beyond imagine at the prospects of his sister drinking such a concoction. So much so, that he fell twice when he ran back over to his seat.

And so it went, with each ingredient after that, one of the children would run over to the shack, yell something to their parents, then race back to the wood pile hoping not to have missed anything. For nearly an hour it continued this way while Brooklyn prepared two tonics and a salve. Then as the sun began to set and darkness crept in around them, Brooklyn announced it was time.

For her part, Tatiana already seemed spellbound when her parents carried her out of the shack and placed the little girl down upon the palm fronds. Over the last couple of hours they tried everything they could to lower her fever but she still dripped with sweat and now twitched and sometimes jerked with seizures. If possible, Kyle thought her leg looked even worse than before and doubted she would survive the night.

As the ceremony began, Kyle could see everyone's face from his vantage point. He noticed how Brooklyn's eyes beamed with brilliance and his eyebrows danced upon his forehead in rhythm with his chants. The expressions on the children's faces seemed to rise and fall within this cadence as well with their eyes at times about to bulge out of their sockets – especially when the shaman squished ushuh berries upon their sister's body to create a complex but decorative pattern of red triangles and zigzagging lines similar to the ones on his own body. Only the rumpled up faces of Ocho and his wife seemed to be in discord with the mystery and pageantry.

At one point KP closed his eyes and just listened as Brooklyn spoke in his native tongue of Saran Tongo and summoned several spirits to come to his aid. The shaman first called upon his own grandfather to stand beside him and guide him with his wisdom. Next he called upon Oa Emana Ta, the fierce jaguar god, to battle the evil spirit that had entered the little girl's body and force it to leave. The shaman then thanked Bobo Unata, the god of the forest for providing the plants and animals used in making the different medicines and humbly asked that their magic be used to heal the little girl. Finally, Brooklyn called upon the spirits of Tatiana's own ancestors to hold her soul to her body and comfort the undoubtedly frightened little girl.

When the wondrous oracle ended and Kyle opened his eyes he found Ocho and his wife standing in front of him. Abashed emotions flickered upon their faces more than the flames within the fire. They languished in agony over the thought of losing their daughter but at the same time struggled with the very meaning of this ritual.

"Earlier I consented to this but now, now I'm not so sure," Ocho relayed to Kyle as they watched Brooklyn force Tatiana to drink one of the tonics. "Our faith in the Lord has always been the one thing that has seen us through difficult times but now, now we stand by and watch as your friend summons spirits."

"We all view things differently," Kyle interrupted trying to diffuse the situation. "It's true – my friend is convinced there are spirits and that something miraculous happens during these ceremonies. I on the other hand believe the power to heal your daughter will come from the plants we collected. There's really nothing magical about it and if there were, who's to say it wasn't God lending a hand?"

"But my children are already singing the praises of this witch doctor."

"Listen – right now there's magic sparkling in their eyes but don't second guess your own convictions," the ethnobotanist implored. "Earlier you said that your prayers had been answered. I can't tell you I believe that – or that I even have faith in a god, but as long as you still believe that than so will they."

"No," Ocho Jesus Candido blurted when Brooklyn began to dance wildly around Tatiana's body. "We should have never agreed to this ceremony but rather accepted God's will without question. We must stop this and ask for his forgiveness."

"There's no sin in wanting your child to live," Kyle Preston countered. "Nor have you turned your back on God," he added while holding them back. "Let my friend try – let him believe what he wants and you believe what you want, and let your daughter have a chance to live – please, let the ceremony continue."

8
ANSWER

When Kyle awoke the next morning, his tired eyes opened to find the teeth-riddled grin of a caiman just inches from his nose. Without thinking, he hollered a string of expletives then scrambled backward on all fours until plowing into the woodpile. From all around him, the ethnobotanist heard laughter and as he regained his wits, Kyle Preston realized he once again fell prey to one of his friend's practical jokes.

"Brooklyn," Kyle yelled as he rose to his feet. "Brooklyn, Where are you!"

KP's vexed howls only brought on more laughter. Contagious titter at that – some extremely high pitched and giddy, more filled full of nose-crinkling snorts and eye-popping hoots, as well as the rolling baritone laugh of the shaman.

"Ha," Kyle smirked after his eyes fixed upon Brooklyn who stood with a dried caiman skull in his hands. "Maybe I—"

Just then the shutters to one of the shack's windows creaked opened and everyone fell silent. They had all slept outside while Ocho and his wife returned to the shack with Tatiana, but not before allowing the healing ceremony to continue. The ritual lasted late into the night and had been one of the most remarkable things Kyle ever witnessed. Even so, he seemed just as captivated right now as he looked over at the shack and wondered what would happen next.

"Come," Ocho uttered without an inkling of emotion in his voice.

Slowly Kyle walked over to the window while Brooklyn and the children remained behind. With each step, KP envisioned the most horrible and bleak scene his mind could conjure. So much so, by the time he reached the window, the ethnobotanist couldn't bear to look into the room but instead focused on Ocho.

For what seemed like a lifetime the two men stood there face to face. Each of them looking at the other for some hint as to what the other was feeling. A gaze so strong – so deep, as if they could see the very soul of the person standing across from them. Then finally, as a tear rolled down his cheek, Ocho moved a few steps back from the window and Kyle looked inside.

In the corner of the shack where he first saw Tatiana, the little girl rested curled up beside her mother. Through the window the morning sun illuminated them both. A simple scene of just a mother with her child, and yet to Kyle, nothing less than a miracle.

9
ARIAU JUNGLE TOWER

Within two hundred meters of turning up the Ariau Creek, Kyle caught a glimpse of the Amazon Towers Hotel. The lavish and exotic resort, comprised of a dozen or so buildings, had been built on stilts and nestled amongst the treetops of the forest. The resort's reputation revolved around its remote location while pandering to the delicate needs of the rich. Needs that included a heliport, aerial swimming pools, and two world-renowned observation towers that rose nearly fifty meters into the air. All interconnected by an elaborate catwalk that stretched nearly seven kilometers long as it fanned out into the jungle and down to the Rio Negro.

For Kyle, after spending the last two months cutoff from the rest of the world, such a place seemed surreal. Located just east of Anavilhanas at longitude $61.85°$ west and latitude $2.05°$ north, the Amazon Towers Hotel bedazzled the mind as it stood out from its surroundings as if some embellished shrine to a lost civilization or an elaborate outpost carved into the frontier. With Manaus still sixty kilometers further downstream, the hotel drew scads of tourists from around the world into the heart of Amazonas.

The insatiable appetite of those eco-tourist to experience firsthand anything deemed primitive reared its ugly head when Ocho brought his dugout alongside the hotel's main boat dock. All at once people swarmed around them. Several mauled Brooklyn as if a rock star and forced him to pose for countless pictures until some of the hotel's staff intervened.

"Attention everyone, we need to stay on schedule so please get back in your groups," one of the tour guides shouted as loud as he could. "Those of you going to the indian village need to move down to the far end of the dock. Everyone going piranha fishing should head over towards those boats over there. The rest of you follow me down to this corner for the jungle trek."

"Frank, if any of them speak English ask how much they want for that," a lady yelled in a thick New York accent while pointing to Brooklyn's pouch. "If not just grab it then waive a dollar in front of their noses because I want that for Theresa's little boy – you know how much he loves playing cowboys and indians."

"Reckon he's got any bloomers on beneath that?" another lady, this one with a British accent, asked to no one in particular as she bent down and scrutinized Brooklyn's breechcloth.

After ten minutes of sorted mayhem, the guides finally managed to get all of the tourists reorganized and seated into several motorized canoes. A few people still snapped pictures and talked up a storm over the unexpected encounter but by now most of them seemed eager for their next adventure. They smiled and waived to their friends who watched from the veranda above while the tour guides started up the engines to the boats. Then one by one the canoes embarked and disappeared around the bend.

"People, people, people," Kyle repeated shaking his head. "People can be so stupid at times," he added. "Is it always this crazy?"

"I don't know the hotel discourages locals from stopping," Ocho replied as he helped Brooklyn get Cleto out of the dugout. "They say it's bad for business and that things wind up missing when someone does stop. Several of us tried to barter for their leftovers but they would rather the animals eat them than us. Even now, they are watching, waiting around to make sure I leave."

"Damn bigots," KP griped after looking over his shoulder at two men keeping a watchful eye on Ocho just as he said. "And we call ourselves civilized. I'm going to say something."

"No, no – I must go, but thank you," Ocho insisted. "Thank you – thank you for saving my Tatiana. Thank you both."

"I should be thanking you," Kyle said as the three men exchange heartfelt embraces. "Meeting you and your family – well, its meant the world to me, especially after everything that's happened. You've reminded me why I'm here – for that I'm truly grateful."

After climbing up a steep set of stairs to the veranda, a hotel worker directed Brooklyn and Kyle over to the receptionist's desk. Without going into gory detail, the ethnobotanist explained their circumstances and asked to use the phone. The receptionist rolled her eyes in amusement then explained neither conventional nor cellular phone service were available due to the resort's remote location. She did however arrange passage for them on the next transfer ship then mentioned breakfast was still being served over in the community torre.

With their cylindrical shape and conical roofs, each torre, or tower resembled an enormous primitive hut. In actuality their wooden facades gave way to rather contemporary and posh accommodations. Most stood three stories tall with the larger ones decked out with close to fifty rooms. In all the resort encompassed six towers – four with guestrooms, one which served as the community building, and another grand torre with an auditorium on the first floor, a cultural museum on the second level, and an elegant dinning room at the very top.

The cafeteria the receptionist had mentioned took up the entire second floor of the community tower. Inside, over twenty rectangular mahogany tables garnished the mess hall with each capable of seating up to a dozen people. For the moment though, about thirty people still sat around enjoying a late breakfast. An eclectic group of tourists given the different languages Kyle heard as they entered the room.

Stationed in the middle of the room buffet style, a spectacular parade of food awaited the two weary travelers. An entire table crammed full of bananas, pineapples, mangos, papaya, citrus, melons, grapes, and guavas greeted them first. Next to the fruit sat steaming chaffers stuffed full of scrambled eggs, crisp bacon, sausage patties, fried fish, and hash browns served with spicy peppers and onions. Then on the next table they eyed baskets piled high with pastries and breads – some sweet, some tart, some hard, some soft, some round, and some flat. Then finally, the last table sagged from the weight of the carafes of sweet tropical juices, jugs of milk, and cambros of fresh-brewed coffee.

"Say goodbye to roughing it," Kyle Preston said after grabbing a plate. "I can't remember the last time I had bacon or scrambled eggs or a croissant, and mmm – smell that coffee."

"I smell only you," Brooklyn remarked while holding his nose.

"Maybe we should sit away from everyone else," Kyle Preston conceded after taking a whiff of himself. "They gave us a key to a room in case we wanted to freshen up," he added after sitting down at an empty table. "After we eat I'll see about getting a change of clothes and a shower."

After three trips to the buffet and five cups of coffee, Kyle finally finished eating. No slouch himself when it came to sweets, Brooklyn indulged himself by wiping out an entire basket of scrumptious chocolate brioche, which he washed down with a carafe of chunky white cupuacu juice. Of course this feeding frenzy did not go unnoticed by the other guests.

Afterwards Kyle retreated to the guestroom and thirty minutes later emerged showered, shaved, and wearing clean clothes borrowed from a hotel worker. Brooklyn and Cleto were nowhere to be found but Kyle wasn't alarmed. The worst thing he imagined happening here to his friend was for the shaman to be mistaken as an hotel employee dressed up in costume like a mascot at a theme park. Besides, the ethnobotanist relished the thought of finding some place secluded to be alone for awhile.

As he climbed the stairs to one of the observation towers, Kyle found himself going around and around and around with the tower narrowing a few feet after each flight of stairs. Slowly he labored upward. At times he stopped to catch his breath and look over the edge at the ground far below. Then, when finally at the top, he relished his reward.

Ten meters higher than the tallest trees of the upper canopy, Kyle looked out over a storybook bastion of dense and majestic greenery. To the north the Rio Negro resembled a lake of precious silver more than a river as it sparkled and shimmered. Above him the sun shined golden like a fiery wheel of Helios' fabled chariot. A scene worth savoring for a lifetime but it wasn't just the view that meant so much to Kyle but rather the viewpoint.

Seeing everything together gave him hope that he would find a place in his mind where he could see both the good and the bad he encountered during this expedition and weigh them evenly. A vantage where the joyous occasions balanced the heartfelt sorrows. A balance struck much the same way he saw the jungle, and the rivers, and the sky of Amazonas. He might regain that magic that he had lost.

Then on the stairs below him the ethnobotanist heard a commotion and a few seconds later a woolly monkey climbed over a side rail holding onto a camera. Kyle watched with amusement as the creature sniffed then tossed the booty aside because signs posted in several languages warned that wildlife inundated the resort's catwalks. Already in his short time there, KP saw several species of monkey as well as acouchi, agouti, cati, and countless species of birds. In this case the monkey, a female like Nonie but slightly smaller, seemed exceptionally bold and in fact came over to Kyle without hesitation and leaned up next to him.

For nearly an hour Kyle stayed there in the top of the tower looking out over the rainforest while petting the monkey's neck. From time to time somebody would join them, snap a few pictures, and say something but Kyle never responded. Even the monkey at times grunted at him but KP just continued to toil in a trance as he tried to come to grips with the past few days.

At a few minutes before noon KP spotted a stout two-story ship appear on the horizon and watched as it made its way upstream. For a second he thought it might pass on by but the boat tooted its horn and turned up the Ariau Creek.

With that, Kyle Preston knew it was time to leave. Time to be on his way again – on to Manaus where he would have to say goodbye to Brooklyn, then meet up with Selena at the airport for the long flight home, then finally return to UNC and walk into the Boiler Room where Rook would inevitable be waiting. The three of them together again in Stephen Lowery's lab – one shy of their perfect team.

10
GATEWAY TO AMAZONAS

Kyle awoke to the rumble of a jet flying only a few thousand feet overhead on its way to landing at Manaus' Edurado Gomes International Airport. Brooklyn still sat next to him with Cleto down at the shaman's feet while most of the other passengers onboard the boat already stood. They gathered along the outer railings and waived to passing ships or pointed to landmarks within the city.

Nestled on an immense and ancient sandbar, Manaus jutted out into the Rio Negro as a gateway to Amazonas. The river swung sharply south around the mountain range of concrete and glass then looped back in line with its previous course. With a population of over a million people, trade coursed as the city's lifeblood with seafaring cargo ships slipping in and out of its deep-water harbor.

"Woowoo – I can't believe it," the ethnobotanist shouted ecstatic to be back. "We're here – finally."

"Yes," the shaman chimed but without the same enthusiasm. "Here."

"What's wrong Brooklyn – afraid someone else is going to try looking under your breechcloth," Kyle joked even though he could tell by the tone of his friend's voice something truly troubled him.

"Good to be afraid," Brooklyn declared as he gestured with his hands out towards the city. "To see these huts taller than the trees, and canoes bigger than islands, and machines in the air instead of birds. It is good to be afraid."

"It's unavoidable with all the people," Kyle said just as the boat broke from the main channel and headed towards shore.

"This too I fear," the shaman spat. "More and more come. More and more with no love of the forest. More and more like those that attacked us."

"That's not entirely fair," Kyle argued even though deep down he shared some of his friend's sentiments. "Not everyone is like that – remember you were wrong about Captain Jack – you two had a lot in common but you never gave him a chance," he added as the boat reduced speed then jostled up against a lone dock. "Sometimes looks can be deceiving."

"Sometimes I wish I had remained in my village and never became a shaman so that my heart was not so heavy by the sight of such a place," Brooklyn confessed as he reached down and rubbed Cleto's ears. "The bliss I never knew I had."

"For me as well," Kyle echoed in agreement but from the other side of the argument, "but then I would have never met you my friend or known the wonders of the jungle or seen with my own eyes the power you possess. Power that you used to save that little girl. Power that these people must be taught to understand and respect as well."

After the crew finished mooring the boat, Brooklyn and Kyle fell in line behind the rest of the passengers. Once onshore Brooklyn took Cleto for a walk along the beachhead while Kyle followed an elegant stone pathway through a colorful flower garden full of single and double blooming Hibiscus. Further ahead, the path encircled a white marble fountain with water trickling down several tiers into a pool filled with duckweed and night blooming Antares. Then the trail disappeared in the shadows of several Banyan trees and their aerial roots but eventually reemerged at the back entrance to a majestic looking building.

"Welcome to the Hotel Tropical," a baby-faced doorman dressed in a white, button-down collared shirt and a pair of sleek maroon pants greeted the ethnobotanist as he approached.

"Obrigado," Kyle said thanking the man. "Which way to the front desk?"

"That way Sir," the doorman replied as he pointed to a grand hallway off to the right with a nod.

Located north of downtown Manaus near Praia da Ponta Negra, the ritzy, five-star Hotel Tropical pampered its guest in a way no brochure could do justice. The three-story, six hundred room hotel resembled a grand Spanish casita with white plaster walls, a terracotta tile roof, and viga beamed ceilings in the guest quarters. Within the inner courtyard of the main building, an enormous fan shaped swimming pool awaited hotel's guests along with two Jacuzzis, several wooden gazeboes, and scores of lounge chairs in which to bask all day long in the tropical sun. Several breezeways with elegant arch openings connected the main building to luxurious shops, fanciful restaurants, and a world class tennis club. The most alluring yet audacious amenity of the resort however was a zoo full of exotic animals captured from the jungle.

"May I help you," a voluptuous woman standing over at the front desk inquired when Kyle entered the room.

"Yes, I had a reservation under Preston, Kyle Preston," the ethnobotanist replied. "Unfortunately I missed it along with meeting a colleague of mine, Dr. Selena Crotalez. Can you tell me if she is still here?"

"I'm sorry but she never checked in," the receptionist replied after thumbing through the files.

"Really, we were to meet here and spend the night before flying back to the States" Kyle said as he tapped his fingers against the desk a couple of times. "Sort of a 'treat' to ourselves after being out in the field."

"I'm very sorry but Ms. Crotalez never arrived."

"What about messages – are there any messages for me because this isn't like her?"

"No – there's nothing," the receptionist said after scouring the office. "But if you like, I'll phone the airport – what was your flight number?"

"That's OK," Kyle declared downplaying his concern for his colleague. "She probably called and found out I wasn't here and just caught an earlier flight. I hate to admit it but I have a reputation of being late."

"We can still accommodate you Mr. Preston," the receptionist proposed. "If you like I'll have someone show you to your room. Maybe schedule a massage before dinner?"

"Thank you but no," Kyle answered still confused by Selena not showing up. "You can't imagine how appealing that all sounds."

Kyle again thanked the receptionist then turned around and walked back to the dock. Once there, he explained to Brooklyn that Selena never checked into the hotel without leaving word that her plans changed. Plans Kyle knew she would not have changed unless in trouble.

"Why can't things go as planned anymore," Kyle posed as the two men started walking along another of the hotel's path.

"What must we do?", the shaman asked as they strolled into the zoo and past a cage full of squawking double yellow headed parrots.

"First we have to go to IAR," Kyle answered as they approached the next cage. "Selena's gear should be in our office there if she made it back to Manaus. Maybe a note as well."

"Where was she?" Brooklyn inquired while watching an enormous capybara root around in the dirt of its pen."

"East of here over near the deserted town of Bensonvia," Kyle replied while looking in at the pig-sized rodent as well. "She's been studying a group of people known as Rednalsi off and on again for the last five years. For this latest expedition their shaman finally agreed to take her along with him while gathering plants. Hopefully, everything went off without a hitch."

"And if not?"

"Let's just get over there," Kyle found himself saying as if the thought of something happening to Selena seemed too painful for him to accept. "If nothing else, at least I'll be able to contact the lab back at UNC and find out what's going on. You know, they're probably worrying about us by now."

11
THE INSTITUTE OF AMAZON RESEARCH

Created in the 1950s, the Institute of Amazon Research resided on a tract of virgin jungle only fifteen kilometers from the city's downtown district. Over the years the institute's original mission to inventory the plants of the Amazon grew to include teaching new researchers. From those early days, the original A-frame cottage remained but to meet its present-day demands, IAR had blossomed into a complex array of buildings with catwalks, stairwells, and towers for easy access to the surrounding canopy. A place, with the addition of the Shaman's Apprentice School, that truly symbolized a storehouse of information for all people and the generations to come.

Several universities like UNC maintained an office at the center as a jump-off point for their Amazon expeditions. Cramped at times when in use by more than one group, the second-floor office contained low-tech as well as some of the most modern equipment available. A bank of four computers connected to a K2 line linked the researchers to the school and its databases. Bookshelves along one wall sagged from the weight of field guides, maps, GPS units, and journals. Another wall stood overrun with canteens, backpacks, raingear, hammocks, tents, and rolls of mosquito netting. Another wall resembled the shelves of a pharmacy. There were even an half dozen rifles and pistols registered to the school tucked behind inflatable raft in a closet. Researchers needed only to arrange food, water, transportation, guides, and bring along any specialty equipment required for their field of study.

Upon entering the office Kyle passed by a ragged old couch he knew all too well and went over to the lower drawer of a desk by the window. He shoved a few papers around then pulled out an half-filled bottle of Chivas Royal.

"Damn, I never thought I'd see you again," Kyle said as he opened the bottle and took a swig then offered some to Brooklyn.

"Amoni boyu," the shaman replied in his native tongue then took a swig.

"Amoni boyu," Kyle repeated. "I don't know about you but I'd say we're entitled to a couple of shots after this trip. Definitely one for the crew of the *Anna Maria* and any reason after that we come up with."

After taking another swig, Kyle scanned the room. Inch by inch, he scrutinized the place for any inkling that Selena had been there even though the receptionist downstairs already informed him to the contrary. Despite their plans, the last time anyone remembered seeing Selena at the center was a month ago just before leaving for Bensonvia.

"Nothing," Kyle finally said then took another swig of whiskey. "No gear! No note! Not a god damn thing!"

"Could she just not be back yet?" Brooklyn asked.

"I don't know – I better check in," Kyle replied visible upset. "Maybe they've heard from her back home."

Brooklyn said nothing at first then reached out and grabbed Kyle by the shoulder. "Whatever you find my friend – we face together."

12
POSITIONING OF PAWNS

"Get on a plane," Rook told Kyle straight out. "Get on a plane then call me once you're at Raleigh Durham. Deborah and I can be there in less than fifteen minutes."

Ronald Oliver Knell never minced words. Bound to a wheelchair because of Multiple Sclerosis, he stood tall and played the tough-guy by never sharing his inner feelings but expressing commentary about the world around him. His two older brothers dubbed him with the nickname of Rook years ago as a pun on his initials and the fact he used that piece in chess to beat his opponents. Even now, as a graduate student and Dr. Lowery's lab assistant, the name stuck with him because of his addiction to the game. He played as many as a half dozen games at a time and followed professional matches with the same zeal and enthusiasm that a football fan might watch Monday Night Football.

"Is that what you'd do – just leave?" Kyle asked while fiddling with the computer's camera.

"Yes," Rook replied. "I would, especially after what you just told me about those thugs obliterating that boat and its crew. You might not know it but there has been a dramatic increase in pirates attacking ships along the Amazon – they even killed a millionaire aboard his yacht."

"I think Ocho was right," Kyle voiced with one eyebrow raised while thinking back to what the Caboclos said when rescuing them from the island. "They were probably smuggling contraband of some sort and we were just in the wrong place at the wrong time."

"And if it wasn't for Brooklyn you'd be dead," Rook reminded him.

"I know," the ethnobotanist replied then turned around and looked at the shaman as if to say thank you.

"Do you – well then act like it and get back here."

"But what about Selena?" KP asked. "You can't expect me to leave until I know she's alright."

"Look – I told Lowery the same thing I'm about to tell you," Rook replied stumbling a bit when saying the professor's name. "Selena's a big girl. She can take care of herself."

"Then where is she?" Kyle asked. "She should have been back by now."

"Kyle listen to me – let the authorities handle it."

"I don't get it – what's the harm in staying until she shows up?"

"And if she doesn't – what then?" Rook jeered. "Are you going to march out to the Rednalsi village and asked them where she is?"

"If need be," Kyle Preston said.

"Have you taken a look at yourself lately?" Rook spouted. "You look like shit man – I mean a big pile of poopie only a dung beetle could love!"

"Well so do you," Kyle blasted back. "So does the room," he added as he looked in the background. "What happened?"

"Oh that," Rook replied in a matter-of-fact tone. "Yeah, it's lucky you haven't tried to get in touch before now. I just got clearance this morning by the fire marshal to re-enter this part of the lab."

"Fire Marshal?" the ethnobotanist repeated as he realized soot covered the wall behind Rook.

"It can wait," Rook replied. "You can see for yourself when you get here."

"Rook – tell me now!" Kyle demanded.

"Alright already," Lowery's lab assistant answered tight lipped at first but then loosened up as he recounted what happened that night. "Deborah and I just finished dinner at the Pink Armadillo when I got word the professor had a stroke while at the girls' soccer match. I went back to the lab hoping it might put my mind at ease. I don't know – distract me somehow. God I still can't believe it – so much for the 'perfect team' now that he's gone. Anyway, and I tidied up for awhile then realized somebody needed to get word to you and

Selena about what had happened. Well, right after that, I looked up and saw a gas cylinder riding on a wave of flames headed right towards me."

"Christ," Kyle said with his jaw jarred wide open. "That's unbelievable."

"No biggie," Rook professed while tapping his lucky chess piece attached to his chair's armrest. "Still, I thought for sure I was dead – hell, should have been – if it wasn't for that shatter-proof glass between the two sections of the lab I would be and I doubt Moorhead Hall would still be standing."

"Any idea on how the fire started?"

"The fire marshal seems rather tight-lipped and won't let me back into that side yet," Rook confessed. "All he would say was that the point of origin was around the ICP in the corporate lab. Something to do with a seated explosion near the instrument and the burn pattern on the adjacent walls and ceiling. He also said it must have blown with a lot of force to send that cylinder flying across the room like that. Needless to say it didn't hit me and because of the separate air handling units the smoke wasn't a problem either. Once I got over the initial shock I called 911 and by the time I slipped out an emergency exit and wheeled around to the front of the building, the campus police were already on the scene."

"It wasn't intentional was it?"

"Arson," Rook replied as if the mere word disgusted him. "What would be the point?"

"Maybe someone had an axe to grind," Kyle proposed. "A student bummed by their grade. It wouldn't be the first time."

"I guess that's possible?"

"Makes more sense than somebody being after you," Kyle said in jest.

"Like I'm important enough to kill," Rook scoffed. "Besides, unless someone was following me, nobody knew I was there except Deborah. Hey, there's a thought – after all it was our anniversary – maybe she wanted to break up but didn't have the heart to tell me so she decided to kill me instead – That's a real possibility. She's always been jealous of my chess playing – and my partners – hey maybe she planned the attack on you – watch out buddy – nothing is as treacherous as the scorn of a woman."

"All kidding aside I'm just saying maybe it was no accident," Kyle claimed.

"To be honest," Rook said as he leaned back in his chair, "it's been one hell of a week. I went from being excited about those Pico de Neblina samples and planning a surprise party for your return to utterly broken-hearted by the funeral, the fire, and the two of you missing. That's why I want you back here. I feel overwhelmed right now, sort of helpless like a pawn – sitting there out in the middle of a chessboard just waiting to be plucked off."

Without replying, Kyle got up from the computer and picked up the Chivas Royal then walked over to the window out of Rook's view. He took another swig, maybe two, then stood looking at a group of researchers standing outside on a catwalk – three men and a woman standing there admiring a cluster of rare truncated bromeliads. As he watched them it reminded Kyle of how Lowery, Selena, Rook, and he huddled together at times in the Boiler Room and talked about their work. The "Perfect Team" working together to make a difference in the world. A world that now seemed far more brutal and unfair than it did just a few days ago. A world, like Kyle's thoughts, teetering back and forth between sense and nonsense.

"Kyle," Rook called out after several minutes of silence. "What are you going to do?"

There was no reply – only the sound of the now empty bottle of Scotch being tossed over onto the couch.

"Kyle," Rook pleaded, "What are you going to do?"

13
ZONA FRANCO

Well after sunrise the next morning, Kyle awoke with an annoying crick in his neck, a walloping hangover, and a heart-tugging decision to stay. For him, it was the only choice he could make because, despite Rooks pleading and his own desire to return home, Kyle Preston knew he would never be able to live with himself if something happened to Selena. Something he could have prevented had he only stayed to look for her.

That wasn't to say KP felt at ease with his decision. Unlike his recent expedition in which he failed to bring back samples from the liana jungle, in this case his colleague's life quite possibly hinged on him. The slightest mistake or delay might cost Selena her life. A gut-wrenching position to be in because it not only put himself in harm's way but also Brooklyn. True to his word the shaman would go with Kyle to search for Dr. Crotalez even though they had never met.

Rolling off the couch and wrestling to his feet, Kyle staggered over to the bathroom and splashed some cold water on his face. He spent the next few minutes washing up then afterwards dug through a box of orphaned clothes that had accumulated over the years until finding a shirt that fit. He also managed to scrounge up a pair of thick socks to replace the hole infested ones he had been wearing, as well as a pair of new laces for his boots. Once dressed, Kyle wandered over to the window where he noticed Brooklyn sprawled out in a hammock strung out over the catwalk.

"Let me guess – my snoring again," Kyle stated as he came outside then took a deep breath of fresh air. "That's one thing you won't miss when you go back to your village."

"Even here you still sound like a pack of wambis," the shaman kidded while whittling away on a new flute for his son after losing the other one in the ambush. "No word yet?"

"I hoped she'd be here when I woke," Kyle said as if Selena personified the princess in a fairy tale. "Guess now we'll go down to the Port Authority and talk with them."

"Perhaps they will tell us something?"

"I hope not," Kyle grimaced. "That might mean they've found her boat abandoned somewhere or even worse her body."

As they made their way towards the Port Authority, Brooklyn and Kyle watched in amazement at the flurry of activity over on the docks. High above enormous cranes lifted and moved bulk cargo carriers as if mere toys. Piles of mahogany, ipe, and teak being stacked upon the decks of the enormous ships resembled toothpicks rather than logs. While at the customs storehouse, stevedoring gangs attacked pallets of coffee and boxes of bananas as ants upon piles of sugar.

Located out on a dock set apart from the ones used by the freighters, the Port Authority was housed in a magnificent, one-story garrison built with flawless blocks of imported blue pearl granite. The building, like much of Manaus, stood as a reminder to a time when the city had been dubbed, the 'Paris of the Tropics'. A time of the rubber barons and when the whole world knew of Manaus.

Once inside and seated at the harbormaster's desk, Kyle recounted what happened to the crew of the *Anna Maria* and also expressed his concerns for Dr. Crotalez's whereabouts. The magistrate eyed both Brooklyn and Kyle with suspicion but eventually stated one of his inspectors would check into both matters then excused himself.

Despite that assurance, Kyle knew it would be a matter of weeks and not days before anyone would get around to doing something. Furthermore, he knew the Port Authority was far more adept at inspecting ships laden with freight or deciphering their manifest than investigating reports of missing persons or running down a band of murderous pirates. Still, no one reported seeing

Selena's boat abandoned or finding a body matching her description. News deep down Kyle expected to hear.

With the fiery tropical sun towering above, Brooklyn and Kyle left the harbormaster's office and headed towards Manaus' business district. They crossed the Avenue floriano Peixtoto then walked past the Igreja de Matriz Cathedral and over to a nearby bank where Kyle picked up some money he asked Rook to wire him. Then, with that in hand, they walked a few blocks further east to the city's open market where Kyle planned to arrange transportation to the Rednalsi village as well as buy enough supplies for a week in the jungle.

Overwhelming was the word Kyle always thought of whenever he came to the city's open market. Down by the river a collection of old cast iron buildings from the turn of the century and adorned with stained glass comprised the inner core. From there the market fanned out with no real end in sight. An entanglement of wooden booths, tents, and at times mere crates overrun with an eclectic stash of wares with each irresistible and compelling in their own right.

Anything imaginable could be bought if one knew where to look for it. That was the hard part though – swimming through the endless sea of people clogging the market's alleys. Another essential skill involved ignoring the constant banter of the merchants. Their voices deafened at times, especially when expounding a true bargain was at hand. For the moment though, as Brooklyn and Kyle inched their way down one of the congested alleyways, they could hear a girl's honey-sweet voice carrying over the others.

"Fresh fruit, fru-i-t, fr-u-i-t; fresh fruit, fru-i-t, fr-u-i-t," she sang out, changing both pitch and inflection when saying the same word again and again. "Fresh fruit, fru-i-t, fr-u-i-t; fresh fruit, fru-i-t, fr-u-i-t."

"Over there," Kyle stated as he pointed to a small fruit stand off to the right.

"Aye, my Carolina sweetheart and boyfriend the shaman – so good to see you both," the girl flirted then bent down and let Cleto lick her face. "How's my puppy?"

"Good to see you too Louisanne," Kyle replied as he stood there waiting for her to finish with the dog so he could give her a hug.

Louisanne appeared far more delicious than any of the fruit she sold. Her big brown eyes twinkled with both mystery and mischief. Her smile curved seductive and crooked when she told one of her countless but harmless fibs. More than anything though, she had a glow to her that drew people to her stand, and even if they did not buy anything, they still came away with something delightful. She remained bright and cheery, even on the darkest of days.

"I didn't expect to see you so soon," the girl commented then felt compelled to explain why. "I remember you saying once your expedition was over you would be heading back to the States. To be honest, I thought you already left."

"Should have," Kyle stated awkwardly, "but something has come up. I need your help in rounding up supplies for another trip. Same stuff as before but just a week's worth this time – can you do that?"

"Yes – of course," Louisanne replied, "but why? Did something happen out there?"

"I'd rather not say," KP asserted, "but I do need your father's help."

"Really," Louisanne marveled with obvious shock, "but you swore never again."

"I know," Kyle conceded while remembering back to the last time he flew with the girl's father. "Believe me – I wish there was another way."

"Pops is probably still down near the fish market haggling with the guy that sells the rocks he likes," Louisanne stated while still wondering what could be so important to make Kyle get in a plane with her father again. "If you like I can show you where?"

"That would be great."

"As would you buying some fruit," the girl proposed with a broad inviting smile. "How about a red pineapple or some juicy mangos or one of these papaya – they're the best you'll find."

"Thanks but not right now," Kyle confessed. "I really need to speak to your father."

"Come on – it's the least you can do for all the customers I'll miss while away getting your supplies."

"All right – How much," Kyle asked as he grabbed two of the mangos and held them out in front of him as if judging them for a county fair.

"Two," the girl asserted.

"Dollars," Kyle teased. "When did you get so greedy?"

"Sweetheart," Louisanne declared, "a girl's gotta make a living."

"Take it," Kyle said as he gave her close to seventy dollars – money not only for the fruit but also the supplies he wanted. "After all, a girl's got to make a living."

Set aside for the local fisherman to bring their morning catch to market, the stained glass building nearest the river stunk of fish. The scores of booths inside equaled the number of different varieties for sale. In one row alone six species of piranha lay on display. Equally as impressive were the booths piled high with Pirararas, an enormous red tailed catfish as large as a person. Even electric eels seemed to be quite commonplace along with caiman, anaconda, stingrays, dolphin, and turtle eggs. Anything in fact found in and along the Rio Negro, whether legal or not, eventually wound up for sale here.

As Louisanne led Brooklyn and Kyle through the rancorous piles of fish, they got brief glimpses of two men arguing just outside the far entrance. Without question the man with his back to them was the girl's father because Don Zito had the peculiar habit, one of many in fact, of always wearing black. In this case he donned a long sleeve shirt tucked halfway into a pair of polyester pants worn far too high, and a ball cap that hid his balding head. Then as they got closer and came around to the side they could see a pair of horn-rimmed bifocals resting halfway down his giant bulbous nose.

"Look at him – he's such a nut," Louisanne professed about her father as they walked up behind him. "Tell you what – I'll start gathering those supplies while you break this up – good luck."

Despite his quirks, Kyle Preston knew Don Zito was a damn good pilot. That wasn't to say he made it easy to look past his antics. On the contrary, KP found it impossible at times. Antics so off the wall and ridiculous, especially when Zito flew, that Kyle felt certain Louisanne's father teetered on the edge of lunacy. So much so, Kyle swore never to get in a plane with him again.

"Zito," Kyle barked as if calling out a gunslinger to a duel.

"Science Officer – get over here and look at this," Zito said while gesturing with his hands for the ethnobotanist to come over and examine a piece of quartz under a jeweler's eyepiece. "Tell this man what you see. He refuses to admit these pieces he sold me are flawed."

"Some things never change," Kyle chuckled, refusing outright to be drawn into the dispute. "You're still up to the same old games."

"Games," Zito scoffed as he pushed his glasses back up his nose. "I can't use this junk. Why, by the time I smoothed out these imperfections, there wouldn't be anything left to use. How can anyone—"

"Don, listen – I need your help," Kyle interrupted.

The ethnobotanist then went on to tell the bush pilot

everything that happened the last few days – how terribly wrong the expedition ended – the dreadful events back in Chapel Hill – and the disappearance of Dr. Crotalez. He held back nothing including his tears, as well as his hope of finding Selena alive at the Rednalsi village.

"So are you in?" KP asked.

"Have you tried going to the embassy?"

"I thought about it but she's a Brazilian national."

"So they won't lift a finger," Zito stated as he played with the bill of his hat. "When were you thinking of leaving?"

"The sooner the better," Kyle asserted. "We have no way of knowing what's waiting for us."

"Alright – but just so you know, there's a good chance we'll fly right over her and not even know it."

"I know but I can't just wait around – I've got to do something."

"You don't have to explain," Zito insisted. "If it was Louisanne out there, I'd be doing the same damn thing."

14
TO BOLDLY GO

In an older section of town, still near the Rio Negro but away from the port and open market, a lime green, convertible Karman Ghia barreled down one of Manaus' main drags. Louisanne seemed unconcerned that the car's tachometer stayed pegged at the redline. Whether she drove this way all the time was unclear but by the smirk on her face she enjoyed the look of dread on her passengers' faces.

"I was wrong," Kyle howled as the antique roadster zigzagged its way between two trucks then veered over to an exit ramp.

"How's that?" Louisanne shouted as she slowed somewhat to round a bend then shifted back up into overdrive.

"I always thought your father was the crazy one in the family."

"He is," the girl laughed as she mashed the gas pedal

and passed the car in front of her. "I'm just getting you ready for the flight."

"Unnghh," Brooklyn uttered as the Karman Ghia crossed a humpback bridge over one of the city's many canals. For what seemed like an eternity the car hurdled into the air then landed with a thud, spraying sparks everywhere from where it scraped the pavement. "Bo moa tu nanado ejama."

"What's he saying?" Louisanne yelled to Kyle.

"You don't want to know," Kyle insisted without translating. "Just be glad he likes you!"

A few minutes later Louisanne darted onto a dirt driveway and fishtailed to a halt in front of a large wooden barn with giant double doors. Several broken-down cars rested nearby in a field of dandelions along with a mammoth pile of scrap metal. Closer to the building there appeared to be the landing gear assembly to a plane.

"Never again!" Kyle commented as he pulled himself out of the car.

"Where have I heard that before," Louisanne mused after popping the hood to the car. "Besides, I got you here didn't I?"

"Yeah – we're here alright," Kyle Preston moaned then grabbed some of the gear and set it down next to the barn. "I swore to myself I'd never come back here again."

Despite the ethnobotanist's misgivings, Zito's workshop seemed a pleasant enough place although somewhat peculiar. Inside, a cornucopia of mills, lathes, drill presses, and die cast machines filled the barn. Shelving lined both side walls the entire length of the barn stuffed full of tools, tubes of various diameters, machine parts, and box upon box of pieces of ground and polished quartz. Over in the far corner, a huge workbench sagged buried underneath astronomy magazines with a staircase next to it leading up to the loft where dozens of telescopes hung from the barn's rafters.

"You didn't waste any time getting here," Don Zito said as he came down the stairs carrying one of the telescopes in his hands.

"Your daughter had something to do with that," Kyle smirked with a disapproving look at Louisanne.

"It's not her fault," Zito proclaimed. "The car is not exactly standard issue – I bore out the heads and replaced the carburetor with the fuel injection system from that ninety-one Honda Civic over there. I also switched out the points and rotor for an electronic ignition."

"I know it's not," Kyle replied. "She's got your genes."

"Easy sweetheart," Louisanne broke in smiling, "remember – the best is yet to come."

Behind the barn tied up to a makeshift dock jutting out into the river, a single-engine Cessna 182 bobbed up and down on two pontoons as waves rolled in towards shore. For some reason, Kyle remembered the plane as being bigger. Not only that, it looked far more weathered and frail than before with new panels of aluminum riveted piecemeal into place almost as shadily as the tin roof to Ocho's home.

"I know what you're thinking," Zito proclaimed as they all walked out onto the dock. "She's more than sound," he added as he pushed his glasses back up his nose. "I've got this engine putting out almost two hundred and fifty horsepower at twenty-four hundred rpm."

"This isn't the same plane as before," Kyle asked before setting down the gear he was carrying.

"Are you kidding," Zito snapped back while reaching up and touching a strut to the wing. "Of course this is my baby – I'd never get rid of her – she's perfect."

"You're digging your own grave," Louisanne chimed as she opened the cargo door and climbed inside the fuselage so she could start stowing away the gear. "Pops, how do you want the weight distributed?"

"Towards the nose," Zito responded. "I'm going to have to carry extra fuel in the reserve tanks in order to have enough to get back. Also, make sure that telescope I brought down gets stored up over the door."

"What about Bones – I guess he's out this trip?"

"No," Zito protested with his glasses about to fall off his nose. "He stays put!"

Inside the plane's cockpit sat a mannequin resembling Leonard McCoy, the doctor from the original Star Trek series. The full-sized figure wore black nylon pants and a long sleeved, tight-fitting, turquoise pullover trimmed in black. The dummy also had on a pair of polished black boots and a gold broach shaped like a

Capital A pinned to its chest. With its porcelain eyes and one of the plane's headsets holding in place a black wig, it looked rather realistic, especially to Brooklyn.

"Zito – you're not still dragging that thing around – are you," Kyle scoffed then noticed some more Star Trek hallmarks and emblems strewn across the plane.

"Of course he is," Louisanne cut in. "Bones is the only one that actually listens to him."

"Alright," Zito huffed. "For the time being you can stow him in back so that Kyle can sit up front. Now if you don't mind I've got some preflight checks to make."

All kidding aside, Zito knew the ins and outs of his plane better than he knew himself. It showed as he first climbed out in front of the plane on one of the pontoons and checked both the prop nut and spinner. Then he slowly ran his hand up and down the propeller feeling for the slightest nick or crack. Once satisfied with that, he leaned over to one side of the plane then the other to check the action of each wing's aileron. From there he went back to the tail and surveyed both the vertical and horizontal stabilizers as well as the rudder, elevator, and clevis.

"Ready to boldly go where no man has gone before," Zito called back to Brooklyn after climbing into the cockpit then donning a pair of reflective sunglasses.

"Go easy on him would you – this is his first time," Kyle answered for his friend, who was squished into a jump seat and staring at the mannequin across from him while holding onto Cleto even tighter than when in the car.

"Really – a virgin," Don Zito joked as he began to make various checks of the plane's electronics then barked some orders to Kyle. "Go ahead and lock down that GPS unit but also check the compass, then strap yourself in."

"Got everything you need?" Louisanne asked Kyle Preston before untying the ropes holding the plane to the dock.

"No – not really," Kyle yelled as the Cessna's engine roared to life. "I wish I had thought to buy a bottle of Scotch."

"Not to worry," Zito said as he pulled out a canteen from under his seat and took a swig. "I've got some hooch here that makes that seem like Kool-Aid."

15
ENCONTRO DAS AGUAS

Cast as a stone from shore, the plane skipped and skimmed along the water's surface until Zito felt they had gained enough speed. The pilot then pulled back hard on the yoke and forced the Cessna 182 into the air while his passengers' stomachs remained behind. Kyle managed to glimpse Louisanne down on the dock waiving to them but within seconds she shriveled into a dot as the plane continued to soar. Higher and higher it climbed until Zito made a turn in Kyle's direction, banking so hard that the ethnobotanist now looked out his side window at the river directly below.

"You kill me when you do this," Kyle professed.

"I know," Zito said with a smile as he leveled the plane off for the moment at around a thousand feet. "It's fun though."

Less than a minute later, the pilot pulled the same stunt again as they flew over the port and open market. This time Kyle peered down upon the cargo ship he saw earlier being loaded with timber. The freighter had just weighed anchor with black puffs of smoke spewing from its stacks. Three tugboats nudged it along but already the ship's massive propellers churned beneath it with a wake aft that rippled across the harbor.

"Believe it or not, there's a reason for all this," Don Zito shared when he brought the plane out of the turn. "I'm trying to skirt the airspace around the airport, or at least stay clear of the glide path. For some reason, they don't take kindly to me hobnobbing with the big boys."

"Like I didn't expect this," Kyle Preston remarked as he looked over at downtown Manaus with all its skyscrapers, then spotted the famed opera house Teatro with its vibrant dome, and further north at the terracotta roof of the Hotel Tropical. "But why not just check in with the tower?"

"Oh I got rid of the radio awhile back – so many questions – too many rules," Zito smirked as if it wasn't a big deal. "What about your friend – how's he doing?" the pilot posed, nodding towards the rear of the plane. "Has he turned green yet?"

"Better than I expected," Kyle answered after glancing back at the shaman. "Although, he's still staring at the mannequin."

"That's Bones for you," Zito joked while changing headings yet again. "He's a talker."

After finally clearing the commercial flight path, Zito gained enough altitude to circle back to the south-east. By now the plane cruised near six thousand feet at a speed of one hundred-forty knots. Visibility remained good with no inclement weather building along their track. A track that put them back over the river in search of Dr. Crotalez.

"Wow, what a spectacle," Kyle exclaimed a few minutes later when they approached the spot where the Rio Negro and Rio Solimoes came together. "How breathtaking is that?"

"Encontro das Aguas," Zito zipped off as if the name to some exotic nebula. "Otherwise known as the 'Meeting of the Waters'. I liken it to two heavy-weights sparring with one another," Zito mused. "Kind of toe to toe in search of the other's weakness before actually mixing it up."

"How long does it stay like this?"

"Close to six kilometers," the bush pilot noted while aligning the plane over the mixing zone. "Each stream has a different flow rate, density, pH, and even temperature."

"It's amazing the way it does that."

"Mmmm, just physics," Zito professed. "Once you understand the mechanics, it's really quite simple."

"Still – it's beautiful," Kyle proclaimed looking down and watching the two streams finally swirl into one.

"I'll give you that," Zito replied then added, "but it's also great for business – I can make almost three hundred dollars in an half hour by flying tourist out here."

"Speaking of which – you never answered when I asked you how much this trip would cost."

"That's because it's on the house," Zito said as he reached under his seat and pulled out the canteen again then handed it to Kyle. "Qapla!"

"Damn – what is this stuff?" KP asked after taking a swig.

"Romulin Ale – at least that's what I call it," the pilot clamored. "I make it from whatever fruit Louisanne doesn't sell along with some barley. Afterwards, I add a little blue curaçao to give it the right color."

"Its got to be near 200 proof," Kyle remarked while handing the canteen back to Zito without taking another swig.

"It ought to be – it's suppose to be the strongest stuff in the galaxy."

"What is it with you and Star Trek anyway?" KP asked. "Ever since I've known you – you've been carrying that mannequin around, spouting Klingon, and who knows what else?"

"I don't know – I guess I always liked Gene Roddenberry's vision of what we can become rather than what we are," Don Zito answered in earnest. "The world is so full of hatred stemming from nationalism. We're like those two rivers down there – not wanting to share but eventually having to. I just wish we would do it sooner than later. I mean, where is the love?"

"You're right – we should be able to look past our differences and respect one another."

"No – we should appreciate the differences," Zito complained. "I always thought it was great to see the various ethnic groups onboard the *Enterprise*. There's an untapped strength in our diversity."

"I never watched the show enough growing up to get all that," KP confessed. "TV reception at my parents' house in the mountains was bad – we got one channel, sometimes two, and both were filled with static. Besides, I spent most of my time outside playing with my friends in the woods or helping my Granny with her garden."

"Funny but I was just the opposite," Zito divulged before taking a drink. "I never went outside or had anyone to do things with so I always watched TV. I started off by watching Buck Rogers and Flash Gordon back in the fifties, then Outer Limits and Dr. Who came along I think in sixty-three, then Lost in Space in sixty-five, and finally Star Trek in sixty-six. I've been hooked ever since."

"Addicted is more like it but I guess it makes sense you becoming a pilot."

"Really – it shocked the hell out of me," Zito said then dropped the plane down to around twenty-five hundred feet so they might have a better chance of spotting Selena's boat. "I was shooting to be an astronaut with NASA and go to the moon and so much more. Guess I fell a little short both in their eyes and my own because here I am – I'm down here flying this puddle jumper and building telescopes in an old barn instead of back home flying the shuttle and repairing the Hubble."

"So, are they out there?" Kyle then blurted for no apparent reason.

"Who?" Zito asked as he looked down at the river.

"Little green men Zito," Kyle wailed. "Are there little green men out there? Or maybe some of those big ugly Klingons or pointed-eared Rumulins. Either of them up there flying around in ships that have – what is it – warped engines."

"Warp engines," Zito corrected the ethnobotanist then for fun went into an half Cuban eight, looping the plane upside down and heading the opposite direction until performing an Immelman maneuver to come back around to the east. "They're called warp engines. Anything else you want me to explain?"

A little over an hour later, visibility worsened from a tract of land being cleared just north of them. Through the haze they could still see the Amazon River slashing its way through the jungle as well as a tributary leading up towards the fire but not much of anything else. Zito then went into a slipping turn, to steer clear of the downwind smoke. Afterwards they could see piles of brush glowing red-hot surrounded by the doldrums of lifeless gray ash. Kyle found it very disheartening to see the forest wasted like this but then something far more disturbing came into view.

"What's that?" Kyle asked looking further north at an enormous festering crater.

"El Brando," Zito stated while shaking his head. "That means we're less than twenty minutes from Bensonvia and no more than forty from the Rednalsi village."

El Brando had started out innocently enough awhile back when a family squatting on the land found gold along the banks of this black water tributary known as the Rio Manatee. At first they just waded into the water and panned but then word spread and a pit opened up like a cavity, eroding away both the surrounding hillside as well as the original stream channel. Now the mine gobbled up more land than a stadium and harbored around a thousand Garimpeiros with its outside walls crumbling away more and more each day. Decay that with each rain poured hundreds of cubic feet of silt into the nearby stream, clogging the channel and choking the plants and wildlife.

"What a waste," Kyle remarked. "Most of those men will try for years, trudging day after day in that mud only to find they had more going for them before they went there."

"Countless never make it out alive because of all the mudslides," Zito added. "Nameless, forgotten bodies rotting away until some other poor slob comes across them."

"Yeah, and if conditions weren't bad enough, they use cyanide and mercury to separate the gold," Kyle said in disbelief. "Even if they are lucky enough to go home with something they're either mad as a hatter or dead within a few years."

"Fool's gold – isn't it," Zito suggested shaking his head again. "Nothing but fool's gold. Thank god the Rednalsi live upstream, otherwise—"

"Otherwise they'd all be dead," Kyle irked finishing Zito's sentence for him then looking back at Brooklyn with some alarm. "I thought Brazil was cracking down on Garimpeiros?"

"They are – especially in the northwest out beyond Boa Vista but not here," Zito replied. "The ownership of this land has been in dispute for years between one of the more powerful families in Brazil and a non-profit setup on behalf of the Rednalsi. Legally, everyone knows the family doesn't have a claim but they've worked the system to perfection and have tied things up in the courts while finagling backroom deals with politicians."

"And in the meantime the mine stays open – that doesn't make sense," Kyle remarked as he looked down at the devastation. "Both sides should want this stopped."

"Word is, the family takes a percentage of whatever they find."

"While the Rednalsi struggle to maintain their way of life."

"At least Brazil still has some pristine regions where indigenous people have held on to their ancestral lands," Zito commented then checked the GPS to confirm their position as well as note the plane's fuel consumption. "Can we say the same?"

"No we can't," Kyle conceded thinking back to his home state of North Carolina and the Cherokee's "Trail of Tears." "We can't at all."

Twenty minutes later, with still no sign of Selena,

the plane past over the abandoned rubber plantation of Bensonvia. Kyle knew the odds of spotting her boat from the air were far worse than finding a needle in a haystack. For that reason he kept his emotions in check the entire flight. Now though, his hope of finding her wavered somewhat.

"I guess some dreams die hard," Kyle said with a degree of regret looking down at Bensonvia but thinking about Selena.

"Yeah – I bet Mr. Henry Ford wishes he never got that wild hair up his butt," Zito joked. "Anyway – there's the village," the bush pilot added pointing to the northeast at a small clearing and a few thatched roofs. "Good thing too – the sun's about to go down."

"How much further?" Kyle Preston then asked scanning the horizon for a body of water wide enough to land.

"What do you mean?" Zito hollered then turned his hat around so the bill was behind him. "We just flew over it."

"My God – you're kidding – right?"

"No," Zito quibbled with a broad grin. "Let's just hope there aren't any stumps."

After slowing the plane down, Zito circled back over a spot where the river recently flooded its banks into a meadow. Known as an oxbow lake, the water probably stood less than a meter deep in some place this early into the rainy season. A mud puddle more than a lake and both men knew it.

"Hold on," Kyle yelled back to Brooklyn as the little plane dropped like a rock out of the sky and plunged towards the river below. "If we survive this – I'll owe you a whole truckload of Yoo-hoos!"

"Just out of curiosity," Zito asked while gripping the yoke tightly with both hands, "does anyone know we're out here?"

"Like the Port Authority," Kyle Preston replied then looked over at Zito – not so much because of the question but rather the crazed tone of his voice.

"I mean, if we go down, is there somebody that will send word to rescue the rescuers?"

16
PICKING UP THE PIECES

Situated at the corner of Columbia and South road, every year a room or floor of Morehead Hall closed for renovation. Just recently new thermal resistant glass with modern frames patterned to look like the old eight-paned windows had been installed, though the new fixtures couldn't be opened – a noticeable change to a building built originally as a dormitory where students once hung from their windows late at night.

Those days though disappeared quite some time ago – ever since the Chemistry Department gained control of the building and Morehead Hall began to house laboratories instead of students. Dubiously named the Boiler Room from when it held an old coal furnace for heating the building, Dr. Lowery's lab occupied a large section of the basement in Morehead Hall. Despite its location and history, the room had a feel about it Lowery once described as comfortable as worn flannel sheets on a cold winter's night.

For Rook, the last couple of days both tried and taxed him. Normal for him, he told no one, but the shock of Lowery dying, the horror of the fire, and then the disappearance of his colleagues in Brazil had emotionally drained him. Of course his girlfriend Deborah wanted him to talk openly about his feelings but he knew that would only lead to questions about his health. Questions with answers, which would only remind Ronald Oliver Knell of his frailty and so he remained tight-lipped to the woman he so deeply loved. The only person who knew anything, after finally resurfacing, was Kyle but he was still down in Brazil.

From their conversation, it sounded as if Kyle had rebounded from the attempt on his life. Rook disagreed with his friend's decision to stay in Brazil even though he understood the need to look for Selena. Still, the fire marshal's investigation revealed new startling details about the fire that Rook wished he knew when he spoke to Kyle. Details that might have persuaded the ethnobotanist to do just as he suggested and get on the first plane out of there.

Earlier that morning, the fire marshal finally allowed Rook to re-enter the section of Lowery's lab damaged by the fire. He was cleared but not before submitting to spot checks of both his hands and his wheelchair as well as answering several pointed questions.

From the line of questioning, it appeared the investigation continued to revolve around a blast near the ICP in the corporate lab, which they already determined wasn't accidental. The inspector disclosed that picric acid, also known as trinitrophenol and considered a Class A explosive, had been detected in swatches of the floor and walls as well as air samples taken right after extinguishing the fire. Furthermore, residue of the acid was detected in shards of the waste container for the instrument – a highly suspect place to find the substance given its incompatibility with metal analytes – the very thing that the ICP analyzed for.

Because of this, the fire marshal suspected this was not the work of an ordinary arsonist. In fact he felt certain it was someone not only familiar with the explosive nature of picric acid but also the operation of an ICP. As it turned out his suspicions were indeed corroborated by the discovery of a printout from the instrument showing it in operation the night of the explosion. A printout for samples analyzed just after ten o'clock that evening, which contained high concentrations of copper, lead, and zinc – the most incompatible metals with the acid. Irrefutable proof the fire marshal surmised that someone had turned the instrument into a bomb.

Another detail of the printout showed the ICP had been programmed to startup on its own. A feature in the instrument's software that the fire marshal verified with Perkin-Elmer, the manufacturer of the Optima 3000, which would have allowed someone to rig the ICP to explode hours or even days before if no one else used the instrument. Because of this, the arsonist did not have to be at the lab at the time of the explosion.

For this reason as well as the fact the spot check of his hands and chair for the presence of picric acid were negative, the Fire Marshal reluctantly dismissed Lowery's lab assistant as a suspect. Since then Rook worked on cleaning up the place by picking up the pieces of broken glass and wiping soot and dust from the benchtops. As he did, he couldn't help but wonder why – why someone would have started the fire in the first place?

For several exhaustive hours Rook along with two of the University's custodial staff cleaned up around the lab. At times the smell of burnt plastic and spilled chemicals overwhelmed them, not to mention the daunting task of cleaning itself. Most of the damage was related to the initial explosion and the emergency sprinklers kicking on rather than the fire. Although the fire had consumed the chess set Rook and Kyle played their games on.

More than anything though, Rook found Dr. Lowery's desk the hardest to clean. The frame to a picture of the professor with his wife and three daughters laid cracked and pushed to the back of the desk. A stack of singed tests and a half-eaten sandwich sat covered with soot and debris. Yellow message slips from the other day still awaited his return. Then an accidental bump of the computer's mouse lit up the dusty monitor to the professor's computer and revealed a corny screensaver of Stephen and his wife Jean.

"Hey buddy," one of the custodians hollered over to Rook from across the lab, "We're going to dinner – want something?"

"They got chicken fingers today," the other custodian added after throwing a heap of pulverized chalkboard into a trash can. "That's what I'm having – fingers, collards, and corn fritters."

"Thanks – but I'm fine," Rook replied even though he hadn't eaten a thing all morning except Pepto.

"OK, well – we'll be back in an hour."

"More like an hour and an half," the other one joked while brushing the dust off his clothes and stomping his feet. "We've got to stop by maintenance and get a shop-vac. Otherwise we'll be here all day."

"I'm not going anywhere," Rook remarked then watched the two men leave the room. "Nowhere at all – nowhere I want to be."

17
PERSONAL LOG

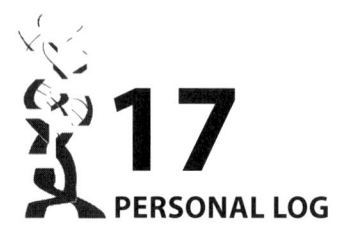

The thought of going through the files on Dr. Lowery's computer did not appeal to Rook. Oh, secretly he had always been curious because the professor spent a great deal of time on the computer. But now that Jake Buckner, the facility president, ordered him to do that very thing, that sense of intrigue disappeared. There might very well be a lot of valuable material to be retrieved but Rook also knew there would be personal things he had no business nor desire to see. Neither did anyone else for that matter, which was why he finally agreed to do it. Otherwise someone else might come in and backup Lowery's entire hard drive and maybe find something that would only hurt the professor's family.

Rook started out by reviewing Dr. Lowery's email. Most were from peers scattered throughout the world, concerning specific molecules and reactions. Others came from companies and organizations inviting the professor to seminars or calls for papers. A few regarded submissions of late assignments by students with lame excuses like their dog or roommate ate their work. Another one Jake had sent asking why he wasn't told about the surprise party on Saturday to celebrate Kyle's and Selena's return. While several more expressed their condolences from well-wishers that heard of the professor's death. But of all the email, the hardest one to read was a note from Stephen's wife on the day he died:

My darling husband,

It seems impossible yet inescapable that our anniversary approaches again. It is a day that I always remember, always cherish, because it is when our lives and our hearts were forever intertwined by the vow made between us almost forty years ago.

From that moment I have always been yours. My body roused by your touch – my mind awakened by your dreams – my soul touched by your spirit. Truly, I am more fulfilled than you can possible imagine.

And yet Stephen, I look forward to the years to come in which to grow even closer to you. Together, hand in hand, reveling in the splendor that God brings forth with each new day. Perhaps a morning spent just sipping coffee with you all to myself down to the last drop. Or a day nestled together back on the tiny beach where we married with the taste of salt on your lips just as it was that day. Or perhaps an evening spent out on the porch rocking in our chairs and watching the fruit of our love with some of its own. Moments made golden because of you my darling husband.

Forever yours,
JEAN
X-X-X
| |
O O

Wiping the tears from his eyes, Rook felt not only ashamed for reading such an intimate message but also so very sad. For forty years Jean Lowery had shared the man she loved with the world, biding her time in which to have him all to herself. Instead, their love affair ended without any of those golden moments she envisioned. Little things people not in love might overlook but the very things Rook knew the professor looked forward to as well.

"Hey buddy – ya miss us," the first of the custodians bellowed as he burst through the doorway.

Rook sighed but said nothing while still thinking about how unfair life seemed at times.

"Coming through – look out," the other custodian teased as he dragged the shop-vac behind him. "We brought you back some Blueberry Yum Yum."

"Sorry," Rook quibbled as he looked up from the computer screen. "This is, at times, very hard."

"Don't dwell on it," the custodian with the shop-vac said after plugging in the vacuum then turning it on even before finishing his unsolicited advice. "Sometimes," he shouted, "all we can do is pick up the pieces and move on – move on because they'll never fit back together again!"

Despite the shrill of the vacuum echoing throughout the room, Rook pressed on. He turned his attention to the most-recent active items listed in the "My Documents" folder. He first opened several PDF files downloaded from the Internet concerning exotic alkaloids to which Rook had no recollection. Two letters sent by Lowery to the National Chemistry Association also showed up as well as an hilarious picture of the professor and his three daughters taken some years back on a camping trip. Next he opened an Excel spreadsheet the professor had created in which to dump data related to the Pico de Neblina samples. Then finally, three more letters – two declining to attend seminars and one accepting an invitation. Nothing of which seemed at all important.

Next, despite running across some other emotional landmines like the email from Jean, Rook went through the Internet Explorer settings. He noted several folders within Lowery's saved "Favorites", linked to various technical sites but nothing he felt the University really needed. Then he opened up the "History" folder and checked the last places Lowery visited, noticing that the majority of the searches appeared related but again not too relevant to their present work.

Afterwards, Rook opened up Windows Explorer and scanned the different names of the folders. He copied the ones that seemed work-related and later planned on going back through and verifying the need for each of the subfolders and files within them. Something he would certainly have to do before handing anything over to Jake.

Over halfway through, little appeared worth saving to Rook. Lowery had used the computer more for personal things and anything that the school might want probably resided upstairs with the department's secretary. Rook however suspected Jake would not be satisfied with that answer and in fact felt certain the faculty president would want to look through the files himself. Something Rook was not about to let happen.

"Hey buddy, is this anything?" the custodian using the shop-vac called over to Rook after shutting the unit down. "It was on the floor over in that corner."

"It's nothing," Rook replied while looking at a small rectangular piece of metal covered with dust the custodian was holding in his hand. "The Fire Marshal made a thorough sweep of the room before letting us back in here."

"Some sort of tag," the custodian guessed after seeing some writing on one side. He then threw it towards the trashcan but missed, sending the piece of metal tumbling across the floor. "Sorry – want me to get that?"

"No – I'll get it later," Rook said somewhat frazzled. "Tell you what guys – can you finish that up tomorrow? My nerves are about shot."

"Sure thing buddy," the other custodian answered after blowing his nose with a rag used to wipe down the walls. He then tossed the makeshift hanky into the trash and started to leave but not before picking up the dusty tag the other custodian found and setting it on Lowery's desk. "We'll be back in the morning and hey – make sure ya eat that Yum Yum. That'll settle ya down – it's good stuff."

An hour later with the lab quiet and all to himself, Rook finished with the computer files. He then contemplated reformatting the hard drive even though school policy stated such action was grounds for immediate dismissal. It would however insure nobody ever found anything that might be on the computer that could embarrass Jean or the girls. Rook felt certain if he cleaned up the files he already copied and turned them over to the faculty president, then told him he had to reformat the drive because of a virus, that would be the end of the matter.

After bringing up a C prompt, Rook typed the DOS command to reformat the hard drive. A message came up asking him if he was sure. Rook stopped to rethink his actions. He glanced around the room and at Lowery's desk for maybe a minute yet afterwards still felt the same. He then brought his hands back up to the keyboard and typed y and slid his finger onto the enter key. He started to press down when—

"I'll be damned," Rook marveled even though he still had to look back over to the corner of the desk just to make sure. He then eased his finger off the keyboard, picked up the piece of metal the custodian found, and wiped the rest of the dust from it. "I'll be God damned!"

18
MAKING THE MOST OF EVERY MOMENT

At a marble bench next to the old well along Cameron Avenue where students came to wish for luck, Deborah Davis waited for her boyfriend to arrive. She vaulted from the bookstore with a customer standing at the register, bundled up, and rushed over after receiving Rook's urgent yet vague phone call.

Not saying what was on his mind was nothing new – something Deborah did not understand but to this point tolerated in their relationship. Tolerated like the frosty wind nipping at her face as she sat there and wondered what could be so urgent. Urgent enough for Rook to insist on meeting someplace they could be alone.

"What's wrong," Deborah asked when Rook arrived.

"This," Ronald Oliver Knell claimed then handed his girlfriend a small piece of metal but not before looking around to see if they were alone. "Read it."

Property of SynRx
LAB BB
Optima 3000
Asset # 230897

"I don't get it," she scoffed. "I thought there might be a problem with your blood work from last week. What's this?"

"It's a placard," Rook asserted. "Specifically, one from the ICP in the Corporate Lab where the fire started."

"You dragged me down here and out in the cold for this," Deborah said getting up to leave. "I've got work to do."

"Wait," Rook pleaded. "Hear me out."

Deborah stopped then turned back to listen. First Rook told her about the presence of picric acid in the fire and then about the printout from the ICP that showed the instrument in operation during the time of the explosion. Next he filled her in about his search of Lowery's computer and how the name SynRx showed up throughout the files – something he dismissed until he saw the placard from the instrument with the company's name on it.

"It's just a coincidence," Deborah argued.

"No," Rook countered then waited for his girlfriend to sit back down before continuing. "Prior to coming over here I checked with one of guys that works in the corporate lab – he said the ICP was donated about a month ago but no one used it because the torch would not ignite due to a bug in the software. They wanted to reload the software but were never given a copy of the program so they called SynRx to see if someone there could help. Eventually, a man got on the line and told them not to worry about it – that he knew there was a problem and that he was in the process of transferring the license agreement over to the University and once that was done, Perkin-Elmer would send the latest revision directly to them. After that, they got busy on other projects and kind of forgot about it."

"So the arsonist is a man and works for SynRx?" Deborah posed. "Not only that – you think he planned this over a month ago?"

"It makes sense doesn't it," Rook replied. "Remember what I just told you the fire marshal said – whoever did this not only knew how to operate that instrument but knew their chemistry as well."

"What about Professor Lowery – how does he fit into this?" Deborah asked. "Was there something on his computer that showed he knew about the fire ahead of time?"

"It's not like that," Rook insisted. "It appears Dr. Lowery had been researching SynRx for several months. There were folders with the company's name filled with information concerning not only their products but also details about their entire operation. He even wrote a letter accepting an invitation to attend an upcoming seminar at their RTP facility."

"What are you saying?" Deborah asked with a look of puzzlement.

"Whoever started the fire," Rook began to say but stopped when startled by footsteps. He wheeled his chair around but saw no one, then realized the sound came from the wind whipping a pile of dry leaves up into the air. He turned back around towards Deborah then smiled and began again. "Whoever started the fire knew the professor was checking into SynRx."

"Isn't that what I said – somehow Dr. Lowery knew about the fire?"

"No," Rook asserted. "It's the other way around. They knew about Stephen so there had to be a fire."

"Oh, and I suppose Dr. Lowery's death was—"

"No accident," Rook proposed, finishing Deborah's sentence for her while nodding his head. "I think Stephen was murdered! Murdered because there's something about SynRx somebody didn't want anyone else to find out about."

"You're insane," Deborah declared. "Utterly insane."

"Really – well there's more," Rook boasted then moved his chair closer to the bench. "The other day someone tried to kill Kyle on his way back to Manaus. Luckily, he's alright but when he showed up at the hotel where he was to meet Dr. Crotalez – she wasn't there."

"You think somehow these things are related?"

"I do."

"And what does Kyle think?" Deborah asked.

"He doesn't know," Rook answered grimacing. "I

just made the connection after going through Lowery's computer so I didn't know any of this when the two of us talked. Making matters worse, he's out looking for Selena. Let's just hope he does what he said he'd do and checks back in once he gets to the Rednalsi village."

"You know what – you should tell the fire marshal or even the police about what you've found," Deborah said as she pulled off a glove then reached over for her boyfriend's hand.

"I can see it now," Rook scoffed as he pulled away from her. "Excuse me officer – can you dig up my boss' body even though his family just buried him? I think he was murdered and this placard proves it."

"Ronnie, I'm on your side," Deborah shot back.

"I'm sorry," Rook replied. "If you only knew."

"I want to," Deborah pleaded as she again reached for his hand, "but you never tell me what you're feeling. It's like there's this wall between us."

"I love you," Rook blurted out for the very first time. "I love you so much."

"Where did that come from?" Deborah asked caught off-guard.

"From behind that wall," Rook admitted gazing into her eyes. "I've wanted to tell you that from the moment I met you but love – love is supposed to be forever and we both know I don't have that long."

"What's wrong with this moment?" Deborah asked as she wiped tears of joy from her cheeks.

"Nothing," Rook replied as the chimes of the bell

tower rang out in harmony with one another until the deep throated bourdon sounded the coming hour.

"Ronnie," Deborah asked with a look of dread, "you don't think the fire was set for you – do you?"

"No – I was just in the wrong place at the wrong time," Rook replied, even though he remembered Kyle saying the very same thing.

"But if you hadn't been there – the whole building might have burned down?"

"Probably," Rook agreed. "And no one would be the wiser."

"But we are," Deborah claimed then dug a coin from one of her pant's pocket and held it in her fist, ready to throw it into the well. "So let's make a wish and do something about it?"

19
BOA VISTA

With the engine revved, Nathan zipped a sporty black BMW out in front of the hangar from where it had been stored. The car screeched to a halt just inches in front of Ian and Rana. Nathan waited scarcely long enough for the two of them to climb into the backseat before he barreled off.

With the rumble of jets overhead, the car then raced across the misty tarmac and onto an access road headed towards the airport exit. Within seconds the BMW reached the gate and after downshifting at the very last second, Nathan slowed the car. Rana lurched forward while Ian anchored himself with his arms. Both the briefcase and Kyle's journal in the front seat fell to the floor. Nathan then spun the car out in front of a dingy dump truck filled with tailings from a nearby sand mine.

Within a mile of the airport the BMW slowed once again and fell in line with several other cars behind another dump truck at an intersection with a flashing red light. The bisecting road, BR 174, was the only north-south corridor through Amazonas. The highway's construction had been a major undertaking by the Brazilian government at considerable cost with even greater expectations. This section of the highway cut a path a thousand kilometers long between the sixty-first and sixtieth longitudes connecting Boa Vista to Manaus.

"Politicians hail this as a "Roadway to Riches," Ian commented as he looked out his window at some children begging for money at the intersection. "Though the environmentalists dub it 'The Pandora Passage'."

"Highway to hell seems more appropriate," Nathan remarked while waiting to move forward.

As Nathan waited for his turn to drive through the intersection, he watched the children in their tattered clothes scamper amongst the traffic. Some seemed barely old enough to walk let alone stand unattended at such a busy intersection. Yet at any given moment, he counted an half-dozen of them working the middle of the street with even more standing at the corners.

"Where did these varmints come from anyway?" Nathan asked pulling within a car's length of the caution light.

"They live in a nearby shantytown, or 'favella' as they're called down here," Ian answered then rolled down his window and handed a few reisle to a brown-eyed boy no more than knee high. "Most of their families were lured from the larger cities along the coast by the promise of free land," he added. "Because of that, thousands upon thousands of people flocked to Roraima. It's Brazil's Wild West."

"Guess you fancy yourself a gunslinger then," Nathan said with some sarcasm. "Although our cowboys and indians didn't get along – unless you count the Lone Ranger and Tonto. How is it you two partnered-up?"

"It's like this boss man," Ian said trying not to smile because he hoped Nathan would ask that very question. "A couple of years back some loggers to the west of here near Santa Rosa hired me to track him down because he kept attacking them. After about a week of lying low and just watching, I finally captured him – it wasn't easy but I got him. Anyway, I tied him up and brought him into their camp but when I tried to collect my money, those sorry, sons of bitches tried to screw me over. I got so mad I cut him loose and together the two of us butchered every single one of them."

"No one likes to be double-crossed," Nathan remarked noting Ian's somewhat tactful threat while sending one of his own.

"At the time," Ian added, "I didn't know it but I was getting a partner because it turns out Yanomamo must believe in a life-debt whenever someone saves their life. Now he just does what he's told. He's my blue chip."

When Nathan's turn came to pass through the intersection, generosity was the last thing on his mind. Even as he reached into his pocket and pulled out a wad of cash his foot never touched the brake. Nor was he overwhelmed with compassion as he cracked his window and let the confetti of bills slip from his fingers. Halfway through the turn, Nathan cut to the inside of the car in front of him then passed another one to the outside using the shoulder of the larger highway. In his rearview mirror, he saw the children grab for the money. Then to Nathan Briers' delight he heard brakes squeal followed by several high-pitched shrieks.

"Jesus!" Ian hollered after turning back around in his seat. "You knew one of those big trucks would not be able to stop in time."

"Of course," Nathan reveled.

"But why?" Ian asked still looking back.

"Why not," Nathan shrugged adjusting the rearview mirror so he could see Ian's face. "Or do you have a problem with that?"

"With what – killing children?"

"Killing whoever gets in the way," Nathan proposed. "You see, I have no doubts about your partner after what you just told me but you – you on the other hand …"

"You're not so sure about," Ian said completing Nathan's sentence for him. "Afraid I won't come through for you?"

"Precisely."

"Don't worry about me – I'm no saint," Ian grumbled unholstering his pistol. "As long as we're clear on the money – we're fine," he added then brushed the barrel of the gun back and forth against the tip of his nose. "Now where's this other job?"

"Relax," Nathan replied even as the car headed away from town. "It's not much farther."

Boa Vista marked the northern limit of the Amazon Basin. To the north and east of the city the ground rose with golden grasslands and mountainous plateaus dominating the landscape. Roads and trails from those directions had been around for centuries with villas and trading post sprinkled in along the way. To the south however, BR 174 tore through lowland covered by rain forest as dense and diverse as any in Amazonas. Forest thought by most to be impenetrable, until the government project started.

To either side of the highway, for as far as the eye could see, charred remnants of that immense forest remained. The burned out stumps of the enormous trees that once formed the canopy littered the ground as hedgehogs on a trodden battlefield. To either side of these piles, fields already abandoned by settlers, eroded even at the mere mention of rain.

Even the road withered from exposure. With nothing around to offer cover, the relentless sun beat down upon the black asphalt, which by midday flowed more as a river of oozing tar than something solid enough to drive on. When relief did come in the form of showers, the rain cooled the road too quick causing it to crack and chip. Only the buzzards overhead, rising and falling on the thermals coming from the road, seemed to find the new conditions favorable.

"Up until this was built, the only way from Boa Vista

to Caracarai, Novo Airao, Manaus, or anyplace south of here was by boat," Ian said as the car passed a marker showing the distances to those cities.

"By boat," Nathan parroted but not really listening because he found the mirages out in front of the car far more interesting than anything Ian said. "Only by boat."

"Yep, down the Rio Branco and then the Rio Negro and all their wonderful winding curves," Ian said sounding knowledgeable about the terrain. "Awfully slow going but it sure beat venturing out into the jungle by foot."

"Prey!" Rana interrupted, speaking for the first time since getting into the car.

"Ohanaa, toa ayaa freem!"

"Ohanaa, toa ayaa freem!"

"Ohanaa, toa ayaa freem!"

"What the," Nathan uttered startled by the indian's outburst.

"There," Ian said as he pointed up ahead to something along the shoulder of the road.

Just another mirage to Nathan at first, the timber truck took on substance only after they were on top of it. Fluffy white steam billowed up from the truck's open hood. In front two men worked on the problem while the rest squatted along the side within the shadow of the rig's trailer to escape the heat. All of them appeared covered from head to toe with sawdust strewn upon them while cutting trees from somewhere further down the road.

Upon seeing the BMW, one of the men sitting on the

ground stood up and started waiving his arms. A second man joined him out in front of the truck while a third climbed up top the giant logs of mahogany stacked on the trailer. All three did their best to flag down the car but Nathan had no intention of stopping as he tightened his grip upon the steering wheel and pressed down even harder on the gas pedal.

In back, Rana smooched his face up against his window with a terrible need. He ground his teeth with a grit that wore at even Ian and Nathan. The Yanomamo balled his hands into fist and pounded them into the seat. He knew these men, not by their faces, but by their action – each with the same name – prey.

"Ohanaa, toa ayaa freem!"

"Ohanaa, toa ayaa freem!"

"Ohanaa, toa ayaa freem!"

"What's that he's saying?" Nathan asked.

"Beats me but I call it his 'word of prayer'," Ian Haleem replied. "In fact, I've never run across anyone that could understand him – not even a missionary that lived with a Yanomamo tribe for a year could translate their language – something about them being 'isolates' and not having anything in common with the other tribes."

"But you said he does what he is told?"

"He does," Ian contended. "He responds to gestures more than anything else but I can tell you this – he says that whenever he's upset – whenever he's going to kill."

20
MODUS OPERANDI

For the next half-hour they drove along the highway and through the vast wasteland without seeing another living soul. Then, after crossing a river choked with silt, trees appeared in the distance. With each passing mile the might of the forest inched its way back towards the rivulet of asphalt until it formed a lush but impenetrable barrier to either side of the road. Then just as it seemed there was nothing around but forest, Nathan slowed then turned onto an unmarked cutoff on the north side of the highway.

"I've been up and down this road a thousand times and haven't seen this before," Ian declared as he leaned forward in his seat, trying to get a better look where they were. "How long has this been here?"

"Too long," Nathan hissed. "Too long."

After a sharp turn onto the cutoff, Nathan Briers drove along an elevated dirt path with the BMW bouncing and lurching more wild than a bronco. Deeper and deeper he drove with an obvious indifference, if not aversion, to the jungle. Ian also grew more edgy while Rana seemed a sea of calmness as he looked starry-eyed at the surrounding trees and bushes.

"This is just a wild goose chase – isn't it?" Ian fretted.

"I assure you it's not," Nathan hissed back just as the car approached a tiny one-room shack. "Listen – they're not expecting me but my ID should get us in," Nathan said before he stopped the car. "If the guards try to question you – don't say anything."

"Guards – why the hell would there be guards out here?" Ian Haleem asked somewhat baffled.

Looking around, the bounty hunter couldn't imagine what could be so important all the way out here. Besides the tiny guardhouse, an eight-foot tall, chain link fence with razor wire fortified the perimeter. A reinforced gate blocked what appeared to be the only the entrance. If someone wanted to break in they would either need to bring some tools along for the job or shoot up the place.

"Remember I do the talking," Nathan Briers turned and reminded Ian. "So just sit there and relax."

Despite Nathan's instruction, Ian Haleem reached over and eased his hand near his gun holster just as two uniformed men rambled out of the guardhouse. The first one out wore a small caliber sidearm holstered at his belt while the second one remained in the doorway with a shotgun at his side. Neither seemed that competent to Ian. Still they had his undivided attention until a calendar hanging inside the guardhouse caught his eye.

For the month of October a picture showed someone in a lab coat pouring a bright yellow solution from a distillation flask into a small beaker. Ian did not recognize the person but the logo on the coat seemed familiar enough – a six-sided ring with the letters "Syn" written within the circle and "Rx" outside but slightly lower. It was identical to the one he saw on the Learjet back at the airport and the one stamped on the briefcase. The very same logo displayed on a flag flown over an enormous plant located in Boa Vista's industrial district, which as it happened, Ian passed almost daily on his way to the bars and brothels on the Rua da Uniao.

"Parada – Este e propriedade confidencial?" the guard closest to the car beckoned after Nathan lowered his window.

Slowly Nathan slid his left hand out of the car and held an ID badge by his fingertips as if a ticket for a valet. Upon seeing the ID the second guard approached the BMW then looked inside the car.

"What business do you have at the lab?" the guard with the shotgun called out.

"Official," Nathan Briers smarted. "So if you don't mind – it has been a long trip."

"We'll notify them you're coming," the other guard said as he handed Nathan back his ID.

"Wait," Nathan implored, "this is suppose to be a surprise inspection."

"No – no surpresa – they'd kill us if we let you in unannounced."

"How about it," Nathan proposed after pulling a box of cigars out from the glove box and offering them to the guards. "Sao Cuban."

Smiles broke out on each of their faces as both guards grabbed a cigar then lit them after biting off an end. Nathan just watched as they puffed away. The smoke lingered around them with its smooth sweet scent – too sweet in fact for an authentic hand-rolled Havana.

"I'll take one of those," Ian Haleem begged Nathan as they drove through the opened gate.

"Entirely up to you," Nathan smirked then waited until Ian held a cigar in his hand and was about to smell it. "You might want to reconsider though – I know those guards would if given a chance."

"Let me guess boss man – it's against company policy," Ian bemoaned while flirting with the cigar on his lips.

"No," Nathan Briers replied. "I want you to stay alive – at least for a little while longer."

Upon hearing those words, Ian Haleem turned around and looked through the car's back window. To his surprise he saw both guards lying on the ground belly up. Their bodies besieged by convulsions as if being shocked over and over again by electricity.

"You Bastard," Ian said dropping the cigar onto the backseat and wiping his mouth upon his shirtsleeve. "Are you trying to kill me!" he added then reached for his gun and pointed it at Nathan's head. "I ought to—"

"Could have," Nathan Briers proposed cutting the handsome bounty hunter off in mid-sentence, "but didn't – so put that away. Besides, you were the one dying for a smoke."

"Dying for a smoke," Ian repeated with Rana watching wild-eyed. "It's a good thing we both have a sense of humor," he said then leaned forward in his seat and jammed his gun a little harder into Nathan's temple. "Somewhat professional too," the handsome bounty hunter added with a glance at the briefcase then re-holstered his gun. "A very good thing."

"Isn't it," Nathan replied as he pulled the car forward. "So let's get down to business."

Up ahead in a clearing, over two acres of the forest had been bulldozed with tons of fill dirt trucked in to raise the ground up above the high water mark. An enormous slab of concrete covered much of the site with three buildings built upon it and rip rap piled at its edges to prevent the pad from being undermined. The main building arose from the slab constructed out of oversized masonry block with no windows, a recessed door, and a flat roof with ventilation ducts sticking up above it. An adjoining corrugated-steel building appeared to house the facility's generators and water purification system. While an enormous three-walled shed sat offset on the back of the pad with trails leading out into the forest in every direction.

For SynRx this particular facility represented a mine full of raw jewels just waiting to be cut, polished, and brought to market. In fact, the company's rise to prominence in the pharmaceutical market came from the introduction of several drugs derived from plants extracted from the surrounding jungle. For Nathan Briers though, the lab struck at a vein he already claimed. The mother lode of all discoveries that he intended to share only with his associates.

"So how does this place tie into the guy on the boat?" Ian pried after stepping out of the car. "Does he work here or something?"

"Who said the two jobs were related?" Nathan Briers quibbled then grabbed the briefcase along with the box of cigars and got out as well. "You assume too much."

"Come on boss man – there's no reason to be so hush-hush," Ian Haleem pressed as Rana stood next to him. I know Kyle Preston was a scientist that picks plants because your associate told me that much. Now we're out here in the middle of nowhere at some lab about to bump more people off – what are the odds?"

"My slut of a wife slept with him and a few others," Nathan spouted. "I want revenge."

"Like a woman would have you," the handsome bounty hunter laughed. "Your money wouldn't buy a poke with the whores I sleep with. Even they need to see something in a man's eyes before they'll spread their legs – something good or bad – something that hints that you either care or don't care for them. With you there's nothing – nothing except ice. My guess is that you're not the 'company man' everyone thinks you are," Ian

Haleem suggested while leaning up against the hood of the BMW and clicking his boot heels together. "Call me crazy but I doubt your boss knows what you're up to."

"See that building over there," Nathan Briers directed, ignoring Ian's comment while pointing to the maintenance shed. "It houses a giant crane used to pluck stuff from the trees. It's not there so somebody is out collecting."

"So," Ian replied, still hoping to bait Nathan. He knew he was right – Nathan wasn't here on any official business. "I'm not saying this company of yours wouldn't put profits before someone's life – Hell, companies do it all the time."

"Just shut up and earn your keep," Nathan clamored while noting Ian's use of the company's name. "I want you to kill anyone you come across."

"Anything else boss man?"

"Yes as a matter of fact there is," Nathan said as he locked the doors to the car. "Once you finish with that – cut off the water to the buildings – understand."

"Got it – and what will you be doing?"

"I'll be saying hello to my dear, sweet wife," Nathan said as he began walking towards the lab with the briefcase and the box of cigars in his hands. "And anyone else inside."

As Nathan Briers turned and started over to the lab, Ian gestured to Rana to head towards the trailhead to their right. One by one they check each trail, walking nearly an half mile each time before turning back, until finally coming upon a beast of a machine. Within the crane's operator's cage Ian could see a man working the controls while a second dangled from a rope near the crown of an enormous ceiba tree.

Bam! Bam! Bam!

Three quick shots crackled loud as thunder, sending Ian's victim to the floor. He then climbed onto the crane and kicked the bloody corpse to the side with his shiny black boots. The handsome bounty hunter then grabbed the control and laughed wildly as he mashed levers and ground gears until figuring out how to control the crane's arm and winch. Afterwards he disengaged the locking pin and sent the man harnessed to the rope into a free fall.

The scientist plummeted over halfway down before Ian stopped the winch. The rope stretched to the point of snapping then jerked the man back up into the air. Eventually he came to rest upside down about fifteen meters above the ground with the rope wrapped around one of his legs. Ian then maneuvered him over to the center of the trail and once again released the locking pin.

The scientist hit the ground dazed by the fall. The Yanomamo stood ready to pounce, watching to see if his prey would try to run. The man staggered to his feet then halfheartedly balled his hands as if to fight. From out of nowhere a rusty metal pipe, roughly four feet long and two inches in diameter, dropped next to the man. Rana looked up just in time to see Ian throw him a pipe as well. The Yanomamo caught it effortlessly with both hands out in front of him and stood with his knees bent poised for battle.

Images of being back with his own people flashed before Rana's eyes. He remembered standing encircled by the other warriors of the tribe and receiving their lofty praise after surviving each of his club fights. Then he remembered how empowered he felt to hear everyone within the village proclaim his fierceness. He stood proud, so very proud of those bumps on the top of his head.

"Ohanaa, toa ayaa freem!"

"Ohanaa, toa ayaa freem!"

"Ohanaa, toa ayaa freem!"

Bam! Bam! Bam!

Three quick strikes thumped hard as thunder, sending Rana's prey to the ground. The Yanomamo then came over and pounded the head into a pile of mush. Afterwards, he tossed the pipe to the side and slid one of his hands down into a gapping hole near what remained of the man's neck. The indian's whole arm disappeared into the torso then re-emerged a few seconds later with a handful of intestines. Upon seeing this Ian realized his partner's intentions and took up the slack in the rope, raising the headless body back up into the air so the entrails dangled below. Then Rana rummage along the ground until he found part of his victim's skull and strung it up as well.

Bam! Bam! Bam!

Three quick knocks rang crisp as thunder, sending

everyone inside to their feet. Nathan flashed his ID badge in front of a surveillance camera then waited for the door to be unlocked. Without saying a word, he entered then walked down the lab's main hallway, noting the number of scientists within the different rooms. Afterwards, he turned to find the head researcher standing in front of him.

"Senhor Briers – what are you doing here?" Carlos Duhanan, asked taken aback to see the company's top scientist standing in front of him. "I wasn't told you were coming – what is wrong?"

"I think you know," Nathan stated without commenting any further.

"Yes – I believe I do," Carlos said while gesturing for Nathan to follow him to his office. "We have much to discuss."

21
THE ROOT OF THE PROBLEM

"Tell me about this mysterious sample?" Nathan asked cutting to the chaff once they were alone.

"Aye yes – the sample," Carlos replied as he sat back in his chair. "Believe it or not my own brother gave it to me."

"And where did he get it?"

"Well," Carlos explained, "my brother is a soldier in the Policias Federais and was in Pico de Neblina with his platoon for a training exercise. While there, they stumbled upon a group of indians living illegally in the park. His sergeant wanted to make an example out of them and told his men to raze their camp. A few of the soldiers got carried away and killed several of them."

"What does this have to do with the sample?"

"Afterwards, my brother went back to help the remaining indians," the head researcher recounted shaking his head in disgust. "In return one of them gave him this," he said then held up a Ziplock bag lying on his desk. "This, I believe, is why you're here."

"That's the root of the problem," Nathan Briers said somewhat incensed while looking at a knurly strand of a vine with plush dark green leaves. "That twig."

"Ironic – isn't it?" Carlos Duhanan commented as he fiddled with the sample for a moment then handed the bag to Nathan. "For such a scraggly thing to contain so intriguing a compound."

"What do you mean?" Nathan asked to assess the damage.

"Well you've obviously read the preliminary report or you would not be here," Carlos replied. "Anyway, as I'm sure you are aware, alkaloids degrade the second they come in contact with oxygen – that's why samples are preserved immediately with some type of organic solvent – to stop their loss. In this case however, all we were given was this cutting and yet we were able to extract and isolate a very large and active molecule – that's what triggered our suspicions – the stability of the thing. Of course once we ran the different phases through the mass spec and then the Bruker, things got even more interesting."

"But you also mentioned something about showing no ill effects of aging," Nathan said as he recited the report almost word for word. "What did you mean by that?"

"Take a look again," Carlos teased as if to imply Nathan overlooked something. "What's wrong, or should I say, what's right with it?"

"Give me a second," Nathan Briers said in pretense because he already knew the answer. "The smell?" he then proposed a minute later after opening the bag and twiddling the vine out in front of him. "There's a sweetness to it," he added thinking back to Dr. Lowery and his lectures on alkaloids, "like a baby's breath – you know, how sweet toddlers are – all that youthful purity."

"In a way," Carlos replied giving Nathan the benefit of the doubt for his momentary digression. "For over a month this bag has been sitting on my desk – and really, my brother carried it around with him for almost two weeks before that. That's almost two months without any sunlight or water or nutrients. With that much time passing this thing should have wilted and rotted and yet look at it – look how fresh and green the leaves still are and how moist the stem still is. It looks like it was cut this morning and yes, even smells the same as when it first arrived. So I ask you – how can that be?"

"Maybe this would be a good time to get all the data and everyone together," Nathan interjected. "I want to hear what your entire staff has to say."

"They would like that," Carlos said glowing. "We rarely, if ever, have visitors."

"Tell me – is this all of it?" Nathan asked as he flipped the Ziplock back on the desk.

"Yes, except for the piece sent to the American University."

"To Dr. Crotalez at UNC?" Nathan asked while already knowing the answer.

"Yes – she was interning there at the time – I thought her input would be invaluable."

"How considerate of you," Nathan forced himself to say.

"By the way, have you found the plant here?"

"Oh no – that in itself will be quite an undertaking," Carlos said as the two men stood up and started walking over to where everyone else was working. "This plant would only grow in what they call a 'liana forest'."

"So I've been told," Nathan bemoaned. "So I've been told."

After a cursory greeting to the other researchers, Nathan Briers began his impromptu review. A charade meant to verify loose ends before proceeding any further with his plan because he did not really care about the supporting analytical data or the other researchers' input. He just needed to shake all the leaves off the tree before burning them as debris.

"This alkaloid appears to be terpenoid in origin," one of the researchers stated, which caught Nathan's attention. "I'll bet it was derived from a classic carbon five precursor."

"Perhaps cyclization starting with the formation of a Schiff base between the primary amino group and the formyl group," another researcher proposed.

"It's an autoinducer that triggers not only the production of helicase but modifies it as well," Nathan blurted as if needing to demonstrate his preeminence on the subject. "The terpenoid chain is the key of course

– it's critical for the reaction to proceed flawlessly. Without it – well – without it the amount and efficiency of helicase present at the replication fork during mitosis isn't optimized."

"There's no way you could know that," Carlos scoffed. "We're still trying to map its structure and determine its receptors. Of course we've theorized on some different pathways but as to its function – that's impossible to know at this point," he said while looking over at Nathan in disbelief. "Impossible for anyone – even you."

"Really," Nathan disputed while staring back. He surprised even himself with his revelation but then again, here was a chance for him to show just how brilliant he was to a group of people that might actual understand and appreciate his genius. "Study Werner's disease and its effect on the eighth chromosome with respect to lipid peroxidation sometime and you'll find I'm right," he added. "Until then, don't tell me, or my associates within the society, what is and isn't possible."

"Chemical Society?" Carlos asked intrigued by the disclosure. "Is that who you're talking about because I can't believe the company would involve them at this point – not without a patent pending. And please Mr. Briers, how long have you known of this? What else can you tell us?"

"Sorry – I swore an oath," Nathan joked to evade answering any more questions. "Those damn secrecy agreements we all have to sign to work within certain circles – I'm sure you understand. Though I can tell you," he added while stroking his muttonchops – "what I've seen here does support our work."

"Then maybe the company will let us work together," Carlos suggested, "because given time, I assure you, we'll get to the bottom of it. And if we can't synthesize the compound – we'll find where the vine grows – even cultivate new plants from that twig we have."

"Well, I applaud your thoroughness," Nathan proclaimed to everyone in the room as he tapped all of the printouts into a neat pile like a teacher just before dismissing their students. "I also want you all to know how much the company appreciates the job you're doing here. I can't disclose the specifics, but needless to say you're all receiving a little extra this Christmas."

"You don't know how much that means," Carlos beamed. "It's nice that corporate knows how hard we've been working down here and to be appreciated."

"Believe me, it hasn't gone unnoticed," Nathan remarked as he grabbed the box of cigars, "not at all."

22
BABY'S BREATH

Indifferent to the lingering cigar smoke and lifeless bodies strewn throughout the lab, Nathan Briers returned his dart gun to the steel-sided briefcase. Afterwards he removed one of the small silver vials cushioned in foam on the other side of the case and held it out in front of him. Gently he shook the vial then brought it up to his mouth. Next he pushed down on the top of the canister and inhaled.

The resulting aerosol intoxicated him with the sweetness of the freshest flowers, or the sugary aroma of a honey-drenched confection, or as any mother would attest to her baby's breath. Nathan licked his lips as if to taste it again. Then he felt a tingling seductive sensation sweep across him that aroused every cell in his body. The euphoria lasted for almost a minute then from out of nowhere, a rush of heat burned behind his eyes as if looking at the sun from just a few feet away.

That flash of discomfort appeared to be the only drawback to Nathan's prized drug he called Baby's Breath. The drug needed to be taken as an aerosol so that it could be absorbed as quickly and evenly as possible. Once inside the lungs it passed from the respiratory system into the circulatory system almost instantly because of the hundreds of capillaries surrounding each alveoli where gas exchange occurred. Then, while in the bloodstream, it flowed into the heart then spread throughout the body within a matter of seconds. The exception to this was at the monopolar cell axons of the optic nerve, which interacted slightly slower with the drug than the rest of the body and caused the burning sensation.

In actuality, Baby's Breath combined two drugs with amazing results. One of the constituents, dimethyl sulfoxide or DMSO for short, was a polar aprotic solvent, considered rather common even though it exhibited some unique properties. Anyone who ever worked with DMSO would have experienced the sensation of both tasting and touching it at the same time. The most intriguing aspect of dimethyl sulfoxide however, was its ability to transport other molecules into the body that would not normally be absorbed through skin or other types of tissue.

In this case, the active molecule hitchhiking on the back of the DMSO was an antioxidant few chemists would have believed existed. Considered a "suicide" molecule, the alkaloid Nathan discovered attached itself to the helicase substrate in such a way that the two molecules fused into one and remained that way for the life of the enzyme. Once attached, the normal operation of the enzyme to unzip the DNA molecule during the creation of daughter cells still proceeded even though the binding sites had been altered. The benefit came from the fact that the modified helicase protected the strands of DNA while being copied against degradation from free radicals roaming within the body. A benefit that meant Nathan Briers would no longer age:

– never turn another day older
– never miss a sunrise
– never fear not finishing
– never die of old age
– as long as he administered the drug on a daily basis to modify new enzymes produced by his body.

23
IF YOU FIRST DON'T SUCCEED

After leaving the SynRx research lab in a smoldering heap of ruin, the powder keg of tension between Nathan and his hired guns continued to build. The handsome bounty hunter tired of Nathan's uppity attitude, continual barrage of snide remarks, and incessant stares with those hypnotic green eyes of his. Meanwhile, the incompetence of Ian, irritated Nathan to no end, especially after finally hearing from his associate. Even Rana's silence fueled the strife. Each of them ready to erupt – ready to explode – needing only the slightest spark to set them off.

"Face it – you missed," Nathan Briers jeered while climbing aboard a boat tied up alongside a private dock in a secluded part of Manaus.

"No I didn't," Ian Haleem maintained as he filed onboard with Rana right behind him. "I know I shot him."

"Even though my associate saw him yesterday," Nathan said after storing the steel-sided briefcase in a small storage locker in the front of the boat. He then checked to see that the weapons and other items he requested were in the main hold before starting up the motor and casting off. "Alive and well I might add."

"I don't see how," Ian huffed looking over Nathan's shoulder down at the cache. "Their boat was riddled with bullets before we blew it up."

"It appears you're not as apt at shooting things as you think," Nathan quibbled as he let the speedboat drift away from the dock. "His indian guide was with him as well as a dog."

"What's so special about this guy anyway?" Ian asked with his ego bruised more by his own words than by Nathan's. "By the looks of that diary he kept, all he cares about is plants."

"I thought you said you didn't read it," Nathan Briers complained.

"Skimmed it," the handsome bounty hunter divulged curious to see Nathan's response. "Didn't find anything though – just pictures of plants with what looked like Greek or Latin written beneath them. A few maps as well. Nothing earth-shattering – nothing worth killing someone over."

"That's right," Nathan said. "Nothing worth killing over."

"Hey – you're the boss man," Ian quibbled. "If you want a silly man who goes around picking flowers dead – that's fine by me – I'll take your money.

"Try to remember that."

"I will," Ian Haleem said under his breath. "I will – at least for now."

"Good, then let's shove off."

"Hey – what about your associate," the bounty hunter asked as he checked out the scope on one of the rifles. "They're not coming?"

"Already in position," Nathan stated with confidence. "It's just a matter of leading Mr. Preston into another trap, but this time," he added with a look of disgust, "I want him dead!"

24
MEDLEY OF MAYHEM

Despite Zito's efforts to shed speed, the airplane still traveled far too fast for such a precarious landing. The bush pilot, however, remained committed to bringing the plane down before the darkness of nightfall made it an impossibility. In a last ditch effort he veered the plane to the right and cut the engine, sending the aircraft into a nosedive. During the awkward free-fall the controls stiffened, but never froze. The fuselage rattled, but never buckled. Then, with only a few meters between them and the water, Zito somehow coaxed the Cessna out of the doomed stall and back on course.

"We're still a little hot," Zito warned after glancing over at the gauges. "Twenty knots," he added. "Maybe even thirty."

"Too bad there's no brakes to slam," Kyle commented while eyeballing the pontoons.

"A runaway rhino on ice skates has a better chance

of stopping," Zito spouted in agreement as he switched the engine back on. "We're just so damn heavy with the extra fuel onboard."

"Any more tricks up your sleeves?" Kyle Preston asked afraid of the answer.

"You're the science officer," Zito claimed with a wink.

"Please tell me you see those?" Kyle beckoned as the Cessna approached two enormous tree stumps that were less than a hundred meters away and jutting up above the water like fangs ready to strike at them.

The next few frantic seconds passed in slow motion for Kyle. He watched in horror as Zito ignored his warning and slammed the plane down right in front of the stumps. A wall of water then swooshed up into the air and obscured their view. Together they listened to the belly of the plane groan followed by a resounding thud back near the tail. With the worse yet to come, Kyle cringed in anticipation of the inevitable.

"Go baby go," Zito pleaded.

"What the hell?" KP shouted bewildered after opening an eye in time to see the plane bounce back up into the air.

"Hey – they don't call these puddle jumpers for nothing," the bush pilot screamed as the Cessna gained just enough altitude to clear the stumps then touched back down again. "But we're not out of this yet."

As they skimmed along the surface, Zito still needed to bring the plane to a stop. Immediately, he set the ailerons on the wings and the tail's split elevators for maximum drag then throttled up the engine. Everyone lurched forward then rocked back into their seats as the pontoons plunged into the water. Afterwards, the Cessna bobbed forward with maybe twenty meters to spare before reaching a dense gathering of stumps that awaited them like tombstones in a graveyard. Zito then turned the plane around and maneuvered it as close as he could to the nearest shore before shutting down the engine.

A few minutes later the two men used a towline to drag the aircraft up far enough into the sand so it would not float away. Kyle then went over and unlatched the cargo door whereupon Brooklyn appeared at the doorway on his knees. The ethnobotanist helped the shaman down, who immediately retreated to the woods and began to retch. In the meantime Kyle climbed up into the fuselage and started loosening the straps used to secure their supplies for the flight.

"Here – make yourself useful," Kyle called out, giving Zito little warning before throwing one of two backpacks at him.

Within no time their gear sat piled up along the shore. Supplies that included not only food and water but also two razor sharp machetes, a lightweight cooking pot, a pocket knife, a fishing bow for Brooklyn, and even a new slingshot for KP to play around with. They also had raided the stockpile of equipment back at IAR and brought along two GPS units, a set of walkie-talkies, hammocks with mosquito netting, and a substantial first-aid kit in case Dr. Crotalez was hurt.

"Seems like a lot," Kyle remarked as he double-checked Louisanne had rounded up everything on his list. "Then again, I'm not sure what to expect," he added once he came across a box of bullets. "Not sure at all."

"Word from the wise," Zito warned while watching Kyle load a small pistol then tuck it back into his backpack. "If you pull that out," he said as reached past the bottle of hooch beneath his seat and pulled out a gun of his own, "be prepared to use it – otherwise someone else will."

"Listen – are you sure you won't come along?" Kyle asked while looking around. "I hate the thought of leaving you here all alone."

"Lions and tigers and bears – oh my," Zito mused as he tossed the gun back under his seat. "I'll be fine – I'm going to check out the optics on that telescope I brought – there's a new moon tonight.

"Zito – I'm serious," Kyle Preston shot back as he grabbed one of the machetes then also stuffed the pocketknife and slingshot into his pant's pockets.

"We both know I'll only slow you down," Zito said. "Besides, I did my part – I got you here – and in one piece."

"If something should happen to you, Louisanne would never forgive me," KP remarked. "At least move away from the water – you're too close – a caiman could easily sneak up on you here."

"Great, now you're mothering me as well," Zito ripped even as he smacked a flashlight into Kyle's hand. "At the first sign of trouble, I'll have Scotty beam me up," he teased. "Now go – you're wasting time – and daylight. This is your away mission – Qapla!"

"It's scary how that stuff just rolls off your tongue," Kyle alleged. "Maybe you missed your calling not as an astronaut but as a script writer."

"If I had worked on that show – Spock would have been hornier than once every seven years and hooked up with Commander Rand because she was bitchin'," Don Zito smirked. "Now go! And I hope you find your friend."

The pilot then nagged until the two would-be rescuers finally headed out. From coordinates taken off a map Selena left behind in the office, the GPS showed the Rednalsi village to be no more than five kilometers from the plane. Kyle knew that meant they should be able to reach the encampment in less than an hour – no matter the terrain. They also spotted signs of a trail during the flyby just south of their position, which KP suspected might lead right to the village.

A few minutes later with nightfall upon them, the two friends walked along the shoreline in search of the trailhead. On several occasions, Kyle took his own advice and shined his flashlight out into the water for the glowing red eyes of caimans. Brooklyn though seemed far more interested in the banter coming from the forest than anything attacking them from the water. Both men though held their machetes out in front of them, prepared to protect themselves from either direction.

"Found it," Kyle called out about fifteen minutes later after spotting several sets of bare footprints in the sand then following them up to an opening in the forest.

"Too dangerous," Brooklyn said after he and Cleto disappeared behind a bend in the trail beyond the reach of Kyle's flashlight only to reappear a few seconds later. "Better to make our own."

"No – the village is due east of here," Kyle commented after checking their position with the GPS. "I think we should take it – Selena never mentioned the Rednalsi being hostile."

"Perhaps – but it is foolish to believe they would welcome strangers into their camp in the middle of the night."

"Then we better get moving," Kyle directed then started to walk off, "because it's still early in my book."

"Wait my friend," the Tirio insisted and pulled his bow down from his shoulder. "We need to go as hunters – not the hunted."

"What do you mean by that?" Kyle asked while looking around with his flashlight.

"Turn that off," the shaman suggested. "Turn your light off and see what you have been missing."

25
BLINDED BY THE LIGHT

With the click of a switch, Brooklyn and Kyle stood at the trailhead in utter darkness. The new moon overhead offered no illumination and while the stars sparkled brilliant in their own right, even they appeared insignificant. For Zito back at the plane with his telescope this would be ideal, but for Kyle the darkness loomed as if the goblin of night had swallowed everything whole. He stood blind – blind and helpless in a black fog of fear.

The only distinction between one direction from another came from sounds. The lapping of water back along the shore and the peeping of frogs tipped Kyle off from where they came. The rustling of leaves swaying on the tree limbs along with the thunderous calling of the cicadas and other creatures told him which way they wanted to go. But the sudden calls from here and there by different animals only added to the confusion. As did the snapping of a twig or the splashing of water.

So much so, Kyle's perception of what was out there – what was happening caved. Everything grew louder almost as if he could see each sound move in the darkness – and always towards him.

Clarity, in more than one way, came to Kyle though as his eyes adjusted to the dark. As Brooklyn suggested they were not only being watched but outnumbered and surrounded – one stood back in the direction of the plane, another further up ahead along the shore, and the third hid behind a palm tree no more than ten meters from where they stood.

"Should we run?" Kyle whispered even though he still held his machete out in front of him.

"That is what they want," Brooklyn proposed even as Cleto growled to warn the person behind them now crept forward.

"How do you know?"

"Because that is what I would want."

"OK – we'll make a stand here," KP shrugged while whispering even softer than before. "I think I can get to that gun without any of them—"

"Don't," the person behind the tree shouted in English much to Kyle's surprise. "Don't force me to shoot."

26
REDNALSI VILLAGE

Kyle heeded the warning and stopped reaching for the gun. He stood there unmoving – surprised the person had seen him – surprised by their threat – surprised even more they spoke English.

"Show yourself," Kyle Preston demanded without thinking, then turned his flashlight back on.

The beam of light shot out to reveal an indian boy of eleven maybe twelve peeking from behind the palm tree. He wore only a red breechcloth like Brooklyn and even had red and blue markings on his body similar to the shaman. By all accounts, the boy looked to be a younger version of the Tirio except for a decorative headdress made from what appeared to be green and yellow macaw feathers.

"Drop the weapons," the boy ordered with an arrow within his bow at its anchor point.

"Tell us your name," Brooklyn asked while trying to keep an eye on the other two people behind him.

"It is what it is," the boy implored as the arrow crept slightly forward. "Now drop the blades and the bow!"

With trepidation, both Brooklyn and Kyle set their weapons down on the ground then took several steps back. As they did Cleto remained out in front of them and continued to snarl. Then from behind, they heard the other two strangers slink to within just a few meters of them. A second later both Brooklyn and Kyle felt the sharp point of an arrowhead pressed into the small of their backs. All along, Kyle kept the flashlight fixed upon the boy out front, who by now stood in the middle of the trail.

"Now what?" Kyle asked with nervous sweat dripping from his body. "Are you Rednalsi – because if you are – we were on our way to your village – we're looking for a friend."

"Toss over the light," the boy demanded easing the arrow from his bow to free up his hands. "Now!"

"Tell us your name and how it is you learned to speak this language," Brooklyn asked again. "Mine is," the shaman began to say in English then switched to his native tongue, "Bruwk a wa lyn."

"Moro," the boy finally announced after Kyle handed him the flashlight. "My name is Moro. Whose dog is this?"

"Mine," Brooklyn replied then whistled two short burst like the call of a red-legged honeycreeper, whereupon Cleto stopped growling and sat down. "Would you like to know his name?"

"He listens well – like m—," the boy started to say but stopped in mid sentence then turned the flashlight off and snapped, "No more talk – just follow the trail – follow the drums."

Within an half-hour of shuffling along the footpath, the faint rhythmic beat of drums permeated through the forest. At first the thumping seemed so far off as it competed to be heard against the creatures in the surrounding trees and bushes. With each passing step though the drums grew in strength while the forest succumbed to its rule, until only one remained.

Bump – bump a – thump – bump a – thump – bump a – thump

Bump – bump a – thump – bump a – thump – thump – thump

Bump – bump a – thump – bump a – thump – bump a – thump

Bump – bump a – thump – bump a – thump – thump – thump

The primal rhythm preyed upon Kyle's sanity. The thumping and the bumping beat even stronger within his chest than his own heart. His pulse raced. His blood boiled. The drums pounded that intense – that enthralling – that maddening. So much so, by the time they reached the edge of the village, Kyle resembled a moth drawn to a blinding light.

"The boy – he has left us," Brooklyn said as the two men stood no more than a stone's throw from over a hundred or so Rednalsi men and women engaged in celebration around a bonfire. "And look," the shaman added, breaking the spell Kyle had fallen under, "they dance naked."

Kyle's jaw dropped as he realized the scores of silhouettes he watched wore only swatches of dark blue body paint. The men also decorated themselves with beguiling masks resembling owls, hawks, and other birds of prey that concealed their identity. In contrast, the women adorned themselves only with a colorful shell necklace. Together, they seemed to be acting out an elaborate mating ritual and in fact afterwards a man and woman would run off into the jungle then return a few minutes later. Whereupon, they would each pass along the mask and necklace to another couple standing along the sideline but only after stripping them of their clothes and decorating their bodies with paint.

After that revelation, both Brooklyn and Kyle stood undecided as to what to do next. The shaman thought it best to leave and return in the morning even though Moro brought them to the village. Kyle on the other hand, despite the orgy, hated the thought of leaving in case Selena was there and needed their help. Either way they both felt uneasy just standing there.

"Friend," Kyle Preston finally called out innocently enough to a toothless old man in the back of the pack. "My name is—"

The old man walked away before Kyle even finished.

"Amigo," the ethnobotanist greeted a second man

in hopes he knew either Spanish or Portuguese only to have the same thing happen.

"Try a few words in Saran Tongo then maybe Arawakan or Cariban," Brooklyn offered.

"Better yet – you try," Kyle sniveled frustrated with the turn of events. "Maybe they'll listen to you."

"Ewe wa nu," the shaman said in Tirio to a young woman to his right who wore only a finger woven sash tied around her waist. "Ewe wa nu."

"I don't get it," Kyle remarked after she walked away as well. "You'd think we were invisible!"

"Perhaps we are," Brooklyn replied. "Perhaps to them we are no more than fleas."

"Hell, even fleas get picked at," Kyle remarked then added, "Moro seemed to see us well enough."

"Maybe he and whoever was with him are not part of this," Brooklyn proposed, "like a patrol so no one can sneak up on the village, especially tonight. Besides, look closely at the eyes of these people – their centers are so very large."

"What's that they're drinking?" Kyle asked as they watched person after person slurp down bowls of a whitish gruel stored in terracotta vats near the bonfire. "Could that be why?"

"Maybe Cassava," Brooklyn replied. "But that alone would not cause this."

Kyle knew Cassava, also known as Manioc or Tapioca back in the States, served as the most important staple crop in Amazonas. Extremely high in starch, its normal preparation started by grating the plant's tubers into a coarse meal then roasting it for later use as flour. In this case though, the Rednalsi chewed the Cassava into a mush, which they then spit into the vats Kyle and Brooklyn noted earlier by the fire, and left it out in the sun for days if not weeks to ferment. A beer nothing like the Black and Tans Kyle downed back at the campus pub but instead one thick and chunky while at the same time stringy from the remnants of saliva. As for potency, cassava beer sported a fairly strong wallop with a bitter aftertaste but would not cause anyone's pupils to dilate.

"Maybe they spiked it with something," Kyle suggested then spotted someone on the other side of the bonfire dancing. "Selena," he yelled at the top of his lungs to get her attention but could not out-compete the noise of the drums. "Selena – it's Kyle!"

Desperate to reach her, Kyle Preston plowed into the crowd. Behind him Brooklyn followed while Cleto seemed content to stay put and munch on a bone someone threw to the dog. Then together, the two friends cut through some of the dancers and past within just an arm's length of the bonfire.

"Selena," Kyle shouted again to no avail with the continual eruptions of the drums drowning him out while she stood with her backside to him.

As Kyle went to spin Selena towards him, only then did he realize his blunder. A mistake made more troubling and confusing when the woman finally turned and he knew her.

27
NOTHING LIKE THE SUN

Savannah Soliel fulfilled an ancient Greek myth of a woman warrior, born from the union of the God of War Ares and the sea nymph Harmonia, whose beauty both astounded and bewitched. Standing five foot nine and wearing only body paint and a shell necklace like the rest of the women dancing, the tall blond stood out – not just for her height, or her golden hair, or her pleasing face, but by the way she moved. The seductive curves of her hourglass body inflamed the fire to burn hotter. Her erotic arms and legs embroidered with muscle swayed each beat of the drums to pound harder. Every move she made tormented her partner the same way her necklace teased the nipples of her firm tan breast – constantly, rhythmically, wildly.

For her part, Savannah Soliel had always been proud of her body and enjoyed the power being so incredibly beautiful gave her over others. A treasure of sensation governed by a clever and calculating mind committed only to the needs of her self-serving will. This dance confirmed her shameless resolve when it came to showing off her wares and using them to get what she wanted. Beauty so spell-binding, like what the Greek myths warned about, that exuded so much heat and burned so hot that sometimes it consumed whatever it touched.

That sense of playing-with-fire only added to Savannah Soliel's appeal as a highly sought-after freelance photographer. With little effort she could sweet-talk her way into the plushest assignments or the most luxurious locations. Sometimes the tall blond did just that but most of the time she took assignments most photographers would never accept. Locations so extreme like the Rednalsi village that would break most people when in fact Savannah not only found them invigorating but somehow, as in this case, ended up in positions to take the most spectacular pictures imaginable. Extraordinary pictures like her, which were highly desirable yet seemingly unobtainable.

Even now as she danced, Savannah gripped a camera in one hand and three rolls of film in the other. She never went any place without being prepared to bring back the "trophy" as she liked to call it. The one shot that stood out from all the rest and became her signature photograph for an assignment. For the moment she seemed content with her current prize – the fastest, strongest, fiercest stud the Rednalsi could offer.

"So your friend is alive," Brooklyn yelled into Kyle's

ear then playfully grabbed Kyle by his backpack and shook him as the two of them stood there. "I am glad all has worked out for you. Although – look at her eyes – she too has drank the Cassava."

"That's not her," KP said while still trying to sort things out.

"Who is she then for she looks like the sun?" the shaman asked even more confused than Kyle.

"Trouble," Kyle said, watching Savannah run off into the woods with her dance partner. "Nothing but trouble."

28
GRANDFATHER

As their luck would have it, no sooner had Brooklyn and Kyle watched Savannah run off, when Moro reappeared next to them. At first KP smiled at seeing the boy because maybe now they would finally get some answers – that is if they could get him to talk more than he had before. However, behind Moro stood four stout Rednalsi males, who seemed rather hardened and serious for a welcoming party and even less likely than the boy to entertain questions. Warriors armed with crude yet sharp knives that could easily carve flesh from a bone and unlike the rest of the villagers engaged in the festivities, these men not only saw Brooklyn and Kyle but wanted something from them as well.

"Grandfather will see you now," Moro announced as a medieval summoner would for his king holding court. "This way," the boy said then turned and walked off.

"Hey – where did you go earlier and how come nobody will talk to us?" Kyle called to the boy then tried to catch up with him but was stopped by one of the four men. "What?" Kyle grumbled as a second man blocked his path as well. "He said to follow."

"Leave your gear," Moro demanded without turning around. "None of it is of use to you here – including whatever you were reaching for earlier."

"Great," Kyle huffed under his breath as he pulled the backpack off his shoulder and set it down on the ground. "That makes two this week I've lost."

"Do as he says," Brooklyn encouraged, "and remember not to let your actions betray you."

Kyle Preston watched with alarm as one of the men enveloping him flipped a knife into the air, caught it, and then sliced through the cord holding the GPS unit onto his belt. The unit fell to the ground with a thud followed by the batteries rolling across the ground. Afterwards, a second man patted the ethnobotanist down and discovered the pocketknife and slingshot tucked away in his back pocket. Then, only after the other two Rednalsi finished checking Brooklyn over, were they allowed to proceed.

Following behind Moro, Kyle felt as naked as the men and women dancing around the bonfire. All along he envisioned being prepared for anything, but in less than an hour they had been stripped of their supplies if not their dignity. It made Kyle think back to his conversation with Rook and how resolved – no, how stubborn and arrogant he had been in deciding to search for

Selena. A macho yet foolish decision on his part it now seemed, which not only put him but also Brooklyn in this awkward position. A predicament far worse than not having clothes because as they walked back further into the village, Kyle also remembered Zito's comment about who knew to rescue the rescuers when the pilot thought the plane might crash.

"Who indeed?" Kyle Preston said aloud as they stopped in front of a small hut built off by itself, "And who is this Grandfather?"

After ducking down and climbing through a small doorway, Kyle saw a lone man mumbling to himself while lying back in a hammock. Seasoned more with salt than with pepper, wisps of hair cloaked his face from view while falling unevenly like a lion's mane over his shoulders. Then, after Brooklyn and the other men crawled into the hut, the old man stood up and flung his hair behind him to reveal a pair of fiery eyes. Eyes which burned hotter than the flames of the bonfire outside, sharper than the blades carried by the four Rednalsi, and more pointed than any arrow Moro might heave from his bow. Eyes that endured as an enigma because they sparkled so bright and powerful despite being surrounded by skin crackled by time.

Indeed, it dawned on Kyle after a quick scan of the hut, the old man Moro called Grandfather must be the shaman Selena came to study. Draped over the beams of the hut's ceiling dangled lumps of moss, clumps of sedges, pieces of roots and stems, strings of mushrooms, and other things Kyle couldn't recognize without further inspection. Satchels made from animal hide hung from pegs hammered into the hut's supporting post along with several blowguns and pipes. A clay cooking pot darkened and glazed from years of use also dangled over a fire pit in the middle of the floor with mats to either side.

"Boro ma tongee," the Rednalsi shaman barked in a deep gruff voice rougher than sandpaper. He then swaggered up to Brooklyn and then over to Kyle, then stood back from them both. "Boro ma tongee," he repeated. "Boro ma tongee."

"I don't understand?" Kyle replied while looking first at the old man then over at the boy. "Moro – tell him I don't understand what he's saying – neither of us do. Tell him I just want to find out about my friend – the one who came to learn from him – then we'll leave. Tell him that for me Moro."

For the next few minutes, Kyle Preston tried his best to explain to the shaman about Selena while also answering his questions. An exchange in which the ethnobotanist never knew whether the boy translated everything as told. In fact, at one point Moro and the shaman debated something without anything being restated in English.

"Grandfather says he allowed the two of you to come this far because he was curious but now you both must leave," Moro snapped with authority beyond his years. "Leave now!"

"That's it?" Kyle rebuffed despite being in no position to argue. "All this way and you can't tell me anything about my friend – whether she's here, or whether she's left, or if she's even alive?"

"Heed his warning because tonight is not a night for outsiders," the boy said motioning for the four men to escort them back out. "The festival of the mischief moon is upon us."

"What about Savannah," Kyle complained then thought to add, "the blond woman I saw dancing – she's not Rednalsi."

"She chose to cross over," Moro replied.

"Cross over?" Kyle asked.

"Remember her eyes," Brooklyn broke in. "He must be talking about the beer and whatever else was in it."

"Yes," the boy said in agreement. "She chose to drink the Cassava and be a part of the ritual. Like the rest, she has crossed over on a night when the moon is darkened by the wickedness of shadows from the spirit world."

"Moro – is there nothing you can tell me?" Kyle pleaded. "If not, at least let me talk to Savannah – surely she knows something?"

"Grandfather said your friend is there next to you," as he nodded towards Brooklyn. "No more can I say."

"What if we cross over?" Kyle asked not that he had changed his opinion about spirits, the supernatural, or the power of God for that matter even after Tatiana's miraculous recovery. "What if," he said with an approving nod from Brooklyn, "we agree to drink the cassava – can we stay?"

Moro at first hemmed and hawed then translated what Kyle asked. Upon hearing it, the Rednalsi shaman rattled off an ominous sounding phrase then once again scrutinized Brooklyn and Kyle, and even shook them both by their shoulders as if sizing them up. He then went over and snatched a small blowgun and one of the satchels hanging from their pegs. Next he opened the pouch, took out a pinch of a rough-cut tobacco, and rolled it into a ball with his fingers. He then loaded the blowgun with the shot and gestured for Brooklyn to come over and sit down on one of the mats.

"Wait," Kyle protested at the turn of events. "I said we would drink the beer – nothing more."

"Grandfather says to find the answers to your questions you must seek out different spirits – more powerful ones that only come forth with stronger medicines."

"Well – then we'll pass," Kyle whined then turned to be led away. "We'll take your advice and leave."

"No – we accept," Brooklyn interjected to both the surprise and dismay of Kyle then walked over and kneeled on the mat. "We accept to seek out these spirits."

"No – Brooklyn – No," Kyle denounced. "I'm willing to go along with drinking the beer and getting a little buzzed but this is different – this is dangerous – this is foolish."

"My friend – I told you before, whatever we find we face together."

"Yeah – I know," Kyle conceded, "but you've also told me more than once not to let my actions betray me

– well I'm not – you're the one who's not seeing things clear now. All this talk of spirits – let's just leave before it's too late."

"This is what we must do," Brooklyn said as he looked up at Rednalsi shaman and allowed him to place the tube up under his nose. "Remember my brother – spirits come forth to those who believe in them – only then will they reveal themselves – only then might you learn about your friend."

"Wait," Kyle shouted once again just as the Rednalsi shaman drew in a deep breath. He then walked over and kneeled on the other mat and reached over and swung the blowgun in front of him. "I got us into this."

"A tu ne," the old shaman said grinning from ear to ear then took another deep breath, held it a few seconds as he stared into Kyle's eyes, and then exhaled through the tube. "A tu ne."

29
SNAKE BITTEN UNDER A MISCHIEF MOON

Before Kyle Preston could even second-guess himself, the Rednalsi shaman sent the shot of snuff into his nose. Over the course of his career he found himself in similar situations but always declined the invitation. Maybe that made him less of an adventurer than others in his field, especially since the experimentation by Richard R. Schultes, the father of Ethnobotany, stood as the benchmark. Nevertheless, there he kneeled, against his better judgement, in that very position bullied by both his kinship with Brooklyn and his longing to find Selena.

It scared Kyle to think about what would happen next and for good reason – there could be anything in the snuff – narcotic analgesics, psychedelics, hypnotics, neuroleptics, or even entactogenics – anything to induce illusions. For the moment though, the effects appeared far more physical.

"Ugh – I don't feel so good," KP confessed as his eyes watered and mucus drained from his nostrils. He then clutched his head in agony, shuddered, and for a moment lost his balance even though he was still kneeling. Afterwards his heartbeat became erratic. His breathing labored. Sweat oozed from his pores more than ever before. "I really don't—"

Succumbing to the potpourri of compounds within the snuff, Kyle collapsed to the ground and blacked out. Several minutes later he awoke and sat back up, albeit no longer in control of his faculties. Despite that, he believed what he saw as real – real beyond any shadow of doubt – beyond doubt of any shadow.

"Got a black magic woman,
 Got a black magic woman,
 Yes, I got a black magic woman,
 She's got me so blind I can't see,
 But she's a black magic woman,
 She's trying to make a devil out of me"

As Kyle swayed to Santana, he watched in amazement as the beads of sweat rolling off his forehead fell ever so slowly into the clay pot next to him. Maybe enthralled described his reaction better because within each droplet Kyle Preston noticed a moment from his life. First a scene of him helping his granny in her garden came into focus from when he was only eight years old. That was followed by the time he rode with his father to the poll and voted for the very first time in an election. Next he saw Angie, the first love of his life.

Drop by drop, these snapshots collected in the bottom of the kettle. Vivid moments captured clearer than any camera could, free falling without rhyme or reason to when the events had occurred or their relative importance. Each so real and lifelike as they bobbed up and down and brushed against one another as if competing to stay afloat. Then, when Kyle decided to reach out and catch a drop of sweat that contained an image of the first time he met Stephen Lowery, something remarkable happened.

Enveloped by the drop and transported back to Chapel Hill on a dog-day of summer where he sat upon a bench near one of the fountains on campus. Just as if there, Kyle squinted from the bright sun overhead, smelled Confederate jasmine in the hot air, and felt the cool spray coming from the fountain. Next to him sat the Professor as he appeared back then with a hefty head of hair, a few wrinkles here and there, and sporting a pair of black, horned-rimmed glasses perched halfway down that big nose of his. Kyle even regressed back to a younger and hipper version of himself. However, as soon as the two of them shook hands, the scene changed to a vision of Lowery's funeral. In it Kyle looked to be back to his normal self while the professor appeared as a haggard spirit. A phantasm, which had clawed its way out of the coffin, and now pleaded with Kyle not to let go. Pleaded while being whipped with a vine back down into the darkened grave by a redheaded man with glowing green eyes.

> "Don't turn your back on me baby,
> Don't turn your back on me baby,
> Yes, don't turn your back on me baby,
> Don't mess around with your tricks,
> Don't turn your back on me baby,
> You might just wake up my magic sticks"

After that, everything went dark and for a few seconds Kyle sensed nothing except the sound of his own voice. Alarmed at first, he then found himself back on the mat in the middle of the hut with beads of sweat still rolling into the pot. By now, the kettle bubbled with twice as many visions as before. Kyle seemed apprehensive though to reach out again because he feared the same thing would happen. Still, when a scene formed of Rook and he playing chess for the first time, Kyle couldn't help but to grab hold of it.

Sent back again into the past, the ethnobotanist found himself this time at the Suds and Duds in Carborro on a frigid Wednesday night during March Madness. A clock on the laundry room's wall displayed it was almost two in the morning as the two of them played chess atop a dryer while doing their laundry and watching UNC play in the tournament. Each donned a pile of quarters, a box of detergent, and cans of Old Milwaukee next to them even though at the time Rook's face appeared covered more with peach fuzz than with whiskers. Unknowingly, that night started a momentous tradition as Rook played white and maintained command of the game. In fact he had just cornered black's queen but as Kyle conceded the move and handed him the piece, they both returned to their present age. After that, Kyle appeared by Rook's side as he handed him back the chess piece before collapsing.

"You got your spell on me baby,
You got your spell on me baby,
Yes, you got your spell on me baby,
Turning my heart into stone.
I need you so bad,
Magic woman I can't leave you alone."

Again everything went dark until Kyle heard his voice and followed it back. When he looked down this time, the memories almost filled the entire clay pot with one of him with Brooklyn dropping down while they lounged on the deck of the *Anna Maria* just before the ambush. Next came an image of his maiden voyage with Zito in his plane almost seven years ago and then the time he mistakenly tried to eat the flesh of a chocolate gourd instead of its seeds. Then a bead of sweat appeared with a vision of Selena inside, which he felt compelled to catch.

As his fist closed around the image, Kyle found himself back in Manaus at IAR three years earlier when he first met Selena Crotalez. They both attended a symposium put on by WWF, the World Wildlife Federation. Of all people, Savannah had just introduced them as a way of excusing herself to mingle with far more prominent people in attendance. Both just shook their heads and shrugged off the photographer's rudeness. Then the scene changed as they exchanged pleasantries and clanged their glasses in a toast to one another. Instantly, Kyle began to age as he had before but this time grew far older than he actually was. Selena, however, remained unchanged while grappling with a rattlesnake coiled around her forearm and poised to strike.

"She's a black magic woman,
She's a black magic woman,
Yes, she's a black magic queen,
She's got you so blind you can't see,
And she's a black magic woman,
You're headed towards catastrophe."

30
DANGLING BY A THREAD

With sounds nibbling at his ears, Kyle awoke and just listened for a moment before doing anything else. Overhead, a light shower caressed the palm fronds in the hut's roof like a mother would its newborn. From somewhere out in the jungle's understory, a pair of melodious nightingale wrens repeated a series of three soothing notes as they called back and forth to one another. Meanwhile, dispersed throughout this sweet broadcast, the sharp shrill of a screaming piha cut in to announce its presence. From nearby, Kyle then heard the pitter-patter and giggles of children splashing around in mud puddles. Telltale signs of a new day well underway before the ethnobotanist even opened his eyes.

When Kyle Preston finally peeked, he found himself alone and no longer in the Rednalsi shaman's hut. Instead he saw women's clothes strewn all about along with climbing gear, camera accessories, and some other electronic equipment. At first Kyle just laid there on his back with a thin blanket draped over him without seeming too concerned. Then, the more he thought about it, the ethnobotanist became alarmed because he couldn't remember how he had gotten there – clueless in every way as to what, if anything, he had seen, heard, or even done, from the time he kneeled down to accept the snuff until now.

Kyle became even more baffled, if not dumbfounded, when he tried to sit up but couldn't. Embarrassed was more like it because, after squirming and wiggling around as a worm for a bit, he realized his arms and legs were tied down to the mat beneath the bedding. Then he noticed his shirt and shorts hanging on a peg over by the door.

"Please let me have them on – please let me have them on," Kyle prayed aloud until he was able to free one of his hands and pull back the blanket. "Oh my God!" he said with his cheeks flushed beet red. "Savannah!"

After freeing himself and searching in vain for his underwear, Kyle threw his shirt on and tucked the bottom of it into his shorts. He cursed Savannah again as he tightened his belt then dashed out of the hut in a rage fit to be tied.

Once outside he noticed Brooklyn across the way sitting with Moro under a tree. The two of them inspected Brooklyn's new flute for his son while the boy's puppy and Cleto played by their feet. Despite that, the shaman, after seeing Kyle, knowingly pointed off to the right over towards an enormous kapok whereupon KP caught a glimpse of Savannah. From the looks of it, the tall blond hung from a rope close to forty or fifty meters above the ground up next to one of the tree's branches bejeweled with epiphytes. The ethnobotanist then looked back and gave his friend a cursory salute, as if to say thank you, before stomping off through the mud puddles in the direction of the tree.

Despite his anger, Kyle admired Savannah Soliel's spirit as he looked up at her through the drizzle. Spirit that showed through as she worked the rope and bounced from one side of the spiked limb to the other while snapping pictures. A sense of adventure even greater than her beauty. Maybe that's why she seemed so good at what she did? Maybe that's why Kyle thought of her as trouble? She did what she wanted – when she wanted – how she wanted.

Almost as if to show Kyle or anyone else watching just how much trouble and a risk-taker she truly was, Savannah climbed atop the branch and disconnected the rope from her harness. The photographer then walked out towards the end of the limb as if a gymnast on a balance beam. The sharp, conical thorns of the branch however made her footing uneven and treacherous – the rain even more suspect. Still Savannah Soliel moved along for almost ten meters before squatting to pluck a tank bromeliad from where it grew. As she did, Savannah even waved down to Kyle, who stood too afraid for her safety to return the gesture. The tall blond then made her way back to the rope and reattached herself to it, but not before placing the plant in between two orchids and snapping almost a whole roll of film of the embellished scene.

"Three years later and you're still getting off on domination," Kyle crowed once Savannah was back down on the ground.

"You didn't seem to mind last night," the tall blond posed as she again unhooked herself from the rope then sashayed over and gave him a playful hug. "Not at all."

"Guess I'll have take your word for it," Kyle replied as he glanced down and felt his wrist then looked over and watched Savannah climb out of the harness. "You look good."

"Of course," Savannah Soliel smirked then added, "I'm getting better with age."

"I'd have to agree," Kyle marveled at how young she still looked.

"You on the other hand have some gray hairs there mister, and what's with that farmer's tan," the tall blond joked as if to let him know last night wasn't a dream. "I didn't recall you having such a white kitandkaboodle. Nevertheless I got some really good pictures of it."

"Could be worse – you could have said 'small'," Kyle smarted back then decided to change the subject. "What are you doing out here anyway?"

"What do you mean?", Savannah rattled off while slinging the rope at him. "Isn't it obvious."

"I mean, how did you end up on assignment out

here – nobody knows about this place and it's damn near impossible to reach?" Kyle alleged. "Surely whatever you're after is somewhere else – someplace closer in – someplace safer."

"Actually, I'm here for two features," Savannah professed. "One is a pictorial on poison arrow frogs that will be in next month WWF's newsletter and the—"

"Wait a minute – since when did you and the Panda make up?" Kyle interrupted in disbelief because he knew the history between Savannah and the conservation group was just as rocky as if not more than his own with her. "I thought they swore you off after you spiked those bananas with Ketamine so you could photograph that troop of howler's."

"Hey – I never said I was a naturalist – just a damn good photographer," Savannah argued. "Besides, we're not living in the past when artist interested in capturing images of the forest canopy sketched them from the ground while looking through spectacles or went around after storms gathering uprooted debris in hopes of finding something still intact. You know as well as I, that no one can be that passive anymore. Kathryn over at WWF understands that now – we've all got to be more aggressive. Honestly, you've got to make things happen."

"Like moving things around as you see fit?" Kyle badgered.

"What's worse – me moving that plant or you shooting it down with that slingshot of yours or someone else peppering the branch with bullets?" the tall blond spouted while wringing some of the rainwater from her hair. "At least I'm not carting it away you plant picker you."

"Still seems like cheating."

"I'm not denying the consequences of my actions," Savannah Soliel bewailed, "Just thinking beforehand."

"There's a Latin phrase for that," Kyle said as he tried to remember it.

"Could be – but you're the academic – not me," the photographer replied. "I just want to take perfect pictures."

"So why move that bromeliad if you're here for frogs?" Kyle Preston inquired somewhat puzzled.

"Because they're in their bull's eye stage," Savannah commented. "Just as bright, and beautiful, and deadly as they can be."

Both Savannah and Kyle knew the presence of bright colors on many animals was not just to attract a mate but rather to ward off would-be predators. A defense mechanism, known as aposematism and based on reverse psychology, where survival depended not on hiding but rather on being seen. In the case of *Dendrobates*, the genus name for poison arrow frogs, some species appeared in solid but vivid shades of yellow, red, and blue. More provocative ones added other colors splattered in patches to form highly decorative patterns. In either case, the frogs looked glossy, if not moist in appearance, because of a mucous exuded by their skin.

That mucous coat protected in more ways than one because it contained a poison of which less than one hundredth of an ounce could kill a person. A toxin so potent that most animals avoided the frogs altogether while the indigenous people of the forest borrowed its propensity to kill by lacing the tips of their arrows with it. A poison Kyle knew the frogs themselves did not produce but rather collected and concentrated it from what they ate – much the same way monarch larva did with the cardenolides in milkweed.

"So you're saying there was a frog on it," the ethnobotanist said as he looked up at the plant then wiped the rain from his face.

"Not at first but they jump you know – jump right when you're ready to snap their picture," Savannah irked.

"And it's not like you can drug them like those monkeys – is it," Kyle quibbled. "Why else are you here?"

"Last night's orgy," Savannah shrugged.

"Oh – I should have guessed that – you and unrestrained sex – or should I say restrained."

"Not nice," the tall blond sniveled. "As I recall you're the charity case here – at least that's what I told myself last night when you showed up at my hut."

"Really?"

"Until you remember otherwise," Savannah Soliel replied with a wink.

"Seriously – why else are you here?" Kyle asked again.

"I told you – the festival," the photographer answered as she began gathering up her gear. "*Anthropology*

Today is including some of Thomas Barbee's work related to the origin of the Rednalsi's mischief moon festival in their year-in-review edition. They asked me to come here and try to capture the scene – of course tastefully."

"Did you – tastefully?" KP asked, "because I seem to be missing something?"

"Oh – is that what brings you out here?"

"For the moment," Kyle replied then added in all seriousness as his thoughts returned to his missing colleague. "I'm looking for Selena," he said assuming the two spent some time out here together. "We were suppose to meet in Manaus then fly back to the States but she never showed up. When's the last time you saw her?"

"Three days," Savannah said taken aback with an air of concern in her voice. "She left here three days ago saying that's where she was headed. What could have happened?"

"I don't know," Kyle Preston replied, "but I'm not going to stop looking until I find her."

"How?" the photographer badgered without really meaning to sound skeptical even though it came across that way. "Manaus is nearly three hundred kilometers from here – that's an impossible task for you and whoever else you dragged out here, let alone a whole army."

"You're telling me," the ethnobotanist bemoaned almost at a loss for words. "We flew over here as low as we could in hopes of spotting her. Now we're going to have to check under each rock and in every hole – starting with Bensonvia."

BABY'S BREATH

"I'll help," Savannah offered without hesitation. "I realize I just said it was impossible and that I don't know Dr. Crotalez as well as you but I can help."

"Thanks but no," was all Kyle said at first then thought to asked, "Got a boat?"

"The Rednalsi have canoes," Savannah offered instead of just saying no. "Kyle," she then pleaded sounding quite concerned for his safety, "don't go to Bensonvia."

"Why?" Kyle asked as a flash of lightning arced across the sky, which was then followed by several seconds of distant yet angry thunder.

"The Seringueiros there – they're not exactly friendly," the photographer disclosed. "Believe me, I know, because when I first got here I was foolish enough to go there. I thought I could pop in and snap a few pictures without anyone minding – boy was I wrong."

"Even more reason to go," Kyle insisted. "Selena could have run into some trouble there."

"I doubt it – she warned me about that place but do you think I listened," the photographer confessed.

"Do any of us?" KP suggested then froze for moment while bothered by several images he couldn't really explain. Hey – I think I just remembered something from last night."

"About me I hope," the tall blond bragged while more thunder loomed off in the distance. "Tell you what though – I've got a satellite phone back in my hut. Do yourself a favor and check in before you head out. Who knows – maybe by now somebody has heard from her."

"Thanks," Kyle said as he gave Savannah a hug. "That almost makes me want to take back all those bad things I said about you earlier."

"Why," Savannah teased, "Last night you said a lot of bad and filthy things to me – and I liked it."

31
DEDUCTION OR ASSUMPTION

"Rook – it's Kyle."

"Dude," Rook cheered followed by a sigh of relief. "When did you get back?"

"I'm not," Kyle answered as he stood just outside Savannah's hut and watched two young boys practice with their bows. "Believe it or not I'm at the Rednalsi village – on a sat phone."

"Sweet – how did you manage that?"

"There's someone else here on assignment but never mind that – Rook, Selena isn't here."

"Damn – all that way for nothing."

"Yeah – but she was here," KP stated while moving around to the other side of the hut after an arrow skidded through the dirt near his feet. "She left three days ago for Manaus."

"Sounds all too familiar," Rook shrugged.

"Maybe she's just had engine trouble," Kyle Preston offered. "There's an abandoned town not far from here. We'll check there first."

"Then what?"

"I don't know," the ethnobotanist replied. "Maybe it was a mistake coming out here."

"There's only so much you can do, especially when the world seems out to get you," Rook said to prepare Kyle for what he was about to say. "Anyway, I've got some news since last time we talked. The fire was deliberate and I think set to destroy the professor's lab. Maybe more importantly, I think the person who set it works for SynRx. Does that company ring a bell with you?"

"No – not really," was all Kyle could say as he tried to make sense of this startling revelation. "I mean they're a prominent pharmaceutical company – other than that. As for Stephen having an interest in them – you know he wasn't one for corporate involvement in academics. Look how hard he fought the University on accepting their donations."

"Do you think it could be as simple as that?"

"People do stupid things for money," Kyle confessed, "but even that seems too far-fetched."

"We'll I'm about to find out," Rook divulged after a long pause.

"Ronald – what are you up to," KP fussed because, even though they were in two different hemispheres, Kyle knew by the tone of his friend's voice that he was up to no good.

"Nothing," was all Rook would say, "nothing that is, that the professor wasn't about to do."

32
CASTLING FOR POSITION

Away from UNC, the brick paver roads of campus gave way to asphalt streets that barreled more than maneuvered through the once quaint neighborhoods of Chapel Hill. South Road itself widened into a major four-lane highway with more and more cars pulling alongside Deborah's rust-encrusted van as she drove. From time to time Rook would look over and give her a reassuring look despite his own doubts.

A few minutes later the van coughed to clear its throat then labored up to speed and onto Interstate Forty headed east towards Research Triangle Park. The park, a nine thousand plus acre industrial site, had been created in 1962 to entice corporations to move into the piedmont. With UNC in Chapel Hill, Duke in Durham, and NC State in Raleigh; corporations within the park recruited each of the school's top students to mold into a skilled workforce. SynRx was just one of many prominent pharmaceutical companies to take advantage of such an ideal location.

"Ma'am, please pull over there so the other cars can pass," the guard instructed Deborah after Rook handed him the invitation to the symposium. "Driver's license and Sir, I'll need your school badge," he added once they parked. "Wait here – this will just take a second."

"What's he doing now," Rook asked straining to look into the guardhouse that blocked the entrance to the SynRx facility off of Page Avenue.

"He's on the phone," Deborah replied cranking her window back up to stop all the heat from escaping. "On the phone and not looking too happy," she added while rubbing the chill from her hands. "Now he's picked up a clipboard."

"Sweet," Rook smarted off as he looked up at a flag flapping above them with the company's logo. "I told you that invitation was a trump card worth playing."

"Ronald – this isn't a game," Deborah said, denouncing her boyfriend's cavalier attitude. "You could get into a lot of trouble. So could I."

"For what – crashing a party?" Rook joked with a wry smile.

"That's crap and you know it," Deborah fired back and was about to voice her opposition again to his ill-conceived plan but noticed the guard hanging up the phone. "Here he comes," she said then rolled back down her window.

"Miss Davis," the guard beckoned while standing just outside the van's driver-side door and holding their identification in one hand and a clipboard in the other, "here are these back and I'll need you to sign in – down on line seventeen."

"Only if you tell me your name," Deborah wooed while holding a pen just above the form. "Or maybe I should just call you captain?"

"Appreciate the promotion Ma'am but I just started here," the guard corrected her outright although the scowl on his face was gone.

"Really – because it looks like you run this place," Deborah teased.

"Who knows – maybe someday – right now though I'd settle for a good cup of coffee and my badge," the guard suggested because they still hadn't given him his identification tag yet. "Now halfway up this drive you'll see a turnoff for the visitor's parking lot. There are handicapped spots near a ramp just off to the right."

"Thank you?" Deborah said more as if asking rather than answering a question.

"Eddie," the guard replied and moved closer to the van.

"Thank-you so much Eddie, and I'll see what I can do about that coffee," Deborah wooed this time with a wink then drove off while Rook bit his lip.

After reaching the visitor's parking lot and unloading from the van, Deborah and Rook made their way through an immaculate courtyard over to the even more lavish entrance into the pharmaceutical complex. The foyer itself dazzled them with its rose marble flooring that bolstered walls overlaid with mahogany wainscot and flowery wallpaper. Deborah took a moment to look at the hardcover novels wedged into several barrister bookcases. Meanwhile Rook wheeled himself over to a curio filled with small amber vials of once mainstay medicines like Calomel, Ipecac, Melarsaprol, and other deadly relics from earlier days in pharmacology.

"The money spent on this room alone is ten times what I owe on my student loans," Rook jeered first.

"What do you mean – most of these books are signed first editions," Deborah declared. "Books like Twain's *Huckleberry Finn*, Fenimore Cooper's *The Last of the Mohicans*, and Nathaniel Hawthorne's *The Scarlet Letter*. Do you know how much a copy of one of these early American classics goes for?"

"Sure am glad the money I shell out for medicine is being put to good use," Rook said in disgust as they left the foyer and passed through a five-story atrium and then into the lobby of the main office building.

Within the lobby, the other guest stood around exchanging pleasantries while waiting for the conference to start. To his surprise, someone recognized Rook and waived him over. Ronald however just nodded and continued to wheel around the room with Deborah by his side. Together they looked for something – something that would help them find the lab from which the donated instrument came from.

"There – by the elevator," Rook noted and moved across the room to review the site map for the complex. "It appears this is the only building outfitted with labs," he said but did not see any names for the rooms. "Maybe once the tour starts I'll be able to figure out their numbering."

"Mr. Knell," the taller of the two guards called out then waited for Rook to turn his chair around while the shorter one came around to the side of Deborah. "Would you mind following us. You too Miss Davis."

"Certainly," Rook replied taken aback because he never counted on any problems with his scheme of slipping into Lowery's spot once through the front gate.

"We certainly don't," Deborah clarified while nudging Rook's chair forward.

"Good morning," a third guard said from behind a desk once they entered the security office. "Of course we're all terribly sorry to hear of Dr. Lowery's passing," he said in between encoding some new employee badges, "but I'm afraid there's been a misunderstanding."

"Really," Rook shrugged then turned back at Deborah for a second but without saying anything despite wanting to. "What seems to be the problem?"

"The invitation is nontransferable Mr. Knell," the guard informed. "I'm sure you can appreciate that fact given the nature of this type of meeting. However, I have been instructed to provide you with reimbursement forms, which once filled out, SynRx will compensate you for your time and mileage. I also have a voucher here for Café Momo so that you and Miss Davis can have a nice lunch before heading back to the university."

"Thanks but we're not here for a free lunch."

"The bistro is no more than ten minutes from here on Highway 54 at the Woodcroft Shopping Center," the guard added despite Rook's outcry and handed Deborah the gift certificate. "I think you'll enjoy it – it's French – cuisine – as they call it."

"Is there any way I could speak to someone?" Rook asked in hope of finding a sympathetic ear.

"I am somebody Mr. Knell," the man mouthed back from his chair as the other two guards looked on grinning. "Been somebody all my life."

"But if we could just talk to the person in charge of the symposium," Deborah pleaded as she walked over to the desk and slapped down the voucher on top of the badges the guard was working on. "Maybe they would make an exception?"

"Maybe," the guard echoed while everyone waiting around in the lobby stood up as a young woman wearing a navy-blue suit appeared from behind a set of large double doors. "Maybe, but looks to me Miss Lee has her hands full already."

"Shit," Rook huffed then turned to head back towards the group despite the rejection.

"Mr. Knell – don't get so bent out of shape," the guard behind the desk teased while the other two reached out and stopped the wheelchair from moving.

"Was that suppose to be funny because it wasn't," Rook howled then raised up in his chair while sprouting hackles. "Don't ever," he said with his voice carrying across the room, "Don't ever make fun of me or someone else in this position because it's not like we had a choice!"

"Gentlemen – is there something I should know," Wendy Lee snapped after walking over to the security office in response to the commotion.

"No Ma'am," the guard behind the desk answered then got up and looked at a bank of monitors displaying live video feed from cameras located throughout the complex. "Nothing a pretty little thing like you should be concerned with," he said under his breath. "Mr. Knell was just leaving."

"Doesn't sound like nothing to me or probably our guest," Wendy Lee countered. "In fact it's quite offensive – like you and your good-old-boy mentality."

"Miss Lee," Rook called out after knocking the guard's hands off his chair. "My name is Ronald Oliver Knell – I'm here to attend the symposium on Dr. Stephen Lowery's behalf."

Rook then quickly explained the situation to her before the guards could intervene. He told her about the professor's unfortunate demise and how he had been Lowery's lab assistant. He then repeated his earlier lie about how the university wanted him to fulfill their obligation by attending today's conference. For her part, Wendy Lee seemed more absorbed in the guards' buffoonish behavior than anything Rook said or the specifics about the invitation.

"We can accommodate you," Wendy suggested while browbeating the guards. "You and your friend both."

"Thank you but no," Deborah declined. "I'll just wait here in the lobby until it's over."

"Are you sure?" Wendy asked again. "Because it's really no problem."

"Don't worry about me," Deborah stated then bent down and gave her boyfriend a kiss while tucking something into his shirt pocket. "If I get bored – I know where to find a good book to read."

A few minutes later, Rook along with the other guest in attendance passed through the double doors and entered a maze of hallways with large, shadow-box windows to the rooms they passed. As they walked along, Wendy Lee did her best to give the names of the different areas and described briefly the process occurring within each room. Of course Rook tried to appear interested in the tour while he tried to understand the labeling of the rooms. So far, nothing even remotely came close to the scheme imprinted on the placard found in the debris from the fire. Then as it so happened, Rook overheard Wendy say to another guest that the last stop on the tour would be a lab back in the main office building.

Twenty minutes later and an elevator ride up to the fourth floor, Wendy Lee led everyone to an open door at the end of a hallway. Along the way, Rook stopped to look at the nameplates mounted on the doors in the hallway. For him, it was like finding the Rosetta Stone because all at once he understood not only where he was but also where he wanted to go.

"Mr. Knell – are you coming," Wendy Lee called from the open doorway because by now only Rook remained out in the hall.

"I can't," Rook replied, already regretting what he was about to say next as he beckoned her over to him. "This is really embarrassing but I soiled myself."

"Oh," Wendy crowed with a squiggle of her nose as if afraid of what she might smell. "Do you need me to call your friend?"

"No," Rook insisted. "By now I'm kind of use to it. If you could – just point me in the direction of a bathroom."

33
BABY'S BREATH LAB

Rook ducked into the bathroom, set the timer on his Ironman watch for ten minutes, and then wasted little time before slipping back out into the hallway and onto the elevator. Once aboard he pushed the button for the second floor then watched the door crawl to a close.

Once at the second floor Rook rolled his wheelchair out of the elevator and into a hallway that aspired to be more than it was. Bicottura ceramic tiles, arranged in geometric forms, bedazzled the floor. Reproductions of notable works from the Impressionist period adorned the walls with track lights in sequence with each painting. Even the doors to the rooms were made of solid oak with engraved gold placards mounted upon them.

If asked by someone what he was doing, Rook knew he would just act lost and ask for help in getting back with the tour. He was determined though to find the room that matched the placard from the donated instrument. To not only find it but also somehow slip inside and find out what he could about the person who turned the ICP into a bomb.

Despite all that, Rook also knew Deborah had been right to say this wasn't a game. Rather callously, he dismissed her earlier concerns while strategizing how to use the invitation sent to Lowery to get inside SynRx. He also joked about how much fun he'd have pretending to crap in his pants as an excuse so that he could roam the halls on his own. Even when his girlfriend suggested that he keep track of the amount of time elapsing, he only agreed to it because of the similarity to a chess match.

Now though, the butterflies in his stomach made it impossible for Ronald Oliver Knell to deny the danger – danger not only of being caught but of what he might find. He had no way of knowing who or what awaited him behind the door as he rolled his wheelchair up to the one marked Lab BB.

tap – tap

No one came.

Tap – Tap

Still no one came to the locked door.

TAP – RAP!!

After the third knock without anyone answering, Rook let out a heavy sigh. He agonized over what he would have done if someone opened the door, because then, he might have been standing face to face with the arsonist and not even known it. Clueless to whether the person across from him, not only started the fire, but also killed Lowery and maybe wanted him dead as well.

"What if I knew them?" Rook quibbled aloud then brushed that thought aside after looking at his watch and seeing that almost two minutes had passed.

As with the other rooms in the building, an electronic locking system comprised of a deadbolt, a magnetic card reader, and an activity sensor controlled access to the lab. An ingenious system designed to be foolproof because in order to release the deadbolt, an employee needed to swipe their ID badge through the reader. Not only that, the cards were programmed to open only certain doors with a record kept of the times and locations of their use. Maybe more importantly, the activity sensors sent a signal to the computer located in the security office, which constantly sifted through the inputs giving whoever was on duty the ability to know both the status and history of any door whenever they wanted.

Perhaps Rook did not realize just how foolproof and effective the system really was as he hovered outside the locked door. While at the security office he focused on pleading his case and not the computer off in the corner or even the live video feed from the security cameras. Nor did it occur to him or anyone else on the tour, Wendy Lee lacked the authorization to enter the rooms they passed. In fact, even the door to the lab on the tour needed to be unlocked ahead of time by someone from security then left ajar for her. Still, Rook did have one thing going for him as he reached down and pulled something out of his shirt pocket.

Whether the adage "great minds think alike" applied here or not, Deborah like Rook had seen the employee badges piled up on the desk back in the security office. At the time the badge on top belong to an Edward Pasquantonio. His picture did not do him justice – at least Deborah did not think so after meeting the security guard in person just a few minutes earlier back at the front gate. Regardless of the bungled picture, Rook's girlfriend lifted the badge when she approached the desk to plead his case, then covered up the theft by setting the reimbursement paperwork and the voucher to the restaurant down on top of everything. After all, maybe Eddie wasn't a captain but his ID badge was probably the one thing they needed in order for Rook's daring plan to work.

Right now, that plan seemed more like a trap because Rook not only heard the bell to the elevator ring but also the sound of a door closing from down the hallway. Quickly he brought the badge out in front of him and swiped it through the reader, which caused a red indicator light to flash but nothing else. Rook tried a second, then a third time but both attempts failed as well. Meanwhile, from just around the corner, he heard the murmur of voices coming towards him while from the direction of the elevator someone in heels approached. By the sound of things Rook guessed he had time for one more try before being spotted.

Cursing himself for ever getting into this fix, Rook raised the card above the reader, started to try again, then at the last second realized he had been putting the badge in the wrong way. Fumbling to flip it around, he almost lost the card but eventually succeeded in reversing it. Then Rook swiped it through the reader and watched in desperation.

"There you are," Rook heard someone huff. "I've been looking all over for you."

"Me too," another person irked. "They told me I couldn't leave until I found out what happened."

Lowery's lab assistant took a deep breath then waited to see what would happen next as a group of employees stood in front of him. He had managed to open the door just in the nick of time and get inside the lab without being seen – at least he hoped that was the case. As he listened to every word being said out in the hallway, Rook wondered who these people were and whether they were talking about him? Moreover, why were they standing right there? Was it just a coincidence, or was one of them about to open the door?

About a minute later, Rook heard the conversation come to a close and the sound of footsteps heading off in either direction. Despite that, he couldn't relax. Not for a second because, maybe they hadn't been, but eventually someone would be out looking for him. Seven minutes had passed and he still hadn't learned a thing.

It took another minute for Rook to stop marveling at both the lab's eloquent design and its enormous capabilities. On a slate benchtop right in front of him sat two capillary electrophoresis workstations extremely apt at separating and detecting several macromolecules including alkaloids and antioxidants. Behind them, on an horseshoe-shaped counter in the middle of the room, were five gas chromatography units, which provided even greater sensitivity and selectivity. Then in two small alcoves, each separated by glass partitions similar to the setup in Lowery's lab, there sat a pair of state-of–the-art mass spectrometers, capable of distinguishing between enatiomers all the way down to the parts per trillion level.

"Hell of a setup," Rook mumbled under his breath as he moved towards the back of the room while looking at the neatly labeled reagents stored in cabinets along a wall. "And rather particular – aren't we."

While at the back of the lab, Rook slid open the door to a safety cabinet. Inside bottles of organic solvents filled the shelves along with a jug of trace metal grade nitric acid. Upon seeing the acid, a light went off in his head because the nitric seemed out of place given the instruments in the room. Rook then looked back across the lab for a spot where an ICP might have been setup and saw an exhaust port hanging down from the ceiling without an instrument beneath it. He closed the door to the cabinet then rolled over to that part of the lab and could see where the tile under the vent not only appeared dimpled from the weight of something heavy but stained yellow. Furthermore, the nearby power outlets as well as quick connectors to lines of argon and nitrogen gas, all pointed to the fact that the Optima donated to the school once sat there.

The final nail hammered into the coffin, as to whether being in the right place or not, came when Rook went over to one of the instruments on the center island. From his pant's pocket he pulled out the placard from the ICP found on the floor of the Boiler Room after the fire. Without having to look too long or hard, he located a similar tag on the GC in front of him.

Seeing them together, with the room number stamped on each a perfect match, Rook's heart sank a little. He knew it was one thing to suspect something and another to see it first hand. To know that somebody lurked out there, going to such great lengths to destroy Professor Lowery and anyone else associated with him.

Afterwards Rook wheeled himself up next to a desk in search of something he could take back to the fire marshal. He wanted a picture, or a Rolodex, or a calendar with a hand-scribbled note, or if lucky a coffee cup covered with fingerprints. He found nothing personal though, not even in the drawers or a nearby bookshelf. No clues at all because, with the exception of a phone and a computer sitting in the back corner, the desk was barren.

"If I had more time I'd find something – I know it," Rook jeered aloud, guessing by now Wendy Lee or maybe even someone from security was out looking for him. "More time – I need more time."

Ronald Oliver Knell realized his blunder as he stared at the blank computer screen in the corner of the desk. He had been so intent on finding a solid lead like a letter or notebook, he overlooked the possibility of something being stored electronically. A careless mistake made on his part, especially given his background and fondness for computers. Nevertheless, he made it.

"Damn you," Rook cursed himself because of the secrets the computer might contain.

Afterwards it occurred to Rook he really wasn't interested in the whole computer but just the files. files kept on the hard drive, a device about the size of paperback book, which could be removed without too much difficulty and, maybe more importantly, rather quickly. He owed it to Lowery, Kyle, Selena, and even Deborah for that matter to try.

From yet another pouch on his chair, Rook reached back and pulled out a set of jeweler's screwdrivers then moved as close as he could to the computer. He did not bother to remove the case cover but instead popped off a faceplate on the front of the tower. Behind that plate, the hard drive sat in a protective metal cradle held in place by two small screws. After backing them out, he slid the cradle towards him, plucked the hard drive from it, and then fiddled around for a second or two with the power and ribbon cords until the drive fell free.

Jingle-ring, Jingle-ring!

The phone on the desk rung out and startled Rook, causing him to drop the screws to the computer. In slow motion, he watched as they bounced like BBs upon the floor then scattered out across the room. Meanwhile the phone rang out again drawing Rook's attention away from the mess.

Rook moved his hand towards the phone because he longed to know who it was at the other end. Somehow the ring even seemed louder to him this time, as if demanding to be picked up. The consequences though of doing that very thing could be devastating – still, the lure was too powerful to ignore. Then, just as Rook went to pick it up, the phone fell silent.

Maybe the call had been a coincidence – maybe not. Either way, Rook knew it was time to get the hell out of there.

34
PICTURE PERFECT

After talking to Rook on the phone, Kyle along with Savannah traipsed through the mud puddles over to the Rednalsi shaman's hut and asked his permission for use of a dugout. Grandfather, as Moro called him, agreed but not before he repeated yet again his warning just to leave. The old man also asked Kyle, quite pointedly in that gruff voice of his, why the ethnobotanist chose to ignore what the spirits revealed to him.

With more questions than answers, Kyle Preston left the Rednalsi village and headed back to Zito's camp along the river. What had happened to Selena mind-boggled him, especially after the Rednalsi shaman and Moro seemed to hold back details concerning her whereabouts. Savannah Soliel's intoxicating effect on him also added to his burden. Furthermore, the startling accusations made by Rook during their phone conversation plagued him because the proposed connection between recent events and a pharmaceutical company seemed too far-fetched.

Of the points raised by Rook, the most baffling

and hardest one for Kyle to accept was that Professor Lowery had been murdered. Of all people – why target him, especially since the professor was so kind, and considerate, and caring, but more than anything – harmless. It just did not make any sense – how could it?

Neither did the idea that someone down here in Brazil wanted to kill both Selena and him. If true, then Kyle Preston must also accept this wasn't the work of an individual, but rather, a coordinated effort between a group of people. After all, the attack on the *Anna Maria* occurred the day after Lowery died, and according to Savannah, Selena left for Manaus the same day.

For the moment though, after returning to the shore of the oxbow lake, the ethnobotanist pushed aside any thought of some grand scheme of conspiracy. Instead he concentrated on finding his colleague. Something already perilous and daunting in and of itself without having to look over his shoulder. Still, in the back of his mind, he wondered if he should not at least tell Brooklyn what he suspected. In the meantime though, he needed to persuade Savannah to go back.

"I see you found her," Zito cheered after pulling his head out of an open engine cowling from where he had spent the last half-hour checking the plane's sparkplugs. "Not only found – but damn – look at her. She's beautiful. I mean Harry Mudd beautiful."

"It's not h—"

"I know I know – it's not nice to cuss in front of a lady," the bush pilot said before the ethnobotanist finished. Zito then escorted the tall blond the rest of the way to the plane while helping with her gear. "Sorry princess but the science officer over there never told me you were such a looker. Otherwise I would have marched into that village and rescued you myself."

"At last a true knight," Savannah mused with sarcasm.

"Zito – not only are you ridiculous but you've got it all wrong," Kyle finally mentioned once able to get a word in edgewise. "This isn't Selena."

"Oh – but you said," the bush pilot started to say then decided to shut up by covering his face with his hat.

"Zito listen – Brooklyn and I are going to Bensonvia to have a look around," Kyle said even as Savannah gave him a disapproving look. "Can you make one more pass over the river south of Bensonvia, then double-back and pick us up there?"

"Sounds solid as a gold coin to me," Zito replied. "I can fly a quick sortie and probably even get there the same time you do. After that though, we'll need to head back to Manaus – otherwise we risk not having enough fuel – even with the extra onboard."

"Hey," Savannah Soliel complained as she strutted over to the ethnobotanist, somehow looking radiant despite the earlier shower. "I know you think I'm not as handy as your indian friend over there but still – why won't you let me come along?"

"Listen – don't take this the wrong way because you're the most capable woman I know," KP said, "but things could get out of hand in a heartbeat."

"The risk is mine to take," the photographer argued.

"Maybe, but there's more going on than you know," KP suggested after being backed into a corner. "I won't say what, but a lot's happened the last couple of days. Things that make me think Selena's disappearance was no accident!"

"Please – spare me the ghost story," the tall blond huffed. "You make it sound like something evil awaits out there when Selena probably just had engine trouble – nothing more."

"Why not let her tag along with me," Zito proposed to Kyle after tiring of the argument. "I could use a second pair of eyes while trying to spot your friend from the air, especially if these storm clouds keep building or that fire downstream from here is still smoldering."

"Kyle, if that's all you'll let me do – so be it – but don't let your precious male ego stand in the way of finding Selena because I'm capable of more than that," Savannah countered. "Remember I've been to Bensonvia so I know what's there and, more importantly, what to expect."

"Alright," Kyle Preston finally conceded after looking at both of them and then over at Brooklyn, who seemed quieter than normal. "You can go," he said then paused for a second before adding, "you can go with us."

"Too bad my dear," Zito smirked then started packing his gear into the plane. "The sights I could have shown you."

"Sorry," Savannah said quite pleased with herself.

"Me too," the bush pilot professed after strapping

Bones into the co-pilot seat and setting the mannequin's hands on the auxiliary controls. "Are you sure you won't come – you're a lot prettier than him."

"Hey – is it bad luck to get a picture of a pilot with his plane before take-off," Savannah asked as she slipped her camera from its case and moved up under one of Cessna's wings.

"Not that I know of," Zito replied then climbed out of the cockpit and down onto one of the pontoons, headed towards the back of the plane. "But I might break your camera."

"Not to worry – oops – hold on – I've got to put a new roll of film in first," the photographer informed Zito while Brooklyn and Kyle turned their attention to the dugout. "It will just take a second."

"Take your time," the pilot announced as he performed a thorough inspection of the tail's stabilizers.

"Ok – I'm ready," the tall blond beckoned a minute later.

"Then so am I," Zito said as he leaned up against the fuselage. "Shoot to your heart's delight." "Not exactly what I had in mind but they'll do," Savannah said as she snapped several pictures of the pilot hamming it up for the camera. "Hey," the photographer asked while pointing to the open engine cowling, "do you want me to close this?"

"Go ahead – I'm finished in there," Zito said as he jumped down from the plane and headed over to speak with Kyle one last time before taking off.

35
BUTTERFLIES BEFORE THE STORM

Zito circled once then tipped his plane's wings before heading south while Kyle and the others started their own journey downstream to Bensonvia. The long thin canoe, borrowed from the Rednalsi, rode low but moved well in the water. Like the Negro though, the tannin-tainted Rio Manatee flowed as a single shimmering sheet, unaccustomed to hurrying or revealing what hid beneath its surface. Because of that, the trip to Ford's failed rubber plantation would take nearly two hours.

"Paddle boys," Savannah cheered as she sat in between Brooklyn and Kyle with her long tan legs stretched out in front of her and two cameras dangling from around her neck. "And let me know if you spot something worth shooting."

"You call that pulling your weight?" Kyle joked while adjusting the canoe's course.

"Whose fault is it there are only two paddles?" the photographer asked. "Not mine," she replied with a glance back at Kyle. "So paddle – paddle to the sea."

"We just might," Kyle rattled off then smacked his oar against the water, sending a wave of spray the tall blond's way. "Besides – everything turned out for the best in that book."

"And so will this Kyle," Savannah Soliel argued. "I'm sure Selena will turn up – you'll see."

"We're bound to find her," the ethnobotanist said in agreement while altogether dismissing things could end different than how he envisioned. "Hopefully sooner than later."

Halfway through the trip, they came around a bend in the river where a paranas, or canal, emptied into the Rio Manatee. At its mouth, a slime-covered mudflat arose just above the water, bedazzled by a swarm of bright yellow butterflies. Hundreds, if not thousands of the exquisite insects roosted upon the shoal with even more descending each second.

Colonies of lepidoptera such as these were common in Amazonas on both types of rivers during their transitions from low to high water marks. Sometimes these swarms swelled so large there would be no end in sight to them. As they moved, the butterflies' elegant wings fluttered in unison as if orchestrated by some master puppeteer. A performance of sorts, which Kyle and the others felt blessed to see.

"Stop – would you," Savannah demanded even

though she was already snapping pictures. "I have to get this."

"You're not on a Carnival cruise you know," Kyle bewailed.

"Trust me I know," the photographer snarled while rubbing her lower back and buttock. "If it were – I'd get a refund then send you the bill for my chiropractor and massage therapist. Don't get too close to them," she cautioned. "Let me out here and I'll wade the rest of the way in."

"Wait," Kyle clamored while looking down at the water and wondering what might lurk within its depths. "Let me drop you off closer. There might be piranhas."

"You're such a wimp Kyle," Savannah complained as she crawled without hesitation over the side of the canoe and into the black water. "What will you do when we get to Bensonvia?" the tall blond asked as she stood waist deep in the river with her cameras held up over her head. "Remember – those Seringueiros won't be happy to see us!"

While Savannah moved towards shore, KP backed the canoe out so as not to disturb the butterflies. Brooklyn and he then watched as the photographer shot picture after picture from every conceivable angle before working her way up onto the shoal. As she did, an enormous yellow cyclone enveloped the tall blond and for awhile it seemed powerful enough to carry her away. Then slowly the butterflies returned to the ground and Brooklyn and Kyle could see the photographer again.

"Isn't this great," Savannah exclaimed as she walked through the mud and over to a large cluster of butterflies resettled along the far bank. "Shows just how irresistible pheromones can make a girl."

"Actually, they're all male," Kyle informed Savannah after bringing the canoe up onto the mudflat. "The females are back in the forest laying eggs."

"So then why are these guys here?"

"This might sound gross but they're feasting on dung left by the birds that roosted here last night," KP explained as he walked towards her. "They're about to migrate."

"Somehow that doesn't surprise me," the tall blond quibbled. "Men are gross like that – you know, real shitheads."

"I accept for all men around the world," Kyle smarted then bowed as if to a crowd.

"Careful it's…," Savannah started to say then watched as the ethnobotanist fell face-first into the mud.

"Slippery," Kyle muttered wiping his face with his shirt as both Brooklyn and Savannah openly laughed at him.

"Aye – does this mean you've fallen for me," the tall blond mused as she stood over him. "Maybe I have my own pheromones at work? Maybe you can't refuse—"

Before Savannah could finish, Kyle grabbed a hold of the photographer's wrist and yanked her down into the filth next to him. At first she seemed stunned then after about a minute of Kyle laughing at her, Savannah removed her cameras and set them off to the side. Then, without warning but with as much force as she could muster, the tall blond impaled herself into Kyle's exposed ribs.

In the mud fight that ensued, neither Kyle nor Savannah showed any hesitation to do what they thought necessary to win. Despite conceding both size and weight, the tall blond seemed quite formidable as she wrapped her legs around Kyle for leverage and toppled him to the ground. Kyle made it a point while down to grab handfuls of mud that he then rubbed into Savannah's hair. Afterwards Savannah chased him, kicking mud with every step she took.

"A ka parach a ne," Brooklyn interrupted a few minutes later when the wind picked up.

"Bo to ne," Kyle replied but not before Savannah threw one last handful of mud at him. "He says that storm has turned this way."

"How come your indian friend hasn't spoken to me," Savannah complained while looking over at Brooklyn who, along with Cleto, waited back at the canoe. "I thought he knew English."

"He does," Kyle declared, "but even when it's just the two of us, hours can go by without a word being said. That's just how he is."

"There's more to it than that," the photographer insisted just before picking up her cameras and rising to her feet. "He doesn't like me."

"Savannah – try to remember Tirio aren't as open-minded as the Rednalsi when it comes to women – especially outsiders," Kyle confided. "In his own way, by not talking to you he's showing respect. Even back in his own village he's not suppose to be alone with a woman other than his wife."

"He has a wife," Savannah remarked somewhat surprised.

"And a rambunctious son," Kyle added. "He's constantly having to keep an eye on."

"Like he does you."

"I wouldn't be here if it wasn't for him," Kyle Preston alleged without going into detail. "He's also why I'm so confident we'll find Selena – he's unstoppable."

"Well I'm envious," Savannah Soliel confessed just before they reached the canoe. "To have a friend like that must be a great feeling."

"It is," Kyle acknowledged just as a bolt of lightning illuminated the menacing sky. "Anyway, let's hurry and cleanup so we can get out of here," he suggested. "Horizon looks bad – doesn't it?"

"Yeah – your pilot friend is probably in for one hell of a ride," the tall blond guessed. "I hope he's alright."

36
AUXILIARY CONTROL

For a pilot in trouble, there could be no better friends than speed and altitude. With speed a plane generated lift and could remain airborne if still maneuverable. Altitude on the other hand bought precious time to react. With both, even a student pilot stood a good chance of putting a wounded aircraft in position for an emergency landing. Zito, however, found himself without either as he approached Bensonvia.

Flying both slow and low in a diligent search for Kyle's colleague, the Cessna 182 hovered no more than five hundred feet above the Rio Manatee when its engine started to cough and sputter. Up until now the massive Continental had performed flawless. Even earlier, while encountering some horrendous storm clouds, Zito merely bullied the plane through the swirls of turbulence without incident. Despite that, the bush pilot knew something catastrophic had happened to his plane.

Keeping his wits about him, even as the engine hacked its lungs out, Don Zito went through his progressions – starting first with his gauges:

Oil pressure – check

Hydraulics – check

Battery – check

Fuel – ch—

"I'll be damned", Zito barked aloud after pushing his glasses back up his nose and seeing the fuel gauge pegged on empty.

Just after take-off, that tank read over half full – Zito felt certain of it. Not only that, given the distance traveled so far, he knew it should have barely dipped, which meant the fuel system had sprouted a leak in flight.

"I told you we were in for a bumpy ride," Zito called over to Bones in between two tremendous jostles from the engine misfiring. "Still – it could be worse."

Zito's optimism seemed inappropriate as the Cessna slogged along within a few miles per hour of its stall velocity. A minute later the plane slipped beneath the lower scale mark on its altimeter and the bush pilot could almost hear the birds calling to one another in the canopy beneath him. Nevertheless, without knowing the true extent of the damage to his plane, Don Zito felt certain he could keep it aloft long enough to reach the abandoned plantation.

That confidence stemmed from shear lunacy as the pilot idolized Star Trek and the way those TV characters managed to get their ships and themselves out of trouble. Whether Spock's cross-circuiting to B, or Scotty rerouting the matter-anti matter stream through Auxiliary Control, or Bones using some backup surgical device to save someone's life; the crew of *Enterprise C* always survived the most harrowing situations by tinkering with secondary systems whenever primary controls went offline. A theme included in each show and one Zito took to heart when making some modifications to his plane, especially those to the fuel system.

Running two-thirds the length of each pontoon, Zito had installed two reserve tanks. Most of the time, like on his short jaunts with tourists to the meetings of the waters, he flew without a need for that much fuel. The added weight also had to be considered when taking off and landing on mud puddles as evident back at the oxbow lake by the Rednalsi village. This time however, his decision to fill those tanks appeared to be a godsend.

With the engine on the verge of dying, Don Zito toggled a switch next to the base of the yoke. Afterwards, several check-valves between the main and reserve tanks opened and sent fuel gurgling through the lines and into the empty tank. As it did, the needle on the gauge never crept upward but nevertheless the Continental regained its thunderous roar.

"I don't like to lose," Don Zito proclaimed just as his idol Captain Kirk would say while facing what appeared to be a no-win scenario. "Not at all!"

37
GATHERING GRUMBLINGS

"Finally," Ian bemoaned after hearing a small plane approach with what sounded like engine trouble. "How about we go out after them?"

"No – let them come to us," Nathan Briers insisted while rocking back and forth in a rickety old chair atop the crumbling porch to an abandoned general store. "To here in fact," he added as he fiddled with the small dart gun he used to kill both Lowery and the scientists back in Boa Vista. "An ambush – right here to finally end this matter."

"You're crazy if you think we can draw them in this far," Ian Haleem said as he looked up and down Bensonvia's defunct main street. "Besides, with all these deserted buildings – they might find a way out. I know I could."

"Not to worry," the SynRx executive declared while stroking the whiskers of his muttonchops. "They will come – to this very spot no less – of that I am certain. And when they do, Kyle Preston will have no chance of escaping. None whatsoever."

"You seem awfully sure about that – how come?" the handsome bounty hunter asked while wiping some mud from his boots. "Is there something you're not telling me?"

"Always," Nathan cooed with delight but did not elaborate. "Just make sure the boat is tucked out of view then keep an eye out for them."

"And if someone tries to leave or they don't come this far – what then?" Ian asked.

"Persuade them to the contrary," Nathan suggested after swatting a mosquito from his neck then wiping the blood from his hand.

"Anything else boss man?" Ian sniveled then risked a quick glance into Nathan's emerald eyes.

"I hope your aim is better this time," Nathan remarked as he swatted another mosquito then brushed away a swarm of gnats that had moved in around him. "Because I have no intention of staying in this hellhole a minute longer than need be."

"Just be ready to hand over that money," Ian Haleem warned indifferent to the insects buzzing him as he eyed the briefcase. "Because one way or another our business ends here."

"How accurate," Nathan acknowledged only after Ian headed back to the boat where Rana awaited his return. "Accurate but not precise."

More so than ever, the tension between Nathan Briers and his hired guns appeared to be at the breaking point. If nothing else, their incessant bickering during the daylong boat ride over to Bensonvia proved that. The SynRx executive's demeanor seemed just as uppity and pretentious as when he stepped off the corporate jet back in Boa Vista. For his part, Ian Haleem continued to live up to Father Mario's admonishment of him being a bastard and grew tired of Nathan's belittlement over not killing Kyle Preston. Whereas Rana still said nothing discernible except with his eyes, which spoke volumes as to the ill will the Yanomamo harbored towards everyone.

The presence of the metal briefcase brewed this gathering of grumblings. Nathan carried the case wherever he went with his beloved Baby's Breath inside. That behavior only reinforced Ian's false belief the briefcase contained all the money promised him. Rana on the other hand had no idea as to its contents but was keen enough to see the interest the other two shared in it and therefore coveted the case as well.

Of the three, Ian wavered on the verge of snapping. Maybe because for nearly a week now he had toiled deprived of any of his vices. Of course, going cold turkey like that was not his idea but a demand put upon him by Nathan. Normally, the handsome bounty hunter relied heavily upon a drink or a smoke or a romp with a whore to mellow both his highs and lows. Without them his nerves popped as much as his gun with him far jumpier than he should be. On edge in fact, the way Nathan wanted him.

Needless to say, making Ian Haleem wait much longer for things to play out might well put him over the top. Then again, that was of no real consequence to Nathan as he sat there in the rocking chair. Once Kyle Preston was indeed dead, the usefulness of the bounty hunter and his partner would come to an end – or at least in a way in which they needed to be alive.

All along in the Society's elaborate plan to rid themselves of Lowery and his colleagues, it had been paramount that each untimely death appear unrelated. None could draw the suspicion of anyone back at the University. That was why the Professor's murder needed to look like he died of natural causes in front of thousands of witnesses at a soccer match. That was why the fire in his lab had been devilishly set to look accidental. And why everything taking place in Brazil painstakingly mirrored recent news stories concerning the brutality of pirates within the Amazon basin.

Unbeknownst to Ian and Rana, they had been handpicked to play the leading roles in this ruse concerning pirateers. Leads scripted to end tragically for them while their deaths added credence to the cover story. Their corpses, after mysteriously making their way to the authorities, would have several notable items planted on them able to be traced back to the University and its professors. Proof no less that Lowery's colleagues had indeed been attacked by these bandits. Evil men who, not so unfortunately, must have ran across someone that finally gathered up enough gumption and saw fit to rid the world of their miserable souls.

The plan seemed worthy of the forethought and logic subscribed to by the Dialectic Society throughout the centuries. One detailed to flawless perfection. Carried out by Nathan and his associates like those that came before them by shrouding it within the darker elements of society. A scheme without suspicion, which now hinged upon the gauntlet, set in place here at Bensonvia.

Before getting up and finding a place within the store to wait out Kyle Preston's arrival, Nathan Briers looked out at the now defunct plantation. The place disgusted him with its stifling hot and humid air after spending most of his days in the comfort of his air-conditioned lab. A place easy to despise as a swarm of gnats encircled him and mosquitoes sucked his blood. It did not take much for him to detest the decrepit old buildings or the jungle as it re-staked its claim on the land. Most of all, Nathan Briers loathed this place for what it represented.

The decaying town portrayed an example of how someone out to harness the power of nature did so with reckless abandon. The type of person that would scour the ends of the Earth in search of the liana that the Dialectic Society struggled to keep under wraps. The Society feared someone like Lowery discovering the vine's potential then making it as commonplace as the ornamental Baby's Breath found in flower shops.

That was precisely why it must end here and now. Nathan knew it and so did the others within the society's inner circle. They all saw the vine as a weed and not a flower – a blight and not a blessing – a plague equal to any within Pandora's box never to be set free upon the masses. The madness they foresaw if everyone lived forever.

Maybe it was fitting then for Ford's failure to be the place in which the Dialectic Society admonished this problem. To once and for all dispense with Kyle Preston and leave him behind to rot like the plantation's abandoned buildings. For the potential of the vine to be just as buried and forgotten as Bensonvia. And for the power of immortality to be back tightly within the Society's grip just as the jungle had reclaimed its hold on this land.

Yes, Nathan knew this was the place to finally put an end to it all. To bury it in the past then move forward and fulfill Socrates' vision. For them alone to have an eternity no less, to unlock the laws of the Universe. To eventually become all powerful and knowing. To one day reign as gods over the masses.

38
JACARE NOIR

With power restored, Zito made one flyby of Bensonvia then eased his Cessna 182 down out of the sky. The plane skimmed across the water and into the ghost town's main harbor. Zito then turned the plane down a side canal, cutting through a flock of diving cormorants while heading towards the southern shore. Up ahead he could see a dock along with a boathouse, which he thought looked like an ideal place to wait for Kyle and the others to arrive.

Thirty meters out and aligned with the pier, Zito shut down his plane's engine and drifted the rest of the way in. Before climbing out of the cockpit and onto one of the pontoons, he closed the valve to the reserve tanks to conserve fuel. Next, while tying up to a rusty pylon, he looked down at the water and noticed several black-pebbled logs floating nearby. After seeing two of them disappear then reemerge within just a few feet of him Zito realized what a precarious spot he had chosen.

Built with reinforced steel, the pier's foundation agonized in rust but otherwise appeared sturdy considering it was nearly fifty years old. The wooden timbers upon it however bowed badly despite being dipped in tar while thick knurly vines strangled most of the dock's surface. Over the years the jungle growth had loosened and even split several of the boards. In fact, despite being mindful of where he stepped, a plank disintegrated beneath Zito, causing his right leg to dip knee deep into the water – water where the black caimans still hovered.

"Go on you damn crocs," the pilot shouted after regaining his balance. He then picked up a piece of the broken board and hurled it at the biggest of the reptiles swimming towards him. "I doubt I even taste good!"

Afterwards Zito returned to his plane and decided to check around for the gas leak. The strong odor of fuel tickled his nose and even made his eyes water. In fact, Zito's fingers soon dripped with it after feeling all around the engine block. Then, when the pilot finally discovered where the fuel was leaking from, he realized how lucky he was to still be alive.

Wedged within the throttle gear atop the carburetor, a small, diamond-tipped file had chewed away at the regulator. Zito grimaced perplexed as to how it could have gotten there because he did his own maintenance – did it all and always accounted for his tools. More disconcerting to him though, as he pulled the file out, was that it did not belong to him. He had never owned anything like it – after all he was too cheap to buy such an expensive tool even for building telescopes.

While twirling the file between two fingers, Zito tried not to think about how easily his plane could have caught fire and exploded. What bothered him more was when and how the tool had gotten there. Nagged at him because he remained adamant the plane's fuel consumption had been perfect before this flight. That meant the file must have—

Wham!

A large crash over at the boathouse caught the pilot's attention as if something big just fell. He reared his head out of the engine cowling just in time to see someone duck inside the building. Or did he? It happened so fast.

"Who's there?" the bush pilot yelled after pushing his glasses back up onto his nose.

For a minute he stood there listening for a reply but no one answered.

"Dr. Crotalez – is that you," Zito called this time after grabbing his gun and stepping back onto the dock.

Reluctant at first, Zito inched his way towards the boathouse. As he did each forgotten plank of the dock moaned and every rusty nail used to secure it groaned. If he hoped to use the element of surprise he stood little chance. Still, the pilot continued on and eventually found himself standing at the building's open doorway.

When Don Zito peeked inside, his eyes popped wide open amazed at how poor the boathouse had faired over time. The front door and the glass for the windows appeared to have been scavenged years ago. The tin roof was gone and in its place vines dangled from the rafters. By far the floor had taken the worst of it because wads of straw, shell-like debris, and thick mud covered most of the boards while those still visible lay scarred with scratches.

Enn – enn.

Zito heard what sounded like a baby crying from inside the building.

Enn – enn.

Looking back at his plane, Zito hesitated yet again but then stepped inside intrigued by the sound. He stopped in the center of the room to listen for the cry again. As he waited there, the bush pilot bent down and felt the scratches in the floor.

Enn – enn, enn – enn.

"Dr Crotalez is that you?", Zito called out again because this time it sounded more like someone grunting with a gag in their mouth than a baby.

Enn – enn, enn – enn.

With that last call, Zito determined the whining came from behind a half-rotted rowboat, which leaned sideways up against the back wall. Next to the boat an oar lay on the floor that the pilot suspected had fallen and made the initial noise he heard. Then something cried again but this time it did not sound like a baby, or someone in trouble, but instead a bird.

Only after rolling back the boat did Don Zito realize how bad an idea it was to come into the boathouse.

One – two – five – seven – nine, he counted. Nine baby caimans encircled by a massive nest of mud and grass. Everyone of them adorable in their own right but each chirping away no less for their mother.

The pilot turned and started towards the doorway, hoping to reach it before being cut off. He clutched his gun but doubted it would slow down one of the monsters outside, which he feared was at this very moment rushing – rushing to her brood. The signs seemed so obvious now as he passed by the scratches on the floor. They were everywhere – how could he have missed them.

"God damn ugly crocs," Zito quibbled once he reached the safety of the doorway with his plane back in sight. "Whatcha got to say for yourselves Doc?" he yelled out to the mannequin, "Letting me go off like that and—"

Thump!!

The blow to Zito's stomach left him gasping with his gut twisted and knotted. He flew back into the room as if a mule had reared up and kicked him. He eventually landed on his knees, catching himself with both hands just in time before hitting his head upon the floor. His gun slid through the mud and all the way back over to the boat. No sooner had Zito somewhat recovered, when he looked in front of him and saw, not the tooth-filled grin of a jacare noir, but rather, a pair of shiny black boots.

Thump!!

"And what do you have to say for yourself," Ian Haleem sneered after jabbing the pilot a second time in the stomach with the other oar to the rowboat. "Because neither I or my partner ever tire of killing people – especially friends of this plant picker Kyle Preston."

"What about Kyle?" Zito squeaked once he caught his breath. "And what is it that you want?"

"What do I want – what do I want?" Ian Haleem repeated several times as if really thinking about it before answering. "I want a cold beer," he said as he flipped the oar from his right hand to his left. "And a hot whore," he added as he flipped the oar back to his right hand. "And a smelly cigar followed by a big bottle of Quervo." He then tossed the oar back and forth between his hands as if a hot potato. "Hell, I'll even take a hot drink, a cold smoke, and a smelly poke, and just a shot of Tequila at this point," he joked while cracking a smile for a moment before his face re-hardened. "But that's because most of all – I want my God damn money!"

39
TWO TO BEAM UP

Knocked out and dazed for nearly twenty minutes, Zito awoke to find himself no longer in the muddy bowels of the boathouse. Instead dozens of beds surrounded him with each in different stages of decay. His offered only a shred of padding with the bed's rusted springs poking into his back. Still, the bed's frame supported his weight – supported him, as well as held him there, albeit against his will with his hands and feet tied to the post.

After testing those bindings then seeing a stockpile of weapons near the doorway to another room, Don Zito wondered if he stood a better chance back wrestling the reptiles than he did now. Although woozy, he remembered all too well the thrashing by a man wearing shiny black boots. Something he would not soon forget because his ribs still ached from where the bastard poked him with the oar.

"Hey – is there a doctor in the house?" Zito called out after reading a sign dangling half-kiltered on the far wall that stated patients to the infirmary must sign in before being treated. "Oh Nurse – Nurse Chapel – where are you."

After his foolish outburst, Zito heard someone in the other room stomp upon the tired wooden planks of the floor. A second later, Ian Haleem shot through the doorway trailed by Rana. Both rushed towards the pilot as if answering a page from a patient in desperate need of attention.

Whack!!

"What was that for?" Zito cried out after receiving a solid backhand across the face.

"Just my bed-side manner," Ian Haleem contended as he leaned in and checked the bindings. "You should know better than to cry out like that. You might get hurt."

"OK – you've made your point," Zito said after spitting blood from his cut lip onto the floor. "Now, why am I—"

"I ask the questions," the handsome bounty hunter informed the pilot after shutting him up by raising his hand as if to deliver another blow. "Where's Kyle Preston and don't try to act like you don't know who I'm talking about, or by god, I'll let my partner tear you from limb to limb!"

"He'll be here – along with the authorities – soon – so you better let me go," Zito responded with guile.

"Gosh," Ian said at first then picked up a dusty tongue depressor from the floor and thumped it a couple of times against the tip of the pilot's nose. "Maybe I should let you go – I, I wouldn't want to get in trouble," he insisted while laughing. "Do you want my umbrella – it looks like a bad storm is moving in. I'd hate for you to get wet."

"Before landing I radioed in," Zito mentioned in passing while wishing it were true. "So by now there's several groups alerted to my position – alerted and on their way."

"Neat trick," Ian crowed then disappeared into the other room for a second only to reappear dragging a mannequin behind him. "Neat because when I checked your plane I didn't find a radio – just this. A little old for dolls – aren't you?"

"Look who's talking," the bush pilot jeered back after being caught in the lie. "You're playing doctor, cops and robbers, cowboys and indians, or whatever game this is. You're wrong though if you think you can get away with this!"

Whack!!

That remark brought a second backhand harder than the first. Afterwards, Ian nodded over to his wild-eyed partner who stood nearby, drooling for a turn at this prey. A turn which came, as Ian Haleem moved out of the way and over to a window with a clear view of the general store.

"I suppose that means it's your turn," Zito barked at the indian, who had crept to within just a few inches of the pilot.

"Ohanaa, toa ayaa freem!"

"Ohanaa, toa ayaa freem!"

"Ohanaa, toa ayaa freem!"

The Yanomamo's feverish words set out from his lips and into the infirmary as a war party intent on a massacre. Their tone wrung with alarm, chasing down the walls and beating down the ceiling. Each time he repeated it, the phrase gained in strength while closing in on the silence in between. Soon, the entire room resonated with the chant. A call without denial to its menacing message – death now encircled.

For several minutes Rana chanted with a vengeance equal to that in his eyes. Then the Yanomamo lunged forward quicker than an ornery snapping turtle and latched onto one of the pilot's ears. His teeth chomped through the flesh and cartilage without any sign of letting go. Even as blood streaked down his chin and neck Rana held on. Held on with the pilot helpless to do anything but endure the attack.

"Enough," Ian Haleem finally clamored as he walked back over. He knew his partner did not understand what he said and yet Rana stopped.

"I owe you one," Zito found himself saying with his blood pooling beneath the bed.

"Don't thank me just yet because I still might let my partner finish his 'word of prayer' with you," the bounty hunter declared while rechecking the bindings. "But first, I've got some unfinished business down at the store with your friend and one of my own – so don't go anywhere. Then who knows – maybe the two of us might strike a deal?"

"What makes you think that?"

"You're a pilot with a plane while I'm – well," Ian Haleem started to say but then just flipped his pistol out of its holster and aimed it squarely at Zito's heart. "Surely you can see the benefit of such an arrangement," he said then just as quickly re-holstered the gun. "Think about it and have an answer ready when we return because this is the only time I'm asking."

Zito watched while the bounty hunter and his partner divvied up their stockpile of weapons for the impending attack. Besides his handgun, Ian armed himself with an assault rifle, several rounds of ammo, and two serrated Bowie knives. Rana on the other hand seemed satisfied to keep just his machete and blowgun. Then, just before leaving, Ian Haleem picked up a discarded heap of moldy bandages and stuffed them into Zito's mouth.

Once alone, Zito tried in desperation to free himself. Over and over again he wiggled as a worm, testing the restraints, hoping they'd break or loosen. However, they were far too strong and tied too well. He wasn't going anywhere. Nor was the gag – or at least, not anytime soon as he worked on moving one end of the wadding around to the front of his mouth with his tongue.

"Damn it Bones," Zito rambled almost an half-hour later after finally spitting the filthy rag from his mouth. "I could use some help here," he added while looking over at the mannequin. "*Enterprise* – come in – two to beam up."

40
FORD'S FAILURE

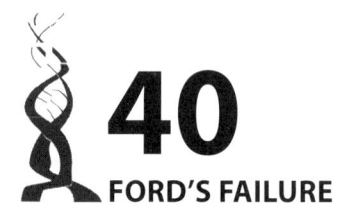

Bensonvia exemplified the last of three follies abandoned by Henry Ford and destined to fade into the past. A ghost town, like Fordlandia and Belterra that preceded it, left for the jungle to reclaim. Its once quaint cottages now fit only to house birds and its main-street shops to store bugs. The machinery left behind corroded long ago into heaps of rust. The once bustling streets full of people and even cars, now stayed jammed only with trees that sprouted up through the cracks between the brick pavers. A place just as lost and forgotten as the auto tycoon's ambitious vision, and yet for the moment clearly on the map.

With a tempest brewing behind them, Kyle smiled, glad to finally reach the deserted plantation despite its scant condition. The menacing storm had already cut short their stop at the mudflat and now nipped at their heals as they paddled into the harbor. Coffee black clouds hung low in the sky. The wind, brewed just as strong, whipped the water into frenzy. While in the not so far off distance, lightning percolated through the dense air more brilliant than fireworks. Each display followed by the rumblings of thunder, which grew ever closer.

"Hard to believe it's almost high noon," Kyle commented as they made their way over to the where Zito's plane remained docked.

"This will not hold back much longer," Brooklyn warned with a watchful eye to the sky while tying up to the pier. "We should find cover."

"Looks like your pilot had enough sense to come in out of the rain," Savannah chimed after stepping onto the dock and throwing her pack up over her shoulder. "He's probably in there," she added pointing to the boathouse. "Not that it's much to look at."

"Yeah but enough nonsense to take the mannequin with him," KP remarked after climbing aboard the plane. "I worry about him."

"I still have no understanding of this," the shaman confessed as he grabbed their gear and Cleto out of the canoe. "Was this Bones once alive?"

"Hey watch your step," the photographer warned feeling the planks beneath her give a bit as she walked. "This thing is a deathtrap."

After baby stepping along the derelict dock and over to the boathouse, Kyle peered through the doorway while Brooklyn examined a hodgepodge of tracks going in and out of the building. Near shore Savannah noted fresh footprints and the telltale sign of someone being drug away but said nothing.

"Zito," Kyle called out while standing in the open doorway. "Zito we're here!"

"Keep it down," Savannah fretted coming back over to the boathouse. "Remember the Seringueiros."

"Yes my friend," Brooklyn warned as well. "We must not draw attention to our presence. Perhaps after the storm passes, I alone should go look – look for your friends while you both stay close to the boat."

"Wait a minute – I'm the one who has been here before," Savannah countered. "If anyone – I should go."

"No ones going anywhere – at least not alone," Kyle Preston told them both then stepped inside the building, searched both rooms then came back outside. "First Selena and now Zito," he complained after finding only the baby caimans. "Where could he have gone?"

"My friend – over here," Brooklyn beckoned after discovering the tracks Savannah saw earlier. "I fear your friend has been taken," the shaman said while pointing down at the trail.

"But why?" KP complained. "Why would they do that?"

"They're ruthless," Savannah insisted. "I told you I was lucky to escape."

"Nonsense," KP said in disbelief. "I've worked with rubber tappers before – followed them around the jungle for days while they went about collecting sap. Some even showed me how they turned the latex into rubber. I mean – they're not bad people."

"These are," the photographer warned again. "Their ancestors were forced to move here decades ago to work at this plantation. When it went belly-up they stayed and continued to work the trees. They've raised their families here, and now the government says the land has reverted back to it and sees them as squatters but they refuse to leave."

"They can't be that ruthless."

"They are," Savannah shot back. "Even the goldminers from El Brando, as desperate and cut-throat as they are, stopped their salvage runs to here. These Seringueiros play for keeps – remember that," the photographer said looking over towards the town. "So don't underestimate them."

Kaboom!!

A brilliant flash followed by a tremendous crackling sent them all to the ground. Seconds later another bolt of lightning hit a coconut palm across the harbor splitting its trunk in two. Afterwards a third strike hit back on this side of the water whereupon each of them felt the remnants of its discharge and smelled the stench of hot ozone within the air.

"Follow me," Savannah said without giving Kyle a chance to dispute her.

The tall blond then scurried towards town with both men along with the dog in chase. As they ran another tree splintered apart – this time bursting into flames.

The ensuing thunder rattled the ground beneath their feet followed by two powder-keg explosions to either side of them. At that point Kyle dared to look back only to regret his courage because the storm seemed to take exception as hail began to fall.

"Christ," Kyle whined after following Savannah into the first building they came to. "I've never seen a storm like that before."

"Relax ya big baby," the photographer snickered as she checked the condition of her gear. "I'd of shot your best side if you hadn't made it, then sent it to all the major papers back home. I can see the headline now, 'Scientific community mourns the loss of – what was your name again?" she joked. "Or how about, 'Mother Nature fights back – pummels plant picker for plundering planet'."

"Funny," KP said moving further back into the room as Brooklyn and Cleto came flying in. "And now we're stuck here," he added as the rain finally began to fall. "Stuck here listening to your smart ass until this stops."

"We should use this storm to our advantage," Brooklyn suggested unaware of the teasing going on. "To look for the pilot without running into anyone."

"And Selena – look for her as well," Kyle Preston added with agreement. "But the lightning."

"We should stay put," Savannah insisted then tossed her backpack onto the building's wooden floor and plopped down next to it. "Wait out the storm – maybe even wait here until dark then look for them."

"Maybe you're right," Kyle agreed as he took a precarious seat on a dilapidated staircase leading to the second floor. "At least until the lightning stops."

Thirty minutes later Kyle and the others remained holed up in the building waiting for the storm to pass. By now the lightning had moved on except for an occasional outburst while the hail had stopped altogether. The rain though still fell in an endless sheet that blurred, if not blocked at times, their ability to see outside. The wind also continued to blow, scattering debris in every direction while howling between the buildings.

"Some storm," Savannah marveled after a piece of the rusted tin roof above her broke free, forcing the photographer to move her pack for the third time because of all the leaks. "Maybe you really did piss off Mother Nature."

"Yeah, yeah," KP bemoaned as he peeked out the front window of the store. "OK Miss Smarty-pants, what else do you know about these Seringueiros or even this place?" he asked. "Anything we can use to our advantage?"

"Not really," Savannah replied. "I mean they had guns of course, and seemed to fly out of the trees from every direction when I didn't expect it," she added as she came over and looked out the window as well. "There's about a dozen buildings on this main street with a few more on side alleys. Oh yeah, there's a church at the top of a slight hill."

"They probably do have it pretty good here," the ethnobotanist contended after thinking about it for a moment. "By now any trees that survived the initial planting would be full grown."

"Yeah whatever."

"Well, you've got to collect from nearly a hundred trees to end up with a latex ball big enough to take to market," KP explained. "The hevea might be indigenous to South America but they grow sporadic in the jungle. But with the trees as dense as they probably are here – that makes this place pretty valuable to a rubber tapper."

"My people collect the sap also," Brooklyn added as he sat there listening to the conversation. "During the dry season we might travel up to three kilometers in a day going from tree to tree."

"Your people are big on gum – are they," Savannah joked at the shaman's expense.

"Never mind her," Kyle insisted. "What are some of its uses?" he asked albeit wishing he hadn't lost his journal.

"It has many," Brooklyn professed. "If cut while out in the jungle, fresh sap stops the loss of blood. When Tuomara root is added it stops diarrhea. Cooked – it is used to coat the inside of our canoes, or hold the top of one plant to another."

"Why not just chew it," Savannah Soliel joked again but then became distracted by something outside. "I see someone," she said while pointing to the porch of a building up a block from them. "It's a little hard to see but there – right there on the corner – where the lane comes through and it says general store. I see someone."

Much to Kyle's surprise Savannah was right. Despite having to look through the heavy rain and several trees growing in the middle of the street, the ethnobotanist could make out a body lying next to a rocking chair. A body that did not appear to be moving.

"That's Selena," the ethnobotanist insisted while leaning out the doorway. "We've got to go get her!"

"Wait," Brooklyn warned just as he had back at the oxbow lake when he sensed Moru spying on them. "Don't rush in."

"Well I've got something for them," Kyle announced as he went over to his pack and dragged out the gun.

"Do you even know how to use that," Savannah asked in all seriousness while grabbing a hold of the ethnobotanist's arm. "Listen to your indian friend – something isn't right."

"Damn," the ethnobotanist jeered as he brushed aside the photographer's grip on him. "Let me go."

"You fool," was the only thing the tall blond had time to say before Kyle leaped outside and into the storm after a bolt of lightning lit up the sky. "You fool!"

41
MODUS TOLLENS

Once outside, Kyle Preston darted over to one of the larger trees growing in the street and slung himself up against it. He stood there still as a statue, until the next flash of lightning finished streaking across the sky, then scampered over to a second tree. Afterwards he waited for another strike and the sky to dim before moving again. Time and time again he repeated this maneuver until reaching the last tree big enough to hide behind.

Looking around, the ethnobotanist tried to gauge his progress. He glanced back behind him for Brooklyn and Savannah but the trees blocked his view of the building. He then peeked forward only to discover he had covered less than a third of the way to the general store. As he scanned the buildings to either side of him, KP also realized just how many hiding spots there were from which someone could be lurking.

"Damn," KP said as he leaned in tighter up against the trunk trying to decide what to do next.

Without realizing it yet, Kyle Preston had taken the bait and stepped into the trap Nathan Briers set for him. Regardless of the distance left to go, whatever decision Kyle now made put his life in jeopardy. It did not matter what he did because several pairs of eyes were already fixed upon him – fixed and poised to strike just as soon as he took his next step.

Of those watchful eyes, the nearest belong to Ian Haleem and Rana positioned in a building once used befittingly as a butcher shop. The handsome bounty hunter hid in a second-story room with a window facing the street and a clear view of the general store. Beneath him Rana stood by the doorway within the shadows, waiting for his chance to erupt. Each of them drooled in anticipation of the kill.

Watching just as intently but from his vantage point within the general store itself, Nathan Briers stood poised to strike. If need be, he could move onto the porch without being noticed – although Nathan did not expect it to come to that. Still, his green eyes sparkled at the thought of killing Kyle Preston.

Indeed for a second, all eyes focused in upon Kyle Preston when he finally moved out from behind the tree. A moment where Ian Haleem saw his mark within his rifle's crosshairs and could look beyond to all the money promised him. A lifetime in which Rana saw his prey right where he wanted it and could envision ripping away at its flesh. An eternity no less in which Nathan Briers saw his mouse within his mousetrap and could see all the troubles of the Dialectic Society put to rest. All of this within a second but a fleeting one at that, because it was gone before any of them could act upon it.

The storm drowned out the sound of the speedboat's engine from over in the side canal until it raced up onto shore. A bowling ball on course for a strike, the boat passed through the lane, slid across the muddy pavers of Main Street then hooked squarely into the general store. It hit so hard and with so much force the whole right side of the porch flew apart as a set of pins with the boat coming to rest at the front door. All too quickly flames then spread throughout the speedboat with the person driving slumped over the helm. Seconds later a horrific explosion occurred. The ensuing fireball rose up well above the two-story building, which diverted everyone's attention towards it.

Spellbound, Kyle Preston stood frozen in his tracks while looking over at the mayhem. The flames mortified him as they melted the person in the boat into a shapeless figurine. His heart then sank even further into his chest as he watched a man and a woman battle one another upon the porch. A fight which ended with the man connecting on a punch and standing in triumph over the woman's body. After which, another explosion erupted and a few seconds later when Kyle could bear to look again, he saw just a man out in front of the burning building.

"Selena," Kyle cried out as he leaned up against the tree while the store toppled down upon itself.

With the inferno a towering backdrop, Nathan Briers walked straight towards Kyle as a shade escaped from Hades. His blacker than brimstone silhouette moved swiftly and purposely with the rain drowning out the fire in his footsteps. Steps, like the gun concealed by his side, he took in stride to commit murder.

Only after another explosion back at the store did Kyle Preston notice Nathan Briers. By now, the two stood no more than thirty meters apart with their faces lit up for the other to see. An unexpected snapshot, in which each saw what they feared most – proof that the other existed.

Without hesitation, Kyle Preston lifted the gun from his side and aimed it at the shadowy figure in front of him. His finger slid along the trigger and into position. He then however, relaxed his hand even though the gun never fired. Afterwards a blast from a nearby window knocked the gun from his hand and sent it into oblivion. Two more shots then slammed into the tree next to him, causing the ethnobotanist to duck down.

More shots then rang out but this time from back behind the ethnobotanist from the direction of the town's main dock. Turning to look, Kyle saw muzzle flash from at least four or five weapons. He buried his head into the ground and expected the worse but never heard a bullet hit near him. Afterwards he listened to someone return fire from the building where the shooting first started.

Despite the volatile eruption of gunfire, the whereabouts of the man he saw troubled Kyle more. He wondered if the man had been forced to retreat or followed him into the clump of trees. Either way, Kyle Preston feared him – feared his coldness – feared his inhumanity – feared his power – feared what he saw within the man's hypnotic green eyes – feared what he felt in his own heart.

Woosh!!

Without warning, a pencil-like spike imbedded itself in the tree just above Kyle's head. After seeing the dart, KP looked in vain for whoever shot it. He then slithered behind a different tree, and then another, and then another, not knowing if he should stop.

"Look out," Brooklyn warned as he flew towards Kyle just as Rana let loose a second dart.

Woosh!!

The second dart hit the backpack Brooklyn carried, piercing both the canvas flap and a couple of the dehydrated meals but nothing more. The shaman then drew back the makeshift shield while Kyle stood up and spun around to look again for the shooter. As he did, KP gasped, not because of the blurred portrait of the indian he saw grinning in the background, but rather the sharper, and much closer image of a machete twirling end over end right for his head.

The blade shaved Kyle's head and plunged into the tree behind him. Afterwards the ethnobotanist ducked unable to react any faster. As he did, he felt his hair being ripped away. Brooklyn then grabbed him by the shirt and together they bobbed and weaved through the trees and off of Main Street to where Savannah and Cleto waited for them.

"We're cut off," the tall blond informed them as they hid along the side wall of a building.

"By who?" Kyle asked with the sound of gunfire all around them.

"Who do you think," Savannah muttered. "I told you these Seringueiros were sons of bitches!"

"Shh," Brooklyn demanded after Cleto growled to warn someone approached. "We must go."

"Where?" Kyle whispered in dismay. "Where do we go from here?"

42
THE KOBAYASHI MARU

"Where?" Selena mumbled as she came to. "Where am I?"

"Someplace safe," Zito assured her despite his own doubts.

"You – you hit me," she said almost as a question while remembering their fight back on the porch.

"I'm sorry but I had to get you out of there," the bush pilot offered in his defense but Selena passed out again before he finished apologizing.

For the last ten minutes Don Zito hovered over Kyle's colleague worried what he would say to her when she woke up. He felt bad for hitting her. Ashamed more than anything but he needed to get past that guilt because he had just saved her life – hopefully Kyle's as well. Besides, he needed to tell her so much – starting with what just happened.

After being left unguarded, the bush pilot eventually realized the diamond tipped file, which he found wedged in his plane's engine, was still in his shirt pocket. He then snared the tool with his teeth and used it to cut through his bindings. Once free, he sneaked out of the infirmary and slithered through the mud while dragging his precious mannequin behind him. He eventually made his way over to a building opposite of the general store – the place he remembered hearing where his friend was to be gunned down. Then after inching his way up the lane along the building, Zito spotted Kyle in a clump of trees at the far end of the street.

The bush pilot had intended to work his way down to his friend and warn him but then saw someone lying on the porch of the store. A woman left out in the open – bait Zito realized – bait luring his friend into the trap, which meant she must be Kyle's colleague.

Mortified by the events unfolding, Don Zito found himself in a position even more difficult than anything he had faced so far. Far harder in fact because the lives of two people teetered in his hands. Their fate balanced against one another as weights upon a scale with no way for him to warn Kyle and rescue Selena. An apparent no-win scenario where the pilot needed to choose who he would try to save.

"Bones – who would you choose," the pilot had asked his co-pilot but of course got no reply.

Zito's incessant drifting in and out of his pretend world of Star Trek could offer him no real answers. Of course the situation reminded him of a Starfleet

Academy test where a captain encounters the *Kobayashi Maru* – a hapless ship in desperate need of assistance while drifting further into enemy territory. A dilemma simulated to evaluate the fortitude of the person in charge because no matter what decision they made, someone died.

Zito, like Captain Kirk, might not like to lose but he needed to face reality. He had no phasers, or transporters, or shields, or any other spectacular devices to fall back upon. He had to decide – decide right then – before it was too late to save either of them.

That's when Zito saw it – a speedboat tucked away behind him in the canal. His first thought was to use it to escape but he then came up with a crazy plan to use the boat as a diversion.

Just before slamming into the general store, Zito had bailed out of the speedboat and left Bones holding onto the controls, giving the appearance someone remained in the boat. After the explosion, Zito and not Nathan Briers had struggled with Dr. Crotalez upon the porch. The pilot startled her at first then tried to explain who he was but with all the confusion it was impossible. Zito felt he had no choice but to pop her in order to drag her off to safety – which he had, albeit to a damp and moldy smokehouse just behind the burning wreckage of the general store.

Since then they had been cooped up inside the windowless shack leaving Zito to wonder what would happen next. Every shot fired made him think a bullet whizzed towards him with his name on it. Each approaching footstep sounded like someone about to walk in on them. Even the rain pounding down upon the roof seemed to be trying its best to get at them. All the bush pilot could do was hope, like the storm, trouble would pass them by.

43
WHAT MATTERS NOW

"Boss man – I thought you said he wouldn't escape," Ian Haleem mouthed off after meeting Nathan Briers out in the street once they had killed the last of the rubber tappers firing upon them. 'No chance whatsoever' I believe you said," he added as he threw Nathan's earlier boast back in his face. "And what about your so-called associate – weren't they suppose to help?"

"Enough," Nathan Briers grumbled, showing some genuine frustration for the first time.

"Oh, was that – accurate but not precise, or precise but not accurate," the handsome bounty hunter mocked. "I get the two confused."

"Just get after him!"

"First – how about a thank-you," Ian spouted while tapping the barrel to his rifle. "Better yet – just throw in a few grand more on top of what you already owe us – call it a bonus for saving your ass," Ian suggested while looking to either side of Nathan. "Hey – where is it?"

"What matters now is Mr. Preston's whereabouts," Nathan Briers replied ignoring the comment.

"Don't tell me the case is gone," Ian whined as he grabbed a hold of Nathan's arm then looked over at the burning building. "All that money can't be gone."

"I assure you – money will never be an issue for you again if you ever kill him," Nathan Briers commented while looking first at Ian's hand upon him then up into the bounty hunter's eyes. "So you might want to hurry."

"You're not coming," Ian noted with a look of surprise.

"You have all the help you need," Nathan Briers insisted.

"Just as well," Ian Haleem grunted then motioned to Rana to start out after them. "I doubt you could keep up."

44
THE ART OF CONVERSATION

The term Dialectics, conceived by the ancient Greek Socrates as he walked the streets of Athens, described engagement with his fellow citizens in conversation. As envisioned, this noble search for truth required both thought and open dialogue. A mechanism where everyone had an equal say just as they did in that city-state's democracy.

Later though, when he fell out of favor and made a scapegoat for the Peloponnesian War, Socrates realized the error in this approach. Such a quest must be undertaken, not by the masses but instead, by only a select few. For this reason, just before his execution in 399 BC, he devised a secret society to unravel the mysteries of the world. Not even Plato knew of the group's existence for Socrates had chosen another student, Soccero, to lead the newly formed Dialectic Society, fearing his more esteemed student seemed far too prolific at writing everything down and would divulge its existence.

"Model thy city on the truth of experience," Socrates told Soccero, "for experience leads to knowledge, knowledge to insight, and insight to wisdom, which in itself is the strong hand of any god." He also went on to recite the following four tenets in order to insure both the group's survival and success:

Modus Operandi:
Conflict is inherent in the search for truth; therefore protect and defend The Society at any cost.

Modus Ponens:
Never be fooled into believing something without actually seeing or understanding it; therefore the only means for accepting its finality is with proof.

Modus Tollens:
Never deny the consequence of an action; therefore plan every move as one would a letter in a word and every word in a sentence so that your outcome is clear.

Modus Vivendi:
Dissention is both vice and virtue; therefore maintain balance by way of a triad and govern by consensus thus avoiding an impasse.

Through the generations the torchbearers of this group never strayed from these tenets in their pursuit of knowledge even when the rest of the world at times fell into upheaval. Quietly, they advanced their respective fields while never venturing into the limelight. Even so, some glimpses of their activities are evident within the pages of history but never the society itself.

For over two millennia since Socrates' death, the secretive lives of those within the Dialectic Society have been an epic far greater than any Homer or Hellanicus or Virgil ever conceived. But now, for Nathan and the other two members of the current triad, no longer would they have to pass their work down to another generation like their predecessors. They stood as the final recruits, the final triad. The ones that would eventually answer the questions always thought unanswerable about the world and even the universe. They would unify the theories, and the postulates, and so much more still beyond anyone's comprehension on their way to becoming all-powerful and all-knowing. They would be the ones to fulfill Socrates' vision.

Then there would be just one question left to answer – how would they rule? Would they embody the virtue and wisdom of a "Philosopher King" or behave more like the petty and meddling gods of Mount Olympus? Would they dispense justice fairly or hold court with irreverence for the masses and the taste of blood fresh on their palates? Would they intervene prudently or act on a whim without discretion?

Would absolute power corrupt absolutely?

45
RUN RABBIT RUN

With Brooklyn leading the way, Kyle pulled Savannah along as the three of them darted from the side of the building for the safety of the jungle. Upon reaching the tree line, both Kyle and Savannah let out a huge sigh of relief. Brooklyn however, knew they remained vulnerable and insisted they keep moving.

Keeping up with the shaman was no easy task, especially as the rain continued to fall. Both Kyle and Savannah found it uncanny in fact, how agile and graceful he seemed compared to them. At times he disappeared out in front altogether only to then stand on a stump or hover near a tree until they caught up with him. Finally though, after an half an hour of running deeper and deeper into the forest, the shaman stopped long enough for Savannah and Kyle to catch their breath.

"What do you think," Kyle asked Brooklyn looking back behind them, "Is anyone there?"

"I doubt it," Savannah offered before the shaman could answer. "Those Seringueiros just wanted to scare us a bit – that's all," she added then propped herself up against a palm tree as she caught her breath. "I told you they'd be that way, but they won't chase us now that we're off their turf."

"I'm not convinced of that," Kyle complained. "Two groups were shooting it out back there – granted one was probably the rubber tappers."

"And the other?"

"There's at least three of them," Kyle replied sticking to what he knew for sure and not speculating like Rook as to who might be behind all of these attacks. "One had these creepy green eyes – he must have been the one on the porch fighting with Selena before the boat rammed into the place. Somehow the thug walked away from that explosion then came at me with a gun. I tried to shoot him, hesitated for a split-second, and then someone else shot the pistol from my hand. After that, all hell broke loose and I ducked for cover behind another tree."

"You're certain it was Selena then," the tall blond asked with skepticism, "because I couldn't tell from where I was?"

"Who else?" Kyle scoffed in disgust.

"I'm just saying."

"Don't," Kyle implored. "I know what I saw so just leave it at that!"

"Well who was in the boat then," Savannah asked.

"I thought maybe one of the Seringueiros tried stealing it but didn't know what the hell they were doing."

"Could have been anyone – even Zito," KP alleged. "All I know is they didn't survive."

"You forget the native," Brooklyn added.

"Believe me I haven't forgotten him," Kyle commented while looking back out into the jungle. "I got a pretty good look at him, even with everything going on. He was dressed in regular clothes but bore a red mark running down the middle of his face."

"Blood stripe," Brooklyn noted then looked back out at the jungle. "Only one tribe wears such a mark."

"I know," Kyle grimaced.

"So," the photographer bewailed indifferent.

"So," Kyle jeered back. "He's Yanomamo or what they call one of the 'fierce people'. Trust me – that's not an exaggeration. They fight to the death even amongst themselves just to prove their worth as warriors."

"Great," the tall blond mouthed as she too looked over her shoulder. "Now what?"

"We make a stand here," Brooklyn advised. "They never expect that from us now."

"There's already been too much killing," Kyle insisted because he knew his friend proposed a fight to the death. "I'd rather make a run for it," he said. "We can't be too far from El Brando."

"Hike where?" Savannah asked as she stretched and tried to work out some of the soreness in her arms and legs.

"A mine to the south of here," the ethnobotanist replied. "We flew over it coming in – there's probably a hundred, if not a thousand men there – between Brooklyn and my GPS – I think we can get there. I think we'd be safe there."

"Why not double back to Bensonvia," the photographer proposed. "We can hide out in one of the buildings again until we see that it's safe. Maybe sneak around like your friend suggested before."

"Maybe I assume too much," Kyle said out of the blue. "I assume I know what the hell we should do, and that there's safety in numbers – that other people want to be treated the way I do – that there's good in everyone – that everything will be fine.

Maybe that's my problem – I assumed I was to search for Selena because it was the right thing to do when that is the farthest thing from the truth. See, once again, I even assume too much – I assume there is right and wrong, and there is truth. I assume more than I should."

46
A REAL ACE IN THE HOLE

Around mid afternoon, they stopped again and hid inside a thicket of terrestrial ferns. By now the storm had passed but the hot and sticky air smothered them to the point they almost wished the rain hadn't stopped. Kyle Preston meanwhile checked their progress on his GPS unit pleased to see they had put almost seven kilometers between them and Bensonvia.

"What's that for," Kyle asked after seeing the tall blond pull out an inhaler from her pack.

"Of all things, asthma," Savannah confessed while lying back on the ground. "Ironic – isn't it. Here we are, probably where the air is the cleanest in the world, and my allergies flare up."

"Don't be too hard on yourself," the ethnobotanist urged after pulling out his canteen to quench his thirst. He then bent down and offered some water to the tall blond. "Brooklyn's pushing us pretty hard."

"It will pass," Savannah Soliel vowed as she closed her eyes and took several deep breaths. "But I don't think I can keep this pace up," she confided after sitting back up. "I know I was the one that begged to come but my muscles are on the verge of cramping, both heels are blistered, and I've stubbed almost every one of my toes. I really can't go much further."

"Sure you can," KP encouraged the tall blond as he sat down beside her. "And if not – well – we'll carry you."

"The two of you will carry me like a princess?"

"No," Kyle admitted as they both watched Brooklyn shimmy up a nearby tree being strangled by a liana with red berries. "You're not royalty but you are a friend," he said reaching out and rubbing the kinks out of her calf muscles, "and friends look out for one another."

"I see that," Savannah marveled looking up at the shaman, who appeared to be scanning the jungle for movement.

"Some of us are just better at it than others," Kyle remarked in admiration of his friend.

A few minutes later the shaman climbed down from the tree but not before picking a handful of the berries. He then took one and sliced through the fleshy pericarp and white aril with his machete, revealing a black seed inside. Afterwards the shaman cracked the seed coat with his teeth and began sucking on it as if a piece of hard candy.

"This will help," Brooklyn pledged as he came over and offered Savannah and Kyle each a seed.

"I'm not eating that," Savannah declined outright.

"They sell this in stores back home as Guarana," Kyle interjected after stuffing one in his mouth. "It's a little bitter when fresh like this but it will keep you going. Think of it as a cup of coffee."

"I don't like coffee," Savannah pouted. "Besides you don't know if that's really safe."

"It's safe," the ethnobotanist repeated as he walked over to the liana and tugged on it just as a car salesmen would kick the tires on car. "The Latin name for it is *Paullinia cupana* but it's more commonly known as 'sleepy eye' because of the shape of its bloom. The seeds contain caffeine along with theophylline, and theobromine. Many indigenous tribes use it to treat a whole slew of symptoms but mainly fatigue."

"Too risky," the tall blond denounced. "I'm afraid it will react with my asthma medication," she added then stood up. "Besides, I'm fine now – really – so let's go."

"You're holding out on us – aren't you Savannah," Kyle insisted while looking up at her.

"What do you mean?" Savannah Soliel snarled far more defensive than she needed to be.

"Wow – some princess," the ethnobotanist remarked after standing up. "I just meant I shouldn't have mentioned we'd carry you – that's all."

"Sorry," the tall blond smirked. "Guess I'm a little jittery even without that stuff in me. Just think what a bitch I'd be with it."

Just before sunset, at longitude 57.0° west and latitude 1.45° north, Kyle and the others came upon a spring bubbling up out of the ground from underneath a brazil nut tree. Over the years the trickle of water had eroded away the soil from the buttress roots on one side of the massive tree, leaving a hollow big enough to park a car. Tufts of stringy moss draped across the opening made it difficult to see just how far back the hole truly went. While in the other direction, a small gully carted the water off through the forest with tall wispy stocks of cane to either side.

Gripping his machete tightly, Brooklyn dropped down in front of the hollow while Kyle and Savannah stood back and watched. After finding only Agouti tracks, the shaman then motioned for them both to join him. Together, they approached the darkened abyss then brushed aside the moss and peeked inside with the aid of their flashlights.

"Know what's missing?" Kyle asked while watching Brooklyn scratch around in the mud. "A leprechaun," the ethnobotanist answered as he crouched down and shined his light upon the water, trying to trace it back to the springhead. "Yep – all that's missing is a leprechaun."

"And his pot of gold," Savannah snickered while shinning her flashlight into Kyle's eyes. "Then I'd be rich and beautiful."

Once satisfied it was safe, Brooklyn then turned and started following the gully through the forest. Kyle meanwhile examined the moss and a few other species of bryophytes growing near the hollow's entrance. Savannah on the other hand just stood there, disinterested in everything, even though the unique setting seemed worthy of at least one picture.

"We stay here tonight," Brooklyn proclaimed after reappearing a few minutes later. "If need be – we can hide in there," the shaman added while pointing to the hole. "There is also a larger stream not far from here we will use to confuse anyone tracking us."

"Finally," Savannah bewailed then plopped down on the ground. "I thought we'd never stop."

"Don't get too comfortable," Kyle Preston implored. "We'll have to get some semblance of a camp in place and, if it's safe enough to have one, go collect some kindling for a fire before it gets dark."

An hour later the three of them settled into their makeshift camp. Given the circumstances, the small fire near the entrance to the hollow was a luxury even though it seemed insignificant compared to the utter darkness that now surrounded them. Still, they needed to be careful not to draw attention to themselves. So much so, they planned to keep the fire going just long enough to dry out some of their gear drenched earlier by the storm and to boil a pot of water for a hot meal.

"I feel like I'm back in middle school and my mom packed my lunch," Kyle complained as he pulled out the dehydrated pouches in his backpack. "Let's see, I've got beans and rice – beans and rice – beans and rice – rice and beans. What do you have?"

"Shrimp Alfredo," Savannah boasted while reconstituting one of her gourmet meals with some of the spring water they just finished boiling. "Maybe I'll let you have a taste of what you're missing," the tall blond teased waving a fork full in front of the ethnobotanist. "Interested?"

"Mmmm," Brooklyn said after ripping open a tub of chocolate pudding Kyle insisted Louisanne get for the shaman because of the impracticality of bringing bottles of Yoo-Hoo.

"Am I the only one who wants to order a pizza," Kyle grumbled almost as loud as his stomach.

"What's the first thing you do want when you get back to the States," Savannah asked while nibbling away at her pasta.

"That's easy," Kyle claimed without giving it a second thought. "There's a Krispy Kreme a block from my house."

"Yes – with sprinkles," Savannah said licking her lips as if sugar remained on her lips from eating a doughnut.

"Nope," Kyle rejected with his hand out in front of him like a traffic cop. "Just glazed."

"What about a hot dog then – New York or Chicago?"

"Definitely Chicago style," Kyle insisted. "It's not really a meal with just mustard and kraut."

"Or edible," Savannah added.

"Hot dog," Brooklyn chimed in while looking over at Cleto. "I never eat dog – too smart – too helpful."

Both Kyle and Savannah glanced over at the shaman then laughed at the seriousness in his voice. Afterwards each made several slap-stick innuendos toward dogs followed up by more laughter. The joking helped to ease the tension in their tired muscles and aching hearts – at least in Kyle's case – at least for awhile anyway.

"This is crazy," Kyle finally professed after forcing down the last mouthful of beans. "I've been coming down here for close to seven years and never the slightest bit of trouble until now."

"Seems like the world's gone mad – doesn't it," Savannah echoed in agreement. "That's where focus and commitment come in," the tall blond insisted after sipping on some water. "Stay committed to your beliefs and anything is possible."

"I agree," Brooklyn remarked. "No matter what happens – I know the spirits are with me."

"Not exactly what I meant," the photographer shrugged, "but I do know that's what it takes to succeed."

"Doesn't hurt to be good looking either – does it Savannah?" Kyle smarted.

"Hey I'm not ashamed of anything I've done," the tall blond countered. "I'm just saying there's a whole slew of people out there so you better know what you want and be ready to fight for it – that's all. Now, you'll have to excuse me," she said after standing up and stretching. "I've got to find the ladies room and powder my nose."

"Savannah – don't wander off too far," Kyle cautioned thinking, not only about the thugs following them, but also how dangerous the jungle turned at night.

"Not to worry," the photographer replied as she clicked her flashlight on and shined it out at some palm trees. "I see it – it's the second one to the right."

"How are we doing?", Kyle then asked Brooklyn once alone. "Any sign of the Yanomamo?"

"We did well," Brooklyn replied, "but so would he."

"I'm guessing we're only a few hours away from the mine," Kyle said as he tapped the GPS unit hanging from his belt. "We put almost fifteen kilometers between us and Bensonvia today – not bad considering we started so late."

"We did well to escape that place," the shaman said while looking into Kyle's eyes. "Though I feel your sorrow. I am sorry for your friends."

"Thanks," KP said reaching over and putting his hands on his friend's shoulders. "I almost joined them back there – except you came through for me – I owe you – again."

"You will do the same for me," the shaman insisted as if already in the past. "I wonder though, why the spirits did not help us reach her in time."

"You know I don't believe in that," Kyle remarked, "I just got high off that snuff – nothing more, because none of what I remember from that night could have prevented what happened to Selena."

"Perhaps," Brooklyn said pausing for a moment to think through what he wanted to say before continuing.

"When we were alone at our camp along the Rio Negro, I told you how spirits only reveal themselves to those they wish to, and yet, even with your doubts, they still came to you – that is very powerful – and so must the visions they shared with you."

"Well if they did visit me – I sure can't make sense of any of it."

"Just remember to keep your mind open," the shaman urged. "Also," he said while standing up and grabbing his machete along with his bow, "when the time comes – use what you have learned and trust the spirits to guide you."

"What – no song?" Kyle said as he watched his friend prepare to go out into the forest. "I bet Savannah would love to hear you," he added while pretending to play a flute. "I promise not to sing along."

"I left it behind knowing the sound would only draw attention to us."

"Maybe next time," Kyle sighed as he let out a yawn that sounded more lion than human.

"Yes, when you need it most – that is when I will play for you again," Brooklyn stated shaking his head in agreement. "In the morning," he added, "I will go gather berries and catch some fish so there will be plenty of food for the rest of the trip."

"Great," KP cheered even as another yawn came over him.

"Amoni boyu," the Tirio then said in his native language.

"Amoni boyu," Kyle repeated just as Savannah came back over to the fire.

"Now what's he up to?" the photographer asked.

"Guard duty," Kyle Preston replied as they both watched Brooklyn and Cleto disappear into the darkness. "He thinks we're doing fine but just wants to make sure," the ethnobotanist said while putting another log on the fire. "Not to worry though – he can tell by the way the jungle sounds if anyone is around."

"Your indian friend is a real ace in the hole – isn't he," Savannah Soliel acknowledged.

"No one better," Kyle boasted in obvious admiration.

"I don't know about that," Savannah cooed as she curled up next to the ethnobotanist. "I feel safe here with you."

"Oh really," Kyle Preston protested even as he ran his fingers through Savannah's long golden hair and sneaked a peek from over her shoulder down at her supple breast and the rest of her perfect body. "Then again – flattery always was your strong suit."

47
SAVANNAH'S BETRAYAL

"Did you plan this?" Savannah asked Kyle as her hands ran over his shoulders, with one stopping upon his chest hairs while the other one moved brazenly lower to his right hip.

"Plan what," KP replied after standing up and facing the tall blond.

"You know," Savannah Soliel contended leaning in for a kiss. "Time alone for some more fun like we had in my hut. I was way too tired last night but now – now you can tie me up."

"Brooklyn should be back any minute with breakfast," KP alleged while pulling away and stoking the smoldering coals left from last night. "I've got to get this going again," he said then threw a log or two on top. "Are you hungry because he'll probably come back with a mountain of fish?"

"I'm starved," the tall blond replied with her hands

now on her own hips, "but I wanted to nibble on you this morning."

"You're not that hungry," Kyle remarked without looking at Savannah because he knew her flirting was more ploy than anything heartfelt.

"You never know," Savannah Soliel countered as she went over to her pack and rummaged through it for a moment then picked up one of her cameras. "Since you're not interested – I guess I'll go freshen up a bit."

"So that's your beauty secret," Kyle joked after seeing what the tall blond took with her, "soap and a camera."

"Hey – there's no telling when that trophy shot might come along," Savannah suggested just before disappearing into the jungle.

As Savannah Soliel strolled through the forest, she came across a break in the canopy where an emergent had been uprooted by the storm and crushed several smaller trees. Looking up through the opening, she could see a troop of red-handed tamarins lounging high above. The small, monkey-like creatures as their name implied, stood out because of their red arms and legs. In all, less than a dozen species of tamarins and the closely related marmosets were known to inhabit Amazonas, making it a rarity to come across them. For some reason though, the photographer continued on without taking a single shot.

Afterwards, from a vantage point overlooking the stream, Savannah spotted Brooklyn no more than thirty meters from her. He stood knee-deep in the tea-colored water with his bow half drawn in search of his next catch. Already an half dozen fish lay upon a palm frond at the bank. Nestled next to them were several small guavas, an avocado, and a clump of a chive-like plant called butara.

For several minutes, Savannah remained hidden and watched the shaman. The photographer found him stunning with his long black hair, decorative tattoos, and red breechcloth. He looked impressive but like the bow in his hands, Brooklyn's lean, muscular body was chiseled with purpose. Savannah saw that as he moved through the shallows without causing a ripple in the water's surface. She sensed an inner quality flowing from the indian and could see why Kyle held him in such high regard.

Then, from out in the middle of the stream, Savannah saw a large fin appear above the water's surface. It approached Brooklyn from behind, swimming quickly on a path right towards the shaman. The photographer could see the outline of a fish as big as a man if not bigger. For a second Savannah lost site of it but then the fin reappeared just a few meters away from Brooklyn, who had turned around, as if sensing its approach.

Now drawn back taunt, the arrow within his bow begged to be released and in a split second it disappeared, plunging beneath the water's surface.

Savannah waited in anticipation as Brooklyn pulled in the line attached to the arrow. The water churned with movement and the tall blond wondered what the monstrous fish would look like. The photographer grimaced in disappointment though, when the arrow re-appeared and revealed something far different than what she expected.

Upon the spear several fish wiggled similar to the ones already lying on the bank. Impressive, Savannah thought, to get more than one with a single shot but she wanted to know what had happened to the other fish – the big fish – the one it seemed that got away.

That thought brought a wicked smile to the tall blond's face because she wasn't about to let Brooklyn get away. She had plans for the Tirio but would have to hurry after looking at her watch. Nearly ten minutes had passed since she left camp and Savannah knew Kyle would soon come looking for her.

While moving through a tall stand of trumpeter's philodendron near the riverbank the photographer heard a loud thump. It rose above the incessant jungle chatter followed by sporadic splatter. Rather rhythmically, the smacking then the whooshing repeated itself with a few seconds in between each other.

Making her way over to a lush but prickly bush growing near the water, Savannah once again gained a clear view of Brooklyn. The shaman hadn't moved much since the photographer started towards him. The only difference Savannah noted were all of the ripples spreading out around the shaman as if something—

From out of no where jumped the enormous fish

Savannah saw earlier. It flew almost a meter into the air before plunging back into the river with a splash. It leaped again but this time she could see that it wasn't a fish but rather a pink dolphin.

Savannah marveled as Brooklyn reached for his arrow and pulled off one of the speared fish then threw it into the dolphin's mouth. Afterwards, the bouto rolled over on its side and made several chirping noises. Then the shaman reached down and grabbed one of the pectoral fins and together they swam as one.

"Have you ever," Savannah Soliel said aloud.

For a moment Savannah Soliel smiled fascinated by such harmony.

She always believed conflict with nature existed in the very psyche of man. The tall blond moved plants and animals wherever and whenever in order to get the pictures she wanted. Her closest associates felt that way as well. They carried on as if above nature – above everyone else for that matter. Maybe that explained why she neglected to take any pictures again – even of something as magical as this.

"Kyle told me I'd find you here," Savannah said a few minutes later as she approached the shaman. "Wow – looks like you're quite the fisherman."

Brooklyn nodded then turned away as customary with Tirio men alone in the forest with a female not one's mate. Immediately he slung his bow over his shoulder and started to wind up the string to the arrow. Afterwards, he moved onto shore near the stockpile of food intent on picking it all up and heading back to camp.

"I'd feel safer if you stayed," the tall blond begged after hanging her camera on the lower branch of a nearby tafe tree. "I just want to freshen up a bit," she added while waiving her bar of soap. "I'll be done before you know it."

Without waiting for a response, Savannah started to undress. She pulled off her boots then stuffed her socks inside them. Next she wiggled out of her shorts and let them fall onto the ground. She then slunk past the shaman bound for the water with only her shirt and the skimpiest of underwear. Once at the river, she took off her white button-down blouse and tossed it aside. Then she strutted into the water, revealing a tattoo on the small of her back – a four inch diameter figure, composed of three curved branches radiating out from a center core.

Albeit begrudgingly, Brooklyn did not leave because like Kyle, he believed in safety with numbers. He knew they had done well yesterday in getting away from the men chasing them but that did not mean they could take their good fortune lightly. There was always a chance of the unthinkable happening.

"I don't bite," Savannah mused between splashes of water and waves of giggling meant to entice the shaman to turn around and look at her.

"Nor do I," Brooklyn replied while still looking away.

"Join me then," Savannah squealed. "I'll wash your back and you can do mine."

Brooklyn turned and gazed at Savannah while tapping the arrow to his bow against his leg. Her long blond hair glimmered gold in the tropical sun. Water beaded off her skin, trickling seductively down her tan shoulders and arms. Her breasts tantalized him even while partially submerged. Everything about her invited his stares but nothing compared to her eyes – they sparkled like sapphires – bluer than any ocean, far deeper than Brooklyn could imagine. Starstruck, the shaman wondered if he had ever seen someone so lovely.

"OK – I'll come to you," the tall blond announced as she climbed out of the water then grabbed her shirt and draped it over her breasts, doing little to hide her nipples and surrounding umbra.

"I cannot," Brooklyn insisted while holding his ground with the tall blond standing all but naked in front of him.

"Make love to me," Savannah pleaded inching forward until sunlight stop passing between them. The tall blond then leaned down and let her warm breath massage his ear. "Come on," she said, "you know you want me."

Mindful of nothing, Brooklyn dropped his weapon and reached for Savannah lost in her sweet seduction. Desire and lust swept through his body like a wildfire. A fire fueled by Savannah's brilliant spark, of which suspicion as for its reason, deserted the shaman far too soon.

Removing her shirt, Savannah twisted it up like a

chord then looped it over Brooklyn's head and pulled him towards her supple body. She dropped the shirt as one of her hands began to travel up Brooklyn's chest while the other one slid underneath his breechcloth and teased his cock. Pulling him even closer, she forced his neck around until he could no longer see her. Then, when Savannah Soliel felt Brooklyn wrap her up with both of his arms, the tall blond knew she had him – knew it and struck.

"Show me," Savannah snickered then stepped back away from the stunned shaman after jabbing him in the neck with a syringe. "Show me some magic."

Three milliliters – that's how much histamine phosphate Savannah had just injected into Brooklyn. A relatively small amount of liquid equal to about half a teaspoon but nevertheless, more than enough of this particular drug to wreck havoc on anyone. An amount equivalent to the body's response to being stung a thousand times – all within his neck!!!

With Brooklyn clutching his throat, Savannah rushed over to the tafe tree and grabbed her camera. By the time she returned and snapped her first picture, the drug had already impacted the shaman's breathing and altogether crushed his ability to speak. She then moved in and around the gasping Tirio, taking picture after picture, reveling in the perfection of her deception. The tall blond even knocked him to the ground at one point so she could capture the anguish on his face as he looked up at her.

After shooting the entire roll of film, Savannah started to cleanup the evidence of her betrayal. The tall blond re-hung her camera back on the tree. She picked up her shirt and put it back on. She also found the syringe that she had hid in her shirt and threw it into the stream. Afterwards, she looked over at the shaman, blew him a kiss, and took a deep breath before screaming for help.

48
POENAS DAREE

Kyle broke upon the stream's edge, baffled but relieved by what he saw. There in front of him his friends appeared to be horse-playing, just as Savannah and he had done back on the mudflat with the butterflies. At least, that's what it looked like to him at first because the tall blond stood bent over the shaman, who seemed to be pushing her away, but not convincingly. Together their arms flopped back and forth with the photographer grabbing at the shaman's wrists. As they fought Savannah kept calling Brooklyn's name over and over again while the Tirio never answered but instead only grunted and snorted.

"Savannah – don't scream like that," Kyle admonished the tall blond after he caught his breath. "I thought those men had somehow caught up. Whew, you just took several year—"

"Get over here," Savannah Soliel commanded, cutting Kyle off. "Your friend – he needs you."

"What – what do you mean?" Kyle asked because he hadn't noticed anything wrong with either of them – that is – not until Savannah stepped back and Brooklyn teetered to the ground. "My God," the ethnobotanist sputtered unprepared for what he saw. "Oh my God!"

In front of Kyle Preston lay a corpse somehow still moving. Brooklyn's pale and mottled face resembled someone fished from an icy pond. The death-white background contrasted by vibrant red blemishes under his skin from where blood vessels erupted. Besides the eerie complexion, his eyes were all but swollen shut and his skin appeared slick and rubbery. Meanwhile thick stringy snot dangled from his nose while drool poured from his mouth. All along, he struggled to breathe.

"What happened?" Kyle demanded after running over and dropping to his knees next to his friend.

"I don't know," Savannah squeaked somewhat hoarse because of yelling for help at the top of her lungs. "I was over there freshening up and he was down here fishing – one minute everything was fine and then the next he was coughing and gagging. Since then I've been trying to calm him down but he keeps pushing me away."

"Brooklyn – tell me what happened?" Kyle pleaded. "Mu potchu?" he asked in Tirio this time as if it would help. "Mu potchu – Mu potchu?"

"Something must have stung him," the tall blond offered while still sobbing.

"But what?" Kyle argued even though he agreed his friend was having an allergic reaction to something.

"His neck is swollen to twice its normal size. And look," the ethnobotanist said while touching his friend's forearm causing the edema building up beneath the skin to ooze out, "what in hell could cause this?"

"Maybe something attacked him in the water?" Savannah then suggested as she squatted down next to both of them. "Check his feet while I look at his back."

"Mu potchu?" Kyle called out again after finding no sign of a wound on either of the shaman's feet or legs. "Mu potchu, Mu potchu?"

"Nothing here," the photographer chimed after pretending to check the shaman's back then watched as Kyle worked his way up to Brooklyn's neck.

"He's strangling on his tongue," KP announced after prying open his friend's mouth. "Jesus – it's the size of my fist."

"What should we do?"

"I'm – I'm not sure," KP uttered vanquished by the sight.

More than anyone Kyle Preston knew what it felt like to be breathless – to extract the last tiny bit of oxygen from the air inside one's lungs then long for another breath. He also understood what it meant to have the will to survive and for it to be meaningless. That sometimes, surviving had little to do with one's abilities or even the skills of others, but instead left to luck, or to chance, or maybe a miracle, or whatever else might counteract the volatility of chaos in the universe. Sometimes, survival depended on a friend.

"Isn't there anything you can do?" Savannah begged.

"Like what?" Kyle whined while watching Brooklyn struggle in earnest. "If only I had thought to bring one of the first-aid kits – maybe an epinephrine stick might counteract some of the swelling."

"Well go get it."

"There's no time."

"Well make something then," the photographer grumbled in defiance and threw her hands up in the air at the surrounding forest. "After all isn't that what you do – make medicines from plants?"

"Damn it," the ethnobotanist jeered as he reached down and grabbed a hold of his friend's outstretched hand. "It's not as simple as that – I doubt anything would work!"

Blind and on the verge of passing out, Brooklyn swiped his hand back and forth across the sand then used one of his swollen fingers to draw a picture. First he made a long sweeping arc about the length of his arm. Next he added a short line coming off of that one, then another, and another, until several identical strands splintered off from the main line.

"I think he's trying to say it's alright," the tall blond proposed as she stood back up and moved behind Kyle. "See – there's a smile."

"I'm not sure," Kyle remarked unable to decipher his friend's scribbling.

Then, whether he meant to or not, Brooklyn started

to draw another line separate from the others but never finished. Never finished because the histamine injected into him by Savannah Soliel had pinched, and squeezed, and finally drained the last of his strength.

"I'm sorry," the tall blond whispered to Kyle in the softest of voices as Brooklyn's body went limp. "Nobody could have survived that though," she commented without really wanting to ease his pain.

Savannah Soliel then walked back over to where she left her clothes and camera, leaving Kyle alone with the exception of Cleto lingering in the margins. Secretly, the photographer wished to capture the whole thing on film. After all, she knew magazines paid top dollar for the type of anguish imparted on Kyle's face from the loss of his friend. Anguish and despair Savannah Soliel inflicted without remorse – no regret whatsoever as she gathered her things and headed back to camp and waited for Kyle's predictable and foolish return.

"I should have been here for you," Kyle repeated over and over and over again as he rocked Brooklyn back and forth in his arms. "I should have – like you were there for me," he rambled while wiping away the tears. "I should have been a better friend – I should have never gotten you involved in this. I was just so sure, together, we were unstoppable. I assumed too much."

Time staggered forward without meaning or measure as Kyle Preston sat on the ground with his friend's head cradled in his arms. Wet anguish from a bottomless well streamed down the ethnobotanist's face. The tears salted his quivering lips with shame. A timeless scene of a guilt-trodden soul in misery while mourning the fallen. A portrait in which sorrow ran amuck, heartache chiseled away at the heart, and the lack of reason drove even the sanest to lunacy.

Eventually Cleto approached as if to confirm what he already sensed. Kyle watched as the dog sniffed the shaman's face then howled sharply several times. Afterwards, Cleto slumped down, resting his head upon the shaman's still chest.

"I know boy," Kyle told the dog as they both sat in misery. "I never got an answer either."

49
WITHOUT FAITH

Dropping a match onto the finished pile, Kyle watched as the clumps of lichen and moss burst into flames. The fire spread quickly from the kindling to the heartier logs, and then to the palm fronds, which Brooklyn's body rested upon. Within no time the entire mass blazed with red-tipped flames that leaped up and lashed out at the night sky. As they did, the air became tainted with the stench of burning flesh and hair, which rolled out over the stream as an eerie fog.

If the men giving chase lingered nearby, this bonfire would allow them to move in and devise yet another ambush. Kyle did not care though because this was something he had to do. An obligation, not only to his friend, but also to Brooklyn's family – even if it put Savannah and him at risk – even if he doubted its legitimacy.

According to Tirio traditions, a body needed to be

burned immediately after death in order for the person's soul to enter the spirit world. Afterwards, the charred remains and ashes were collected in a clay pot and saved for a year in which to mourn the person. Whereupon, in a ceremony held on the first anniversary of the death, the remains were ground up and made into a gruel for the deceased's family to ingest. Only then, could the soul of their loved one move back and forth from the spirit world – a necessity when summoned to come to the aid of the living.

Kyle stood almost atop of the fire with anguish and guilt garrisoned across his face. The wild flames swiped at him but their blistering blows felt trifle compared to the burning loss within his heart. A part of him being consumed while he watched.

"Whatever we find we face together," Kyle said after finally moving back from the fire and sitting down next to Cleto, who never budged from the corpse the entire day. "We told each other that before we ever came out here," he said as if the shaman could hear him.

"What I wrote in my journal seems so ominous now. It was merely the way I felt with the expedition coming to a close and knowing I wouldn't be back anytime soon. I feared you wouldn't be here when I eventually returned. Turns out, I should have left – you'd still be alive then.

Instead that passage turned into a horrible prophecy. A vision come true on this awful day and in a way I could have never foreseen. Could anyone have – I wonder?

That's what makes this even tougher – having no faith. No faith in a spirit world filled with your ancestors which should have warned of this. No faith in a god that would allow such a thing to happen. No faith in a world plagued with so much violence and death. More than anything though, I have no faith in myself because I let you down.

I wish I believed in something right now. Unfortunately, the only thing real, is you are gone.

"Amoni boyu – peace brother."

50
WHAT LIES BENEATH

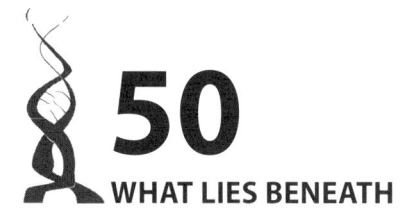

Despite a brilliant sunrise, Kyle Preston's mood remained dim and dreary the next morning. He had spent the entire night in front of the bonfire grieving Brooklyn's death while contemplating his own misfortune and pondering what would happen next. He felt certain it wasn't a question of if, but when – when would something else go wrong and what, if anything, would he do.

Kyle struggled to answer that fatalistic question because it implied everything happened for a reason. If so, then no one's death could have been avoided – not Lowery's – not Captain Jack's and his crew – not Selena's – not even Brooklyn's. It also meant it was no accident Rook survived the fire, or that Ocho came along when he did, or that Tatiana recovered from her wound. Moreover, that meant there was even a reason why he was still alive – at least for the moment anyway.

"It can't be that way," the ethnobotanist sulked as he

sat there all alone. "I'm not destined to succeed or to fail – I have a choice – don't I? I can sit here and let them find me, or I can keep on running, or I can even fight – the choice is mine."

"I went ahead and packed everything," Savannah Soliel announced after popping out of the jungle with her pack already strapped to her back. "I wish things were different," she added afterwards – not to seem too insensitive, even though she appeared eager to leave. "I wish I knew what happened. I wish I could have saved him."

"Me too," Kyle sighed after a long heartfelt pause then crawled over to the ash pile left from the fire. With heartfelt regret he stuffed some of Brooklyn's remains into the leather satchel the shaman always wore. "But you're right – it's time to move on."

"I still think we should double-back," the tall blond suggested while looking back the way they came. "We can slip in behind these thugs then fly out. It shouldn't be too hard, especially if you stored the coordinates for Bensonvia in your GPS?"

"And if Zito's dead – what then – I can't fly a plane – can you?"

"Then we'll head back to the Rednalsi village and hide there," Savannah proposed as if she had considered everything. "I've got a plane coming in less than a week – plus there's the sat phone."

"No," Kyle Preston said after tying the satchel around his waist and consolidating his gear into a single pack. "We stay with the original plan and keep heading south towards the gold mine," he added after turning on the GPS unit and getting a reading. "We've almost reached the first latitude – it can't be much further."

"You still think those miners will help us," the photographer peppered back. "All they care about is getting rich. They'll turn us over if they think they can make a buck."

"Maybe so – but that's my decision," Kyle Preston countered then reached up and grabbed a hold of Savannah's arm. "You don't have to come," he said as he held her. "They're not after you."

"Now what?" Savannah Soliel whined. "You don't want me with you anymore? You're the one that said friends look after one another."

"I've got enough blood on my hands," the ethnobotanist confessed while looking one last time at what Brooklyn wrote in the sand. "I don't want yours as well."

"If you do – then so do I," the tall blond crowed. "Besides, each of us stands a better chance getting out of this if we stick together – I mean, let's face it, neither of us are as capable as your indian friend – right?"

Kyle said nothing but instead tossed the backpack upon his shoulders, whistled for Cleto, then headed out. An hour later, with Brooklyn not there to guide and prod both of them along, they failed to make much progress. Instead they crisscrossed and doubled-back along their own path while trying to follow the stream through the jungle. Making matters worse, thunder rumbled again as another storm brewed overhead just as they reached the edge of a squishy-squashy marsh knee-deep in places with overflow from the river.

"I've got to rest," Savannah Soliel insisted as the sun disappeared behind the clouds for a moment.

"Already," Kyle Preston huffed even though he could use a break as well before trudging through all that mud and water.

"I can't help it," the photographer alleged. "I can't seem to catch my breath – my asthma must be flaring up. Besides, do you really think they're still after us?"

"Yeah," Kyle shrugged as he flicked his machete to the side and brought the GPS out to check their progress. "Yeah, I do."

"Why?" Savannah asked just before taking a hit from her inhaler. "There's been no sign of anyone since that first day."

"It's easy to think you're alone out here when you're not," KP replied. "And these guys don't seem like the type that give up," he added while looking around. "They're out there alright – so we better keep moving."

"First – what was with the bonfire last night and filling that pouch with your friend's ashes?" the tall blond asked while her asthma medicine took hold. "You never did say."

"Just trying to do the right thing and respect Brooklyn's beliefs," the ethnobotanist shared then put the GPS away after not getting a lock. "It's really the only thing keeping me going at this point. Now, can we go – we're sitting ducks here – plus we need to cross that river, especially before it swells anymore from all this rain."

"Damn it," Savannah bellowed after taking only a couple of steps.

"What now," Kyle complained.

"My ankle," the photographer grunted in obvious pain. "It's on fire."

Stranded within the muddy overflow, Savannah never saw the half-buried stingray she stepped on. The ray would have already died from exposure but for all the recent rain. Even in its weakened state though, the stingray had swung its tail and sliced through the photographer's skin.

"Help me with my pack," Savannah howled after hobbling over to a clump of grass before sitting down.

"Let me look," Kyle insisted as he squatted next to the tall blond and tucked his backpack under her leg for support. "Ugh," he said reminded of Tatiana. "The barb broke off under your skin. I'm going to have to dig it out with something and then we'll need to get some antibiotics in you before an infection takes hold."

"I'll do it," Savannah insisted after pulling her boot and sock off then grabbing the first-aid kit from her pack. "Like I trust you with anything sharp."

With her legs crossed and her foot resting on her knee, Savannah took a deep breath then dug at the wound with a pair of tweezers. To her dismay, the barb remained wedged long-ways under her skin and never budged. In the end she resorted to using a scalpel and made a small incision, exposing the trailing end to the mucus-covered spine.

"Finally," Savannah announced and grabbed a hold of the barb then wiggled it out.

Afterwards, Savannah fastened together a syringe and needle from her kit then removed the protective packaging from two drugs. Quickly she drew out 1 cc of Dexamethasone, an anti-inflammatory, and two cc's of the broad-spectrum antibiotic, Ceftriaxone, to prevent the infection Kyle seemed so concerned about. Without flinching, she injected the medicine into her calf muscle. Then she grabbed several Betadine swabs from the kit and cleaned the wound.

Meanwhile, as Kyle squatted there watching, a small symbol on the back of the first-aid kit caught his eye. The red lettering jumped at him along with the manufacturer's logo comprised of a six-sided geometric figure. Something Kyle Preston would never have noticed any other time but now.

"SynRx," the ethnobotanist said aloud then glanced over at Savannah, whose head reared up after hearing the company's name. "Now there's a coincidence?"

"How's that?" the tall blond asked trying to act indifferent while reaching for some bandaging.

"That's the company Rook was going to snoop around at," KP stated while pointing at the emblem with his machete. "Said someone there was behind Lowery's death and the fire."

"Kyle what are you talking about?" Savannah Soliel

clamored once finished dressing the wound. "I remember you calling someone on my phone named Rook," she added while fiddling around inside the first-aid kit then tucking it back into her pack. "But who's Lowery and what fire?"

"There's more going on then I've let on," Kyle Preston said slamming his machete into a nearby stump and walking away from it. "I'm sorry I didn't tell you earlier but that's why I don't think these guys will let up. It seems someone killed a colleague of mine back at UNC and tried to burn down his lab. There was also an attempt on my life before coming out here and looking for Selena. It might all be related. I only wish I knew how or why."

"Now you tell me – but do we really have time for this?"

"You're right," the ethnobotanist replied even though he was having trouble letting it go. "Savannah," he then asked as if he did not remember her answer from before, "whom did you say you were working for?"

"I told you silly – WWF and *Anthropology Today*," the photographer professed while getting her boot back on. "Why?"

"Well – your stuff is all first rate," Kyle remarked. "I mean your climbing gear looked brand new as well as the other equipment back in your hut. Of course it's a given your cameras would be top notch but then there's the satellite phone and now a plane."

"Are you saying I'm not worth it?" Savannah reeled back.

"No – just seems pricey for those organizations – that's all."

"From your perspective I guess it would appear that way," the tall blond countered. "Your school worries more about basketball than anything else, which means you're use to playing second string and not having the best equipment or even what you need – I'm not. Now if you're finished with the cross examination Perry Mason – I can use some help up."

"Sorry," Kyle bemoaned. "I'm just a little—"

When Kyle leaned down, Savannah lunged towards him with the scalpel she devilishly kept out of the kit without the ethnobotanist noticing. She tried to thrust it into Kyle's chest but he reacted quicker than she expected, catching her arm with the blade just inches above his heart. Afterwards, he pried the scalpel from her hand and tossed it aside.

"Why Savannah – why would you do that?" Kyle demanded to know as the two of them stood there face to face. "I don't understand."

"Why what," Savannah Soliel rifled back. "Why would I want you dead – believe me, I have my reasons – only you're too naive and stupid to understand. Although, I have to give you credit, we never thought you'd be this hard to kill."

"Who's we?" Kyle Preston asked while squeezing her wrist harder. "Tell me who's out there! Tell me what this is all about!"

Savannah Soliel nodded at Kyle Preston as if conceding but then rammed her knee into his crotch. As Kyle keeled over, his grip on her gave way and the tall blond reared back and connected with an uppercut that bloodied his nose. She then reached for his machete but Kyle somehow tripped her at the last second. Afterwards the ethnobotanist then climbed on top of her but Savannah managed to flip free.

As they struggled, the two of them rolled next to one of the ponds as if replaying their wrestling match back on the mudflat. Unlike before though, this was no game. Meanwhile Cleto barked aloud while running circles around them.

"Why didn't you just kill me earlier?" Kyle asked after pinning the tall blond to the ground. "You've had plenty of chances, especially that night in your hut?"

"Because you were suppose to be shot," Savannah Soliel snarled as she arched her back then turned over and struggled to her feet. "Besides, I didn't want to have to drag your ass all the way back on my own."

"And Brooklyn – you killed him – didn't you – how?"

"I'll gladly show you," Savannah chimed. "Not that you'd like it. Looked rather painful – didn't it?"

"Bitch," the ethnobotanist jeered as they both reached for the machete.

"You can't win Kyle!" the tall blond alleged. "You must know that by now – if I don't kill you then somebody else will! At least with me, your death will be preserved – remember – I promised you I'd shoot your best side."

"No," Kyle yelled then let go.

Caught off guard, Savannah Soliel stumbled into the pond and fell face-first into the waist deep water. She popped back up but then stood glaring at Kyle for several seconds while thinking what to do next. In that moment of indecision, her boots sank down into the mud. Merely irritated at first, Savannah yanked and pulled but could not break free. Still, she did not think much of it – that is until she noticed a slight ripple move across the water's surface towards her.

Lured by the splashing, a mammoth black piranha stranded in the pond wasted little time in coming over to satisfy its rabid hunger. First it ripped at her wounded ankle where blood had already drained through the bandage and into the water. Then, the foot-long fish pecked at her knee, then her thigh, and then finally at her hip as if sampling before feasting.

"Kyle," Savannah cried while reaching out to him. "Help me!"

"What's this all about," KP demanded as he dangled her backpack just out of reach from the water's edge. "Tell me and I'll pull you out."

"Baby's Breath," Savannah bemoaned as she felt the piranha tear a hole in her belly with its razor-sharp teeth. "It's amazing," she said even as the fish tugged at her innards as if they were cotton candy. "We're going to live forever."

"Who Savannah, who?"

"The Dialectic Society," the tall blond screamed,

breaking an oath that had lasted over two thousand years. "There – now help me – you promised!"

"And you assume too much," Kyle said then turned and walked away without remorse.

"Damn you," Savannah Soliel cried as she slumped over. "Selena said you—"

"What about Selena," Kyle Preston demanded to know but by the time he turned back around the tall blond had slipped forever beneath the water's surface. "What about her?"

51
BEAUTY SECRETS

While sitting on his own backpack, Kyle Preston sorted through Savanna's belongings looking for clues. He brushed aside the camping gear and most of the photography equipment as trivial. To that pile he added her clothes after checking the pockets. Then, to the other side of him, KP tossed all the photographer's rolls of film. In another pile he rounded up all of her necessities like soap, the first-aid kit, her asthma inhaler along with several refills, and an inordinate amount of make-up given their locale.

At first glance what remained seemed of little consequence to Kyle with the exception of a few noteworthy items. A detailed map of Anavilhanas noted two islands circled in red with the exact date of the ambush written next to them. Stored within the memory of a GPS unit, which Savannah never mentioned having, were the coordinates to those islands along with Bensonvia. While on a book of matches from a bar located in Boa Vista were the names, Ian and Rana.

Digging deeper, Kyle went back and read the labels on the undeveloped film. Several rolls seemed benign enough with names he expected to find like "Rednalsi Village," "Festival of the Mischief Moon," and "Poison Arrow Frogs." One though tagged "Fall Guys," and another marked "Selena Slaving Away," left him wondering as to the titles' meanings. While with others marked "*Anna Maria* Ambush," "Brooklyn's Last Breath," and "Burial Fire," the ethnobotanist just shook his head in disgust.

"That Bitch," Kyle implored. "Am I really that naive and stupid," he asked Cleto, who sat next to him. "I must be if I'm wanting an answer from you – hmm boy. I just didn't see this coming – none of it – and she's been in on it from the start."

Kyle then turned his attention towards Savannah Soliel's first-aid kit. As expected it contained general medical supplies like gauze, scissors, tape, the pair of tweezers, a tourniquet, and various over-the-counter medications. The ethnobotanist noted some more elaborate items as well such as anti venom, epinephrine sticks, Lariam tablets, syringes, needles, suture material, lemon-glycerin swabs, and a whole slew of injectable drugs. Of those, only three looked opened; the two Kyle just saw Savannah use on herself and a vial of histamine phosphate.

Holding the histamine in his hand, Kyle scrutinized the label even though he already knew the drug's potential:

Histamine Phosphate

Indications:
> Gastric histamine test:
> subcutaneous administration for determining hydrochloric acid production by gastric mucosa.
> Pheochromocytoma test:
> intravenous administration as presumptive in determining Pheochromocytoma.

Precautions:
> Average or large doses may cause extreme allergic reactions.

Warnings:
> Usage in patients with bronchial, asthmatic or other respiratory conditions may precipitate severe allergic reactions resulting in death.

Adverse Reactions:
> Headaches
> Dyspnea
> Dizziness
> Local or general allergic manifestations
> Collapse with convulsions
> Cyanosis of the face

Kyle's heart sank because looking back, he remembered Brooklyn having most, if not all, of those symptoms. Given the title on one of the rolls of film, Savannah must have snapped pictures of his friend struggling to survive – her calls for help merely part of a vicious but well-orchestrated ruse.

The meaning of what Brooklyn drew in the sand, just before dying, now dawned on Kyle as well. The picture wasn't of the Tirio smiling as Savannah suggested but rather of the rising sun – a reference to the tall blond and the way she first appeared to the shaman back at the Rednalsi village. KP understood his friend's warning now – albeit much too late and yet, in a way, knowing its meaning helped to restore some of his faith in himself.

The problem he now faced was what, if any of the things Savannah had told him, could he believe. Where did the truth end? And the lies start? How much of what she divulged just before her own death could he believe? He feared he'd assume too much.

As Kyle Preston mulled the extent of Savannah Soliel's betrayal, Cleto stood up and cocked his head. The dog growled and the hairs along his back bristled while honing in on something moving along the tree line. Kyle looked but saw nothing even as the dog's growls grew more fervent. The ethnobotanist then turned back the other way when a flock of rust-colored wattled jacana jetted out of the marsh to the south of him. A few seconds later, more birds bolted from the marsh in a panic but this time from only a few hundred meters away.

At first, Kyle felt that same instinct to run away until he remembered what Brooklyn said to him back at the oxbow lake when Moro had stalked them, and then again after escaping from Bensonvia. How not to flee as frightened prey but instead to seek out the seeker – to have the hunted become the hunter – something Kyle Preston knew was long overdue as he retrieved his machete from the stump.

52
DELIVERANCE FROM EVIL

Outnumbered, outflanked, and outgunned, Kyle Preston realized he could not confront whoever awaited out there head-on but instead needed to ambush them with guile. He discarded all of his equipment except for the machete, his slingshot, and the pouch that held his friend's ashes. He then shooed Cleto away, not only for the dog's own good, but also for his own. Afterwards, the ethnobotanist pretended to lay down for a nap but then turned onto his belly and slithered through the muddy marsh over to the river.

Brushing aside his fear of what lurked within its depths, KP slipped into the water. Amongst debris already adrift in the water, he let the meager current drag him downstream, a hundred meters or so, to a point where a downed limb from a ceiba tree jutted out into the river. Despite its spines, Kyle clung to the branch, using it as cover while he crawled onto shore. Afterwards the ethnobotanist scurried behind the tree's enormous trunk then glanced back.

From across the river and looking back upstream, Kyle watched two men pilfer through the gear he had left behind. Even from this distance he could see the bold blood stripe running down the center of the Yanomamo's face. The other man held a rifle, which Kyle assumed to be the sharp shooter that knocked the pistol from his hand. In a way he longed to see again the redheaded man with those disturbing green eyes – to account for him as well.

From his vantage point, Kyle Preston waited to see if anyone else appeared. As he looked on as a fox upon bloodhounds, his confidence grew. Still he grappled with his, as well as his weapons, meagerness to go on the attack. He then realized, as he scrutinized the fallen limb in front of him, how overloaded the branch seemed with seedpods along with orchids, bromeliads, ferns, lichens, mosses, and a few other species dislodged from the canopy high above. Dozens in fact – still intact with their microenvironments.

Mindful of not being seen, Kyle snatched several items off the branch then scampered off into the forest. Armed with more of a foolish idea than a sensible plan, he sliced his way through the undergrowth in search of the right spot to make a stand. A place even he wasn't sure he would find.

53
ABUTOR QUOD TU ABEO DOCTUS

While Rana slinked along its perimeter, Ian Haleem entered a small clearing garnished with a lone tree. With his rifle poised to bring down anything that moved, the handsome bounty hunter inched his way froward. Halfway to the tree he stopped and made eye contact with his partner before proceeding further. Then Ian spotted a small satchel dangling from one of the tree's upper branches.

At first the hired gun assumed Kyle left the bag as a ploy to slow them down. Then, the more he looked up at the bag with its intricate design, Ian questioned whether it had been left by accident. He wondered if it belonged to the plant picker or someone else? He wondered if the bag might contain something the boss man wanted? He wondered what was inside?

As the handsome bounty hunter stood next to the bulbous trunk of the tree, his sheer lust for money consumed him. The same terrible greed that drew him into killing people for a price in the first place. The same overwhelming desire that would not let the hired gun walk away from this job until paid. The same vice that Father Mario swore would be the bastard's downfall.

After setting his rifle aside, Ian lifted himself into the tree and quickly climbed towards the satchel. A third of the way up, he surveyed the surrounding jungle for the slightest sign of trouble while all along prepared to pull his pistol from its holster and unleash a flurry of bullets. He then noticed the small nodules sprouting from the tree limbs and the slits bored into every inch of wood.

With the satchel's strap entangled around the branch, Ian Haleem was unable to look inside. As he grappled with the knot a lone scout ant scampered towards him to investigate the intrusion. About a centimeter in length with fierce-looking jaws attached to an oversized head, it was one of many on patrol. In fact Ian had been lucky not to have run into more of them by now because a cecropia tree such as this one could hold up to a million ants within its loins. Most of them deep inside and hard at work until called upon to defend their home. All it took was something to rile them – something like—

Thump!

From out of nowhere a small rock whizzed through the air and hit solid against the base of the tree. Its impact, although not close to Ian, did resonate throughout the tree. Seconds later another rock hit, then another, and another, like a drum being pounded on a battlefield.

A call to arms that drove the army of ants inside the tree's trunk and branches into a frenzy. The very thing to incite the devil at peace within his garden.

Ian saw his oversight as the ornery insects gushed out of the tree's tiny holes prepared to wage war. The colony moved so quickly and with such naked aggression it seemed truly evil. Still, Ian continued to work on freeing the bag despite the danger because his greed consumed him. He couldn't leave without knowing what the satchel held.

While Ian Haleem fought to free the bag, more and more ants poured out of the tree. Dozens already crawled across his body and tried to drive him away. Their rugged jaws pierced right through his clothes while injecting an acid-like venom up under his skin. A venom that boiled Ian's blood and crazed his mind. Crazed him so much that when he finally did free the satchel, Ian decided to jump despite being almost five meters up in the air with several branches between him and the ground.

The handsome bounty hunter's gamble to jump bankrolled him as the strap to his shoulder holster caught on the first branch down. It pinned him in mid air helpless to free himself or ward off the enraged ants as they inflicted bite after bite upon his body. Still Ian Haleem had one blue chip left to cash in – or did he?

"Rana," Ian screamed as he swung like a piñata. "Get me down," he said while kicking madly with his shiny black boots in hopes of ripping the holster. "Now!"

Despite hearing Ian's pleas, the Yanomamo never

helped. The warrior instead smiled as he watched the ants pick away at his partner's flesh. He knew all along of the army hidden within the tree's bowels, and why no saplings grew in the clearing, and why no vines strangled the tree's trunk, or why no birds roosted upon its branches. He knew all along of the tree's danger, and yet, never warned Ian not to go near it.

For so long Rana yearned to be freed from his life debt – to choose his own prey – to kill when he wanted and how he wanted, and not stop until ready.

Free to do as he pleased, Rana still relished the hunt of this prey. From his earlier vantage point, he saw the rocks being launched at the tree and even admired the tactic, if not the prey more – now that it fought back. Still, the confidence of the warrior never wavered. After all, he was Yanomamo.

With his prey pinpointed behind a clump of palm fronds, Rana slunk through the forest and reigned down upon his prey as a jaguar would its quarry. His fiery eyes remained alert and focused for any sign of another attack even while half expecting this prey to flee. Then, once in a favorable position, he pulled out one of the poison-tipped darts from the pouch around his neck and loaded it into the blowgun. Afterwards Rana lifted the tube out in front of him, pressed it against his lips, took aim, then sent the dart on its way with a whoosh.

Rana waited until the dart hit square into his prey's back then smiled as it stumbled around before slumping over against a palm tree. Afterwards, the Yanomamo approached, excited by the prospect of no one being around to end his defilement of the body.

"Ohanaa, toa ayaa freem!"

"Ohanaa, toa ayaa freem!"

"Ohanaa, toa ayaa freem!"

In the few seconds it took Rana to reach his prey, the dart's poison seemed to already induce paralysis because Kyle Preston did not move. He never tried to escape. Never fired another rock from the slingshot clutched within his right hand. Never brought his other arm up to defend himself even as the Yanomamo feigned delivering several blows to his skull with the blowgun. Instead Kyle remained slumped back against the tree dazed and indifferent.

Seeing that the hunt was all but over, Rana pulled out his machete from its scabbard intent on decapitating this prey much the same way he had the monkey back on the boat. As he bent down to prop the head back for a clean cut, he lost sight of his prey's arms for a second – inconsequential perhaps, but nonetheless a mistake on his part, especially for such a battle-hardened warrior.

After biding his time for just such a moment, Kyle Preston brought his left hand around without the Yanomamo noticing. Hidden inside was a chalky substance the ethnobotanist made by pulverizing several spines chiseled off of the ceiba tree back near the marsh. Kyle waited until Rana drew back his machete then flicked the powder up into the warrior's eyes.

Besides the physical irritation of the thorn's rough

grit, the grounds contained a mild Tropane alkaloid. Used during eye exams, atropine dilates the pupil and causes temporarily blindness by allowing too much light into the eye. Both belladonna and jimsonweed of the nightshade family are two plants better known for this alkaloid due to their distribution and potency. In this case, the crushed thorns of the ceiba worked better than Kyle could have hoped for.

With the Yanomamo blinded, Kyle snatched the warrior's machete and blowgun then tossed them out into the jungle. Next he took his own machete and sliced through the strap to the pouch around Rana's neck and threw it off to the side as well. Afterwards KP stepped back and watched the Yanomamo rant and rave in lunacy for several minutes until finally squatting down next to the ground and chanting to himself.

"I'm lucky you're a good shot," Kyle said as he glanced down at the dart protruding from his chest.

After pulling out the dart, Kyle then unbuttoned his bulging shirt to reveal a bulletproof, or in this case at least, a dart-proof vest made from several skids of a stag horn wrapped around wads and wads of fluffy white kapok gathered from the ceiba tree. KP grinned ecstatic it stopped the dart, while at the same time, seemed just as happy the Yanomamo was a good shot.

"Now what?" Kyle Preston asked, more to himself than to the Yanomamo. "I guess there's no chance of you telling me what this is all about – is there? Because I'd really like to—"

Rana lunged straight towards Kyle after honing in on just his voice. KP tried to wield his machete around in time but the warrior moved far too quick and nimble. Together they fell backwards with Kyle hitting the ground followed by Rana landing on top of him. Afterwards they struggled for the weapon with the Yanomamo gaining the upper hand at first until for some unexplained reason he stopped fighting then collapsed.

"Damn," Kyle marveled after rolling Rana off of him and seeing the dart wedged within the Yanomamo's gut. "Somebody is looking out for me."

With the showdown over, Kyle walked back to the Garden of the Devil to retrieve the satchel filled with Brooklyn's remains. Fortunately, it laid on the ground even though the poor slob, who had climbed up after it, dangled from the tree. The ethnobotanist thought about cutting him down but ants still hovered about in an uproar. Scores even scurried across his own feet as they combed the clearing for more intruders.

"Aye, Mr. Preston," a voice called out from behind the ethnobotanist. "Seems we meet again!"

54
ACCURATE BUT NOT PRECISE

"Can't say I recognize the voice," Kyle Preston replied despite knowing who stood there. "But the face," he said then turned. "I'd never forget your face."

"Then we're past the need for introductions," Nathan Briers mouthed as he motioned with his dart gun for Kyle to drop his weapons. "Now take a step back."

"Does seem rather foolish with you pointing that at me," Kyle countered. "What's this about?" he asked in need of answers. "Or don't you know?" wondering again if he assumed too much. "Maybe you're just someone's pawn."

"A pawn like you," Nathan snickered stroking the whiskers of his muttonchops. "Hardly."

As Kyle stared at Nathan he wanted to believe the person responsible for everything stood in front of him. In an odd way, the ethnobotanist would be comforted by looking into the very eyes of such a devil. Not only to see them but to ask them why – why in the hell would they do this.

"You look the part," KP finally said while eyeing the somewhat charred, metal briefcase situated near Nathan's feet with the SynRx logo still visible. "But heaven help you if you are," he warned. "You have a lot to answer for."

"I'm shaking."

"Your two cohorts seemed just as arrogant," the ethnobotanist remarked while looking up at the ants still pouring over Ian Haleem's body. "So was Savannah."

"Indeed," Nathan professed. "It was good of you to leave my associate's gear strewn around like that – it made finding what I needed that much easier."

"Don't give me that – there was nothing there – believe me I looked."

"On the contrary," Nathan boasted as he tapped the side of the briefcase. "Something rather extraordinary in fact."

"I know about your discovery and your damn society," Kyle Preston clamored hoping what Savannah told him was true. "Immortality – my ass."

"You know nothing," Nathan denounced with some obvious irritation in finding out Savannah broke her oath. "Otherwise you would have known what you were looking for. Instead you left it behind."

"Maybe, but it's amazing what someone will tell you before they die," KP chimed, "but not to worry," he added, although somewhat distracted because he thought he heard something moving through the jungle off in the distance. "Your secret is safe with me – that is, if you really are running the show."

"Accurate but not precise," Nathan begrudged as he lifted the barrel of his gun into the air as if to bid Kyle adieu. "Anything Savannah told you Mr. Preston – dies here – with you – unless," he said with a mischievous sparkle in his eyes, "unless you join me?"

"Join you?" Kyle Preston repeated in disbelief. "Are you crazy? After you've killed everyone I cared for – my friends, my colleagues."

"And you mine," Nathan replied. "And yet, for that very reason, I now offer you immortality – think about it Kyle – you'll never get any older than you are now – never see your body wither away before your very eyes – never have to die."

"How – by being a part of this barbaric society?" Kyle questioned with a degree of interest that scared him.

"A new triad must be formed," Nathan answered without explanation or emotion. "Therefore, I must ask myself – how best to accomplish this task? How best to move forward?"

"You think I'm the answer?"

"The difference between you and I – isn't as much as you think," Nathan suggested. "Our goals are different but not dissimilar – our missions in life distinct but not divergent. It's only a degree of perspective that separates us. A shade of gray within a black and white world."

"You've hunted me like an animal," Kyle snapped

back even as his mind raced with thoughts of never growing old. "All this time you've been trying to kill me and now I'm suppose to believe you want me as a partner in crime."

"An associate," Nathan Briers corrected with a wry smile. "We call each other associates within the society, and yes," he added while still aiming the gun at Kyle, "you haven't realized yet, but with what you know, you are the obvious choice."

"Sorry but from where I'm standing, things aren't so obvious," Kyle said then looked past Nathan because he distinctly heard someone coming through the forest in a rush.

"I'm offering you a chance to be a god," Nathan jabbered because he too could hear someone coming. "Tell me now!"

Cleto broke into the clearing and leaped into the air. The dog slammed into Nathan's chest, sending him to the ground, but not before he managed to get a shot off. At the same time, Kyle dove to the ground then rolled behind the cecropia tree despite the crazed insects. Afterwards, he brushed away an ant that had latched onto his neck then ran, ran as fast as he could into the jungle.

Kyle sliced through the heavy underbrush for several hundred meters before stopping to catch his breath. He then bounced back and forth for some distance along the banks of a small stream to obliterate his trail. Afterwards he felt dizzy and fell down next to the black water and labored to breathe as a whale upon a beachhead. A minute later Kyle forced himself back off the ground. He stumbled forward – moving forward an inch at a time until he stood upon another world.

Void of any vegetation, El Brando resembled a cataclysmic crater on a barren planet. The lip of the mine sparkled and bedazzled in the bright sun but the footing bordered on treacherous. The enormous pit plummeted several stories down with thousands of Garimpeiros inside, climbing around on an endless crisscrossing of ladders from one level to the next. Near the bottom, water seeped from the clay walls to form a thick muddy gruel no miner dared to walk across in fear of being buried alive.

"Finally run out of places to hide," Nathan said when he caught back up with the ethnobotanist. "Oh, I see I winged you," he added after noticing a scratch on Kyle's neck. "Guess that answer doesn't matter now – now that you're going to die."

"Even in hell," Kyle mumbled somewhat starry-eyed while looking into the ominous pit. "See the forsaken souls," he added pointing at the miners who scraped and dug with their bare hands. "Tell you what – let's join them," he said with conviction while rubbing his neck, "how about it – you and me – in hell together – forever."

"Why – when I'm about to leave this miserable place behind and be a king," Nathan boasted as he tapped the case against his leg. "A king no less that lives forever – or rather a god – in part thanks to you. My two Ass—"

"Asshole friends are dead so why not join them,"

Kyle butted in as he grabbed a hold of Nathan then let himself slip over the edge like an anchor to a boat, bringing Nathan down with him.

Together they fell twenty meters before landing upon a small ledge. Somehow Kyle found himself entangled with a ladder that stopped his fall while wrenching his arm out of its socket. He then watched as Nathan bounced past him and off the inner ledge along with his precious briefcase.

"Looks like forever wasn't that far off," Kyle Preston smarted after seeing Nathan land at the bottom of the pit then disappear along with the case beneath the mud. "Guess that means it's my turn,' the ethnobotanist then added as he felt his strength slipping. "At least I had a choice."

Before reaching the edge, Kyle heard a chaotic chorus of hauntingly familiar voices. First the hardy grumbling of Captain Jack told him to cross himself and to shun black magic. Afterwards, Ocho spoke to him about fighting god's will. Next he heard Rook rant at him to come home and also Zito say he would do the same if Louisanne ever went missing. Then the gravelly muttering of the Rednalsi shaman warned him again just to leave. Afterwards, he heard Brooklyn tell him to trust in the spirits.

In the end though, Kyle Preston heard one voice come through louder than the others. A calm yet confident voice that repeated a single phrase again and again:

"Don't let go! Don't let go! Don't let go!"

55
THE JOURNEY HOME

Zito went through the motions of the preflight inspection without his normal enthusiasm. After each system check he readjusted his cap then looked back towards shore before moving on to the next task. Selena Crotalez noticed he stalled but said nothing.

Albeit begrudgingly, the two of them had agreed to stay put for three days before leaving. Time enough for Zito to make repairs – time for Selena to mend a little from her ordeal – more than enough time they thought for the others to return.

"I hate this too," Selena confided to Zito as the two of them strapped themselves in for the flight back to Manaus. "I feel like I'm betraying them."

"It's time," Zito conceded despite looking one more time out at the abandoned plantation. "Though I can't help but feel we're being watched."

After an uncharacteristic sputter, the Cessna's massive Continental engine roared to life with a vengeance. Zito rattled the throttle back and forth and listened for the slightest hesitation. Once satisfied his repair job would hold, he maneuvered the plane away from the dock and into the harbor. Then after one last check back towards shore, the pilot turned the plane into the wind.

"Now what," Zito moaned after spotting a small motorized canoe downstream from them. "They've moved right into out path."

"It's those thugs – isn't it," Selena said. "Turn around and go the other direction before they start shooting!"

"Damn it all," Zito declared while pushing his glasses back up his nose to get a better look. "I can't see that far," he added while keeping the engine throttled up just in case someone on the boat started shooting.

"Maybe they're afraid to hit the plane?" Dr. Crotalez offered. "You told me one of them wanted you to fly them out. Take my word – just go!"

"No – I think someone's waving," the bush pilot said as the boat drew closer. "Hey," he said with some certainty," in the front there – isn't that Cleto?"

"Who?" Selena Crotalez asked confused. "Who's there?"

"The dog," Zito cheered as he cut the engine. "I think I see Kyle as well," he added as the distance between the plane and the canoe closed. "It's him – he's alive! Kyle's alive!"

Despite the delirium from the trace of poison within his bloodstream, Kyle Preston never let go of the ladder. Three brothers working in the mine then came to his rescue before his strength gave out. Afterwards the ethnobotanist spent the night in their care and then arranged passage aboard this canoe.

"You look terrible science officer," Zito told Kyle as he grabbed the dog from him. "What happened?"

"They're all dead," Kyle shrugged without explanation then crawled into the back of the plane with Brooklyn's satchel tied to his waist. "You know what," he said as he took a deep breath and let it out slowly, "I sure could use a shot of that blue stuff?"

"Who's dead," Selena asked while Zito dug under his seat for the booze.

"You for one," Kyle said in utter shock. "I thought you died in that explosion."

"Looks can be deceiving," Selena declared with a wink as she handed Kyle the bottle.

"Tell me about it," KP said then downed two healthy swigs of the so-called Romulin Ale. "Savannah murdered Brooklyn."

"I can believe it," Zito replied after thinking about it for a minute. "She sabotaged my plane," he said, "and right in front of my nose. But why – that's what I want to know – why?"

"Some secret discovery, or society, and some other foolishness if what she said was true."

"What's this about a society?" Selena asked after

coming back to where Kyle sat slumped up against the fuselage.

"I wish I knew," Kyle Preston scoffed. "Savannah said some crazy things before she died – something about living forever."

"Wow – what a lunatic," Selena professed in disbelief. "She never came across that way while at the village but then again, she got there just as I was leaving."

"Believe me – she had me fooled as well," Kyle bellowed as he reached over and patted Cleto. "I should have known better! Hell – I did know better!"

"Don't be too hard on yourself," Zito interjected as he prepared to crank the engine back up. "She had a way about her – I mean even Spock wouldn't be able to resist her."

"Did she say what the name of this secret society was," Selena asked, "or what they did?"

"No," KP replied, "and I can't say any of it makes sense."

"Maybe that's a good thing," Selena said while checking Kyle over to make sure nothing more than his pride needed mending. "Rest now," she then insisted and pressed her soft hand against his lips so he couldn't talk anymore. "We made it – it's over."

56
THE SHAMAN'S APPRENTICE

As the Cessna 182 pulled up into the sky, a young Rednalsi boy holding a bow stood back in the shadows of Bensonvia and watched the plane take flight. Afterwards, Moro moved out to the water's edge and sat down on the dock where Zito's plane had been tied up. The boy then put down his bow and pulled out a small wooden flute – a gift given to him by Brooklyn while the two of them sat the other morning in the rain back at the Rednalsi village.

On that morning, Kyle assumed the two talked about their dogs when in fact, Brooklyn and Moro discussed what the spirits had revealed to the shaman. Images the Tirio saw during his own vision quest far different than Kyle's. Still, Brooklyn swore an oath to his friend that the two would face whatever lay ahead of them together. An allegiance he chose to keep despite the risk and above any sacrifice.

As Moro played, the jungle responded to the flute's simple melody. The resounding roar of the cicadas fell silent along with the peeping frogs and croaking toads. The incessant squawks from the macaws and toucans, and every other bird hidden within the nearby canopy dropped off as well. The monkeys stopped screaming. The tamarins stopped leaping between the trees. Even the coati stopped traipsing through the forest. Soon nothing called or moved except the song of the flute floating through the air.

Moro played this song of peace – and of harmony – and of being one with Amazonas. The same melody played on the nights Brooklyn and Kyle spent around the campfire during the expedition. A motif passed down for tens of thousands of years by the indigenous people of the forest and now to the young Rednalsi boy. One that would take him years to understand and even longer to master.

Nevertheless, a few minutes later a bouto splashed out in the harbor just as Moro stopped playing. The boy knowingly waited until the pink dolphin rose up above the water again, only this time, right in front of him. He then put down the flute and picked up his bow then dove into the water without fear of the black caimans beneath the dock or any other peril in the surrounding shallows. After all, it was time for his first fishing lesson.

57
DAY ONE

Autumn-turned leaves tossed in the breeze and rustled along the tree-lined street as Kyle Preston stepped down from the curb. Amidst the bare trees and withered leaves upon the UNC campus, the ethnobotanist brushed along with far more abandonment and dullness than his surroundings. A man devastated by his losses who retreated inside himself as if hardened as well for a long bitter winter.

A month had past since his return from Brazil and yet only today Kyle ventured over to the school. Once there, he found himself standing long overdue inside the village cemetery at Lowery's grave. At first he stood frozen in front of the marker as if on an icy shoal – alone, bitter, and cold. Frozen for the moment not by the weather but rather his inability to let time move past his recent misfortunes. The loss of his friends loomed as a damnation bound to devour his soul. A doom he intended to remember for the rest of his life. To take all of that pain and hurt with him to his own grave. He would be that doleful – that miserable – that unforgiving. He would become that ghastly ghost he envisioned clawing its way out of Lowery's grave.

Then, as Kyle stood there steadfast in that decision, the chorus of the bell tower filled the cold, harsh air. The warm melody flowed out across campus – just as it always did. Somehow though, the bells rang sweeter and more inviting this time. Something the ethnobotanist tried to ignore but couldn't because he now realized Brooklyn had played the same song on his flute during their time together. The very one his friend swore to play for him again when he needed to hear it most.

"How?" Kyle asked aloud while looking up at the gray wintry sky. "How can that be?"

Whether a fateful sign or nothing more than a coincidence, a crack formed in the icy emotions holding Kyle back. A chance things could be different – could move forward. The choice of whether he faced the end of the road or day one of a new expedition.

58
THE DUBUQUE OPENING

After that first difficult visit, Kyle Preston returned each day to the cemetery until the start of the spring semester. The demands of the first week kept him, along with Rook and Selena, pushed to find even a spare minute in their busy schedules. Rook stayed occupied overseeing the underclassmen using the renovated Boiler Room and helping with arrangements for his and Deborah's wedding. Dr. Crotalez seemed immersed but right at home with the two sections of Organic Chemistry she taught. Meanwhile Kyle's efforts focused around reigning in a new and quirky graduate student, who seemed to be just as passionate about a TV show called "Voyager" as discovering medicinal plants.

It wasn't until the Wednesday of the second week that the three of them found themselves together again in Dr. Lowery's old lab. Without the professor, the room still seemed to be in shambles to them. But then, they all realized, life sometimes seemed more about what one did with the pieces after something fell apart, rather than remembering where they use to fit. A choice to live with the cracks and the rough edges in what still remained or be consumed by the irreplaceable gaps.

"So what did you say once she accepted," Kyle asked Rook as the two of them worked on setting up their pieces for a game of chess on a brand new board. "Was it – Oh Lord, thank-you for what I am about to receive?"

"Funny," Rook shot back after coughing up an oyster of phlegm to clear his throat. "Unlike you – at least there's a woman that will have me."

"Not if you keep that up," Kyle insisted then opened the game by moving his king's pawn forward two spaces. "You sound terrible."

"Damn cold," Rook bemoaned after moving one of his kingside flanking pawns up a square. "I've been fighting it since school started. Of course Deborah thinks I should go get it checked."

"Maybe you should," KP suggested while listening to his friend hack more phlegm up.

"I'm fine," Rook replied as he brought out a handkerchief from his pocket, wiped his mouth, then blew his nose into it. "I'm not running to the doctor every time I get a sniffle."

"You're lucky Deborah finds pigheadedness attractive," KP said as he moved his queen's pawn forward two spaces. "By the way – how's Cleto?"

"Seems right at home," Rook replied while moving his bishop into the hole left vacant by his first move. "We started taking him over to Carborro Park in the evenings to let him chase a Frisbee around."

"Glad that's working out," KP said as he paused and thought back to how much Brooklyn loved the dog. After about a minute of reminiscing, his attention partially returned to the game as he moved his queenside knight inward and up to the third file on the board. "Hey – any word from your friend over in the computer lab about that drive?"

"Matter of fact she showed up this morning with it," Rook replied as he brought the device out of a pouch on his chair and tossed it next to the board. He then moved his queen's pawn up a square. "Evidently it had some sort of tamper-proof encryption software on it. Portia said the thing started wiping files the moment she skirted the password prompt."

"So you broke in there for nothing," the ethnobotanist sighed as he moved his second knight up even with the other one. "It figures," he said in disgust, "whoever he was – that guy was something else!"

"Era louco," Selena commented in Portuguese as she turned around from a nearby fumehood after preparing some standards. She then picked up those solutions along with some new eluents extracted from the last remaining scraps of the Pico de Neblina sample. "Crazy," she repeated in English this time while walking over to the glass partition dividing the lab into two separate rooms. "He was crazy – like the way both of you are over that game."

"You know – we call that eave's-dropping here."

"Aye, but we Brazilians think of that as a good thing," Selena rifled back as she pawed at the door to the partition with a pair of thick protective gloves she wore, then passed through to the other side, and started loading all the vials she prepared into the autosampler of the mass spectrometer.

"I didn't get to finish," Rook announced after the door swung shut. "The thing is," he said while countering Kyle's last move by bringing his kingside knight inward and up to the sixth file, "even though everything got dumped, Portia went back and retrieved some fragments."

"Like what?" Kyle asked after moving his Queenside bishop all the way up to the fifth file.

"Garbage mainly but a few IP addresses I'm hoping will lead to whoever—"

"Rook – when is your wedding again?" Selena asked cutting him off as she came back into the room and started to clean up the mess she had made in the hood. "I can never remember the date."

"The tenth," Rook replied then thought to add, "of April – which unlike the idiot sitting across from me, still leaves you plenty of time to find someone to bring."

"Kyle – maybe we should go together?" Selena suggested after moving a bottle of methylene chloride she used during the extractions off to one side of the hood. She then lifted out a rack of dirty separatory funnels and carried them over to a nearby sink. "What do you say?"

"Don't take pity on him," Rook argued.

"Trust me – I'm not," Dr. Crotalez countered as she washed the glassware. "I know better than that."

"Hey – I can get a date," Kyle alleged after moving his pawn from the first rank up two squares. "Does anyone want anything from the machine?" he then asked while hunting around in his pockets for some change.

"A pack of Marlboros would be nice," Rook joked in between coughs. "Unfiltered," he added as Kyle started for the door. "If I'm going to hack up a lung – might as well do it right."

"Do you want anything or not?" Kyle asked again while standing in the doorway. "Either of you?"

"Eu sou muito bem," Selena replied just before Kyle left the room. She then dried off her gloves with a hand towel and strolled over to the chessboard next to Rook. "Looks like you're using one of Paulsen's defenses on him."

"I am," Rook said taken aback. "I was just about to castle."

"I'm surprised he doesn't see that coming – the Dubuque opening is so obvious," Selena Crotalez said with an unfamiliar air of cynicism in her voice while walking back over to the fumehood – back to where the bottle of methylene chloride remained uncapped.

"The Dubuque, obvious," Rook challenged after

bringing his hanky back out and blowing his nose again. "I didn't even know you played."

"Among other things," Dr. Crotalez replied as she screwed the lid back on the solvent bottle but not before pouring some of the toxic liquid onto the towel she still had with her. "How my associates let him get the best of them I'll never know."

"What do you mean by that?" Rook asked confused while waiting for Selena to return from the fumehood.

"I'm sure Kyle's told you all about the tall blond," Crotalez irked as she slithered her way up behind Rook's chair and locked its wheels so that he couldn't move. "Not that he learned anything of substance about Savannah or the Society for that matter. But then after all, like you, he is just a pawn – like you – just one of the masses!"

Without warning, Selena lunged forward and held the hand towel she had doused with methylene chloride up over Rook's face. The solvent seeped from the rag and surrounded him in a shroud of toxic fumes he struggled not to breathe. A silent and invisible killer that burnt his eyes and tickled his nose as it lingered in wait to wreck havoc on his lungs.

"Don't fight it," Selena insisted as Rook thrashed his head about in an effort to free himself even though he was no match for such a young and vibrant woman, especially one who would remain that way forever because of the Baby's Breath she took. "It will all be over soon – it has to be – you're much more resourceful than any of us thought. I can't take the risk you'll find something on that disk. Too bad though, I was looking forward to your wedding."

After breathing in some of the fumes, Lowery's lab assistant began to cough up phlegm along with blood. As he did, Selena Crotalez reached down and grabbed the hard disk and smacked it against the benchtop, cracking the silica wafer inside. She then placed the broken pieces on the floor to make it look like Rook knocked it off the bench. She then went back behind him, unlocked the wheels to his chair, then pulled off her gloves, and threw them along with the towel inside the hood.

"You bitch," Rook gasped on his last breath.

"No," Selena denied matter-of-factly as she reached over and selected a piece from the chessboard then stuffed it into Rook's dying hand. "You of all people should know – even black has a queen."